# Maxx's Well

## A Dark Anthology
## of Shorts, Sketches, &
## My Descent Into Madness

By: O. W. Maxx
And guests

# Maxx's Well

...

O. W. Maxx

To my family, who deserve so much better.

To Jesse and Amber, Jamie and Claire. All long since departed,
if they ever really existed at all.

To Kim, who obviously still has much work to do.

To the darkness, my old friend.

This is a work of fiction. Names, characters, businesses, places, events and incidents are either the products of the author's imagination or used in a fictitious manner. Any resemblance to actual persons, living or dead, or actual events is purely coincidental and unintentional.

ISBN: 978-0-9993986-1-6

# Imagine

In August 2019 experienced mountain climber Graham Parrington successfully completed the difficult ascent of Mount Rainier in the state of Washington, USA. The day glowed bright and crisp, the unimaginable views stretched forever, and the physical accomplishment brought with it the heady intoxication of euphoria. Imagine such a moment, being atop the world.

But then came the descent.

The snow and ice beneath him crumbled, giving way to an unseen crevasse. He slipped, feeling the evil fingers of gravity clutching him as he began to fall. Flailing helplessly in a futile attempt to catch himself, he plunged instead into an ever-thickening darkness. Deeper, farther, faster, he smashed through layer after layer of melting snow until he dangled precipitously at the end of his fraying rope mere inches above a razor-sharp blade of ice. At the edge of death, he screamed into the void—alone.

Thus, is this collection of writings.

# Table of Contents

# Forward

"Nighttime sharpens, heightens each sensation.
Darkness wakes and stirs imagination.
Silently the senses abandon their defenses.
Helpless to resist the notes I write.
For I compose the music of the night."

Andrew Lloyd-Webber, Music of the Night

# A Glimpse

I must travel this road to the end. Stay this course until it's finished. Every hero faces his trials. But so, too, does every villain. Odysseus and Scylla in the Straits of Messina. Why should I be any different? Grasping at the rotting edges. Pushed unwillingly forward. Paying oh so dear a price. Eyes wide in both horror and hope.

Am I the one who started this journey? Me?

Or did I stumble on an unseen root when the night sagged bleak and starless? A forlorn moment when the sky closed her eyes in shame and left me groping like a blind man on unfamiliar slopes? Tumbling down the precipice. Crashing and hurting and bleeding until I no longer cared. Until I just wanted it to stop.

But I've not yet reached the bottom, and gravity is a relentless mistress.

I caught a glimpse of something more—beyond the shadows. I'm certain of it. For an instant, it shimmered, glowing behind a charcoal veil. From David, Solomon. Then, swallowed anew by the grinding darkness, vanished. Abandoning me to what? My weighty doubts and pathetic reflection, shriveled monster that I am, realizing my own foolishness.

Only God can judge, or redeem, me now.

# Section 1: Below the Rim

"Stars hide your fires.
Let not light see my black and deep desires."

William Shakespeare, Macbeth

"I am terrified by this dark thing that sleeps in me;
All day I feel its soft, feathery turnings, its malignity."

Sylvia Plath, Ariel

## So Happy

There was a knock. My heart stopped, and I stared at my father.

"This is insane," I said. "She's my daughter. I say she shouldn't date until she's thirty." I ran my fingers through my hair. "She's barely nineteen."

"Nevertheless, her beau is waiting. Best go let him in." He winked at me. "And she's almost twenty."

"Think I should scare him away?"

My father shook his head. "Kristin really likes him."

He was right.

My temples throbbed as I opened the front door. There was a tattoo and a mop of shaggy hair on my stoop.

I hated him. I started to slam the door.

My father caught it in mid-swing. "You must be Tommy. Kristin's told us a lot about you."

I didn't move from the breach. My eyes narrowed. I just knew he'd done jail time.

My father placed his hand on my shoulder. "Why don't you let Kristin know that Tommy's here?"

I forced myself to be civil. "I'm Bob Tramble. Kristin's father. Welcome."

The hoodlum came in.

"Thanks Bob." He walked over and sat in my recliner.

He'd called me Bob. Not Mr. Tramble. Bob. Then he'd deliberately sat in *my* recliner. The hooligan! My hand formed into a fist as my eyes bore into the back of his scraggily head.

My father stepped in front of me. "Why don't you go get Kristin." He guided me from my hijacked recliner and toward the stairway. "Tommy, I was just getting myself a soda. What can I get for you?"

I started up the stairs but slowed to watch as the harbinger-of-doom looked at my prized stuffed pheasant. I was sure he smirked. What was that supposed to mean? I obviously couldn't trust him down there. I stopped and shouted.

"Kristin, your—" I couldn't finish the sentence. Her what? Date? Boyfriend? Father of my future grandchildren? I felt nauseous. "Umm, someone's here to see you." I stormed into the kitchen.

My father was dumping a bag of chips into a serving bowl.

"Did you see it? The tattoo? And I thought that hair went out in the 60s." I looked out toward the living room then back to my father. "What a delinquent. He's probably deflowering the vase as we speak."

"Kristin speaks quite highly of him."

"I pray for her future every day, I work two jobs to send her to a respectable university," I rubbed my hand across my forehead, "and she brings home this..." I struggled for the word, "truck-stop reject?"

He placed his hand on my shoulder and smiled. "Son, I'm proud of the job you've done since her mother passed. You've a right to be protective but learn to let go. Like I had to do with you." He handed me the bowl. "Now go get to know him a bit. He's probably not so bad after all."

I carried the chips into the living room. My father was right. Kristin had always shown good judgment with her friends. I needed to give Tommy a chance, or at least to try.

"So," I ground my teeth, forcing a smile, "what are you studying in college?"

"I'm getting into gynecology."

My left eye twitched.

Gynecology?

Was he smirking again? At me?

He wasn't going to be doing his homework with my daughter if I could help it. I reached behind the sofa and opened my gun case. I pulled out my twelve gauge.

"You ever do any shooting, Tommy? I like shooting." The corners of my mouth stretched upward.

He dropped his chips. The smirk vanished. "Uh," his eyes fixed on the steel I held, "where—where do you shoot?"

"Mostly around the house." I stared at him, unblinking.

His jaw dropped.

My father entered with a tray of sodas.

"He's a gynecologist, Dad. Kristin didn't mention that." I stood, my hands trembling. "And he's still in my recliner!"

Tommy jumped from the chair, his eyes wide. "I'm sorry, sir. I didn't know." He swallowed. "I want to be a medical missionary."

My father lurched between us. "Now Bob..."

A soda can fell from the tray and exploded as it hit the floor, making the sound of an echoing report.

Tommy's face drained. He stumbled backward over the arm of the chair.

Kristin came downstairs. She looked so much like her mother that my eyes stung. She took Tommy's hand and smiled at him, really smiled at him. Her eyes sparkled. She seemed so happy.

"Is everything ok?"

So happy.

I set the gun into its case. "Yes, honey. Everything's fine."

# The Homecoming

A lump formed in my throat when the old water tower came into view. I squinted my eyes against the moisture pooling in them.

I hadn't expected to feel like this.

Grandpa steered his old pick-up along the highway. He patted my arm. "Not long now, Jimmy."

No one had called me Jimmy in three years. It felt comfortable coming from him, like a pair of old Levi's. "Are Mom and Dad at home?"

He nodded, "Got a few folks coming over to visit."

"Aunt Lisa, too?"

"I think so."

I hadn't seen them in a lifetime.

It seemed as if I still had foreign dust in my hair and eyes. I could taste it, probably always would. The blood of strangers stained my hands. The chaos of war burned my mind. It was all part of me now. Something I would carry until I died. At least, that's what they'd said at my debrief.

I felt dirty.

But the blue of the sky over Emeryville seemed to have a power, a magnetic presence, a familiarity. I let it bathe me.

I inhaled. The air was filled with the fragrance of corn, wheat, and fertilizer. I smiled. The fields were in sow. The shoots, new again, were fresh and reaching for the heavens.

"You heard they put in a stoplight?"

I hadn't. They'd told me that nothing stays the same. That people had moved on with life while I was away. They said to be prepared, the lights of home will have dimmed.

Three years is a long time.

Sandy had moved away to college in Iowa City the year after I left.

She was one of the guys back then, all barefoot and braces. I'd never thought of her much beyond that, a 17-year-old tomboy. And I was a skinny farm brat fresh out of high school. In the 'Stans, I began to realize what I had back home was special.

I hoped I hadn't lost it forever.

Grandpa turned the corner into town.

The Dairy Queen was still there, faded and peeling just like I'd last seen it. The granary, where Dad had been foreman for the past 15 years, stood majestic and gray. Shar's Daily Drive-in was still missing letters on its sign, leaving only "har-D-ly Drive-n," the way it had been for a generation.

I'd carried memories of these places through mountain passes and across deserts half a world away. They made my 50 pounds of gear seem lighter and the pain of loss feel softer. If time had put a little more rust on them, well, that was ok.

After all, I'd changed, too. My body was lean and firm where softness once reigned. Muscles rippled where before there'd only been potential. Tanned skin had covered my freckles.

And there was the scar.

I hadn't told anyone about the shrapnel that had missed my spinal cord by less than an inch. Nor how I begged the Captain to let me stay in country and finish my tour.

I went to do a job.

I was glad to do it.

The sidewalks filled with people. They were looking at the old truck slowing in the center of Main Street. A banner was strung between the general store and the mercantile. It read, "Thank you, Jimmy! Welcome Home!"

An American flag fluttered beneath it.

Folks began to wave and cheer. Yellow ribbons sprouted from windows and doorways. Red, white, and blue bunting was everywhere.

The bell in the church steeple began to ring.

I hadn't remembered the town having so many people. They spilled into the road and called my name. Their hands were waving and clapping, each movement as if reaching for me, gathering me, holding me. A soothing, healing, welcoming embrace.

Their mouths, drawn into smiles, had uttered countless prayers in my absence. Now they rejoiced with thanksgiving, and their sound touched my heart.

It occurred to me that three years isn't such a long time when faith and hope remain alive.

Grandpa stopped near the park. Mom and Dad held me, weeping.

I stepped into the midst of the people, my people. They patted and hugged me, bringing me near, drawing me home. I was washed with their laughter.

I saw her, Sandy, standing in the back. Her hands were folded beneath her chin as if in prayer. I moved toward her. She was smiling and her cheeks were streaked with tears—for me—my tears.

I was home.

# The Apology

Chill from the doorknob penetrated my fingers and palm, amplifying the sullen weight that already pressed upon me. Air escaped my lungs between flaccid lips, a remorseful prayer for guidance.

I pushed the door, leaden feet stumbling forward.

Our hand-stitched bedspread lay disheveled across the rutted mattress, littered with tissues crumpled and twisted. My wife's lavender pillowcase condemned me through tear-sodden lace.

I hesitated.

Heidi's delicate shoulders bowed against drawn knees; her auburn hair tangled and mussed.

I had been the cause of this.

"Look," I swallowed, the motion tearing my constricted throat, "I didn't mean…" My voice trailed away, lost among boulders of shame.

She rocked to the uneven rhythm of sequestered agony; her moist gaze buried, withdrawn.

I stepped near, trembling. "It wasn't like I…" But the words flickered and died, an insufficient candle in a midnight gale.

She blinked, eyes darting to the floor.

I sat on the bed next to her unyielding figure. "Honey," the utterance struggled past a swelling anguish in my chest, "I…" My cheeks were damp. "I'm sorry."

Her breath shuddered, sniffling. She placed a hand on my arm.

The warmth was healing.

She laid her head on my shoulder.

## Miriam's Song

Wind she blows
Through the trees
Senses fill
With love's togetherness

Wind she blows
Far away
Won't come back
The tree remains

# Curves

T he clouds wispy, soft, like red and gold accents on a master
painting
Your eyes bright, excited
The setting sun blazing behind mountains newly freed by spring
The curve of your palm as I take your hand,
Our first date
Memories of an unexpected introduction

The steeple bells peeling through a shower of rice
Your eyes eager, alive
Candlelight glinting off pearls woven into your gown, soon crumpled
on the floor
The curve of your bare hip as my finger traces your body,
Our first night
Images from a day of wonder

The whispers of an intercom soothing a ceiling of surgical green
Your eyes wide, uncertain
The glow of the fetal monitor as it flashes in the predawn gray
The curve of your womb as our future stretches and kicks,
Our first child
Seeds of our hope-filled expectations

The strobe of red and blue crashing against withering leaves
Your eyes fixated, horrified
The body of our only son near his crumpled bike

O. W. Maxx

The curve of your arms as you helplessly cradle him,
Our first loss
Shards of a dream broken

The relentless slicing of the vaulted fan in a noiseless room
Your eyes swollen, red
My reflection in the darkened window, shallow, lifeless
The curve of your tears as they track pallid cheeks,
The first time I didn't care anymore
Splinters of a shattered promise

The disparaging midnight wind, the frozen clawing of skeletal
branches
My eyes thick, unblinking
The sound of your distant car motor still searing my interminable
consciousness
The indented curve of the now vacant mattress that we'd once
shared,
Our first leaving
Fragments of a failure complete

The shadowed archways, the luminous stained glass
My eyes stinging, searching
The long-forgotten scent of pews and candles
The curve of my stooped shoulders as I crumble at the altar,
My first humbling
Kernels of a desperate healing

# Losing Hope

I was losing Hope.

She lay under crinkled hospital linens, eyes hollow and closed, slipping into another realm. Drops inside IV tubes seemed to count down her remaining moments, like sand in some sort of obscene hourglass.

Nothing more could be done. My wife was leaving me, leaving us, and the impending loss became a palpable weight across my chest.

I sat on the bed, in the curve of her waist, the bones of her hip protruding, and held the hand that once caressed away my anger as I struggled against fitful sleep. I wrestled with the God who'd afflict my soulmate and leave our children motherless. I wanted nothing to do with him.

She'd seen me through the turmoil that battered my faith. She prayed without ceasing, for me, the girls, and our futures.

But she didn't know how deep my spiritual wounds had been cleaved.

I stroked her cheek, sunken and prematurely cold. The corner of her mouth flickered, perhaps a final throb of pain surfacing despite the medication. Or the last vestige of a smile from some distant shore.

*Where are you now? Come back. Don't go.*

A tear coursed hot from beneath my sodden lashes, becoming lost in unshaven whiskers.

I'd promised God to move mountains for him if he'd bring a cure—asked him to take me instead—explained that a father is an income while a mother is life.

When my prayers dissolved into barter sessions, she'd hold me, and we'd cry together. The healing power of her love bathed me.

*I'd rather you healed yourself.*

Twenty years of marriage laid waste by a shattering malignancy. It was over, cut short. Hopeless.

And I was angry. So very angry.

The door of the room inched open in a slow, faltering arc. Juvenile fingers gripped the frame, ushered forward by a nurse with trembling hands. Charity and Peg edged past wilting flowers, eyes pulled wide and steeped in moisture. At 12 and 8, they were old enough to understand but still young enough to scar.

I reached for them. "Time to say goodbye. Mommy will be leaving us soon."

Peg wiped her nose on her sleeve. "Is she... does it hurt, Daddy?"

I stroked the tangles of her un-brushed hair. "No, Princess. The doctors gave her medicine." I nodded to the dripping tubes. "She'll never have to feel pain again."

She sat on my lap, leaning back against my chest. "Can I touch her?"

"That would be good." I said. "You both can."

Charity smoothed the blanket. "Dad, we need to pray." Her voice was even and calm. The tilt of her head, the angle of her chin, the cadence of her voice—all so much like her mother. For an instant, I was lost in a memory—our wedding day, laughter and dreams.

I swallowed, trying not to choke. "I think she'd like it."

"Not to make Mom happy." She blinked and looked at me. "To keep us strong. There's a promise beyond. Mom showed me in the Bible."

"A promise? Yes, there is," I said.

But I didn't have the heart to explain that even promises in the Bible can be broken. That prayers are not always answered. That a ravaged spirit can lose hope as quickly as the shattering of a crystal chalice.

Peg stared at the machines and monitors as they flashed and beeped in an ever-decreasing rhythm. "We get to see Mom again after this." In her voice, a peaceful certainty.

I shuddered; my lungs involuntarily gasping. A simple realization dawned behind the curtains of grief encircling me. Whatever grace had been given me now resided only in my daughters. I'd once believed like them, but how could I now in the face of such tragedy?

How could I ever again?

I was losing hope.

# The Porch Light Flickers

Stray scraps of confetti on our stairs
Shouts, screams, giggles, and song in an unending electric torrent
A disheveled pile of shoes mounded by our front door
The constant stream of dirty dishes unsteadily piled atop our counter
Scratches, chips, stains, and holes
Purpose
Our home was well used and brimming with the energy of unlimited potential

Until it wasn't anymore

Cobwebs cling between tread and riser where nary a foot has stepped in days
Deafening quiet echoes against graying walls
A solitary pair of sandals waits alone behind the chair
Dust settles over unused surfaces, a smothering film
Decay, neglect, forgetfulness, and disregard
Irrelevance
The building shudders like a hollow relic in decline

And yet the porch light flickers above an unlocked door

## Apple-Head Dolls

**D**ust sprinkled down when Grandpa lowered the secret ladder leading to the attic. The rusted springs groaned like ghosts on Halloween. I stared up into a dim world of mysterious shadows.

Mom shooed the floating particles. "Now Dad," she warned, "please don't go filling their imaginations with any of your crazy stories."

"Stories?" I wondered aloud. "About what?"

"Never you mind," Mom chided.

"But I'm nine."

"That's right, young man. And your little sister is only six."

I kicked at a fuzzle on the carpet.

"Don't worry," Grandpa winked while nudging Lissa and me to the steps. His eyes were bright, like he was about to sneak a cookie before supper.

He giggled as we climbed up, up, up.

The room was huge with a peaked roof and beams of wood crisscrossed above our heads. Tattered boxes and old trunks filled the floor and shelves, like a cave overflowing with pirate booty. Spiderwebs drooped from the corners and everything slept under a blanket of dust stretching deep into the darkness.

I took Lissa's hand to make sure she wasn't scared.

Grandpa tussled my hair. "The Good Book says we don't need to be afraid, but sometimes it sure is fun." He flipped a switch. A single lightbulb hanging from the end of a wire began to glow. "Lots of interesting stuff in here. Some from when I was your size."

"That's old!" I blurted.

Grandpa grinned. "It's not so much the age, but the memories."

Lissa pulled her hand from mine and started to explore the room, roaming around the clutter, leaving little footprints on the floor.

"What kind of memories?" I asked.

"Some happy, some silly," he glanced toward the ladder then leaned close to me, "and some a little scary, maybe even dangerous."

"Dangerous?"

Lissa squeaked with fright and ran to us. Her eyes looked like saucers, wide and round.

"Whoa, there." Grandpa comforted her against his leg. "Did you find something?"

She snuffled and pointed to an ancient set of shelves against the far wall.

Grandpa led the way, knocking down old strands of spiderwebs like he was chopping a path through the jungle. He stopped past a broken rocking chair. "Is this what you saw?"

Lissa nodded, scooting half a step back.

I inched near trying to see, my skin starting to tingle. "Ah, they're just a bunch of stupid dolls."

"Are they?" Grandpa's voice grew dark. "Are you sure?" He brushed away more webs, picked one up, and handed it to me. "Take a closer look."

It weighed a lot, at least for a doll. The clothes it wore looked real, not like the glued-on scraps from Lissa's Barbies. But it was the head that made my heart catch. I lifted it into the pale light. The face appeared to be made from shriveled flesh, actual human flesh, with a gaping mouth and gouged eyes. Like the ones in my zombie books. Like the mummies we learned about in school.

Grandpa whispered into my ear. "Some might say that's one of your grandma's old apple-head dolls. But who would make a toy from a piece of fruit? So, tell me, is that a doll? Or is it," I felt his breath against my neck, "a shrunken person?"

"Wha-what do you mean?" I could hardly make the words come out.

He splayed his fingers. "What's this stuff all over my hand?"

I swallowed. "Sp-spiderwebs?"

"Wrong!" He ground his teeth. "They're cobwebs. Not spiderwebs." He stared hard into my eyes. "You ever seen a cob?"

My knees trembled, "Like a corn cob?"

"Yes, yes!" He stood and waved his arms about the dimness. "Like a corn cob but old and dried out. Worthless and cast aside. Angry and hurt. You've found them lying in the fields after the crows are done picking at them. What do you think they do at night? Just lay there?"

"I-I-I'm not sure."

"No. They wander about spinning these." He thrust his fingers toward me once again. "Cobwebs!" He cackled. "To trap people, like us. And do you know why?"

I shook my head in a twitching, jerking motion.

Grandpa raised his chin, the distant light catching his nose and brow, making him appear to be an evil monster. "To dry them out like cobs and shrink them down into one of those!" He gestured to the mummified corpse in my hands, laughing deep and sinister.

I screamed, dropping the body as Lissa ran away. I followed right behind.

"What's the matter?" Grandpa called. "You seem a little stressed."

I flailed my way to the ladder, trying to avoid the cobwebs.

# Grant Park

T he evening traffic stalled. I touched-up my faded lipstick in the visor mirror to kill time and adjusted the heated leather seat. I wanted to reach my fiancé in Skokie before the Canadian front spun off Lake Michigan. The cell phone in my purse chirped; I rummaged beneath my handkerchief to answer.

"Maggs, don't hang up. Plea-please. I'm in trouble."

The voice left me cold. "I don't want anything to do with you, Dad."

"Wait. I-I have a baby."

"What?"

"Meet me at Grant Park. I'll explain. Help me, Maggs." The phone clicked into dead air.

The memory of a lonely girl reflected in a frosted window, forever searching an empty driveway, darkened my mind. I couldn't leave any child with that man. I pursed my lips and caught the 290 interchange heading east.

I found him on a bench, an oversized woolen coat draped about a frame wasted and thin. He faced away from the lake, the winds buffeting his back, causing him to recede into the folds of cloth. He sat alone.

I lifted my fur collar in a futile effort to shield myself from the frigid blast. "What's going on?" My breath froze in short bursts. "Is this some kind of morbid joke?" Homeless alcoholics don't travel with babies.

His eyes glazed over, a sheen of water reflecting the arctic sunset. "Maggs, no. I'm trying to get sober."

My mouth shifted into a doubting smirk. "Sure. What do you want?" I raised gloved hands to show I hadn't brought my wallet.

"I don't want nothing from you." He looked toward the dirt, shame in his hollow cheeks, failure in his motion. "I need your help." He lifted the flap of his coat revealing a knot of tattered blankets nestled against his chest. The swaddle wrapped about a pink ski cap covering most of a sleeping face.

"Oh my God!" My voice caught; the breath ripped from me. "Is she yours?" I shuddered, my mind ground by the glacial remembrance of a seventh birthday party when my father never returned.

He shrugged. "She's more mine than not." He shook his head. "Her mama died a couple months back. I promised I'd look after her."

The ache of a fatherless childhood shivered through me. "Wasn't it enough that you screwed up my life?" My eyes flooded. "Fifteen years I waited for you. I won't let you do that to her too. Give her to me!" I lunged forward and grabbed the girl, bundling her close.

He stood; his hands reached toward me as if he were fighting the urge to pull her back. "Me and her mama were like mar-married. We named her Sunny cause she made us feel warm."

He sounded sincere, but I doubted. "So, you just took the baby? You should've told the police." A gust cut through me, and I turned my back to the wind, stepping beside the man who'd abandoned me.

"What do you want from me, Maggs? I-I gotta try to do the right thing at least once, don't I?" He wiped his eyes. "I took Sunny as my own, just like they tell you in your church, right? Feed the orphans. That's what they say, isn't it? Well, I did that. For two months, I gave all I had."

"A kid's more than a short-term commitment. You seem to have trouble remembering that."

He nodded as the corners of his mouth sagged. "You think I don't know that? You think it don't k-kill me to admit I can't do it? Not for you and now not for her? I done my best, but I'm bone dry. You're all I got left to give her."

Sunny kicked in my arms and cried.

He picked up a crumpled grocery bag. "Her bottle and the last diapers are in there." He pressed it into my hand. "And her stuffed rabbit. She likes rabbits. Just like you did." He placed a hand on her legs and smiled. "Don't cry, Funny-Sunny. It's gonna be ok now." He looked at me. "She's getting cold. You gotta go."

There was something wrong about leaving, and I stood motionless among the swirling flurries and decaying leaves.

He took off his overcoat, wrapped it about his daughters, and turned, stepping into the thickening darkness. "It was good to see you again, Maggs."

Sunny snuggled into my arms and I labored to find a thought or action. "Dad!" He stopped in the distant shadows and faced me once again. "Dad. Call me?"

He nodded and disappeared.

## The Shadow

By Purity Snowe

Stained walls flickered sickly,
Neon ghosts, pallid, fleeting.
Faint projections from the brothel
Through the broken window gleaming,
Off the needles and the bottles
Littering the squalid shanty
Where I sold my body cheaply

The shadow of a stranger
Pressed its way in through the doorway.
Standing, staring in the refuse
At the mattress in the corner,
At the filthy sheets and covers,
At the girl by the window
Sitting, waiting for companions

I stood and faced the shadow
Of the stranger in my bedroom.
He who crept in stealthy, sneaking,
Like a dormant seed that sprouted,
Standing, staring in the refuse
Past the mattress and the bed sheets
At the harvest by the window.

A shudder rippled through me,
Sordid murmurs catching, wheezing.

O. W. Maxx

"Put your money on the table."
And I moved to pull the covers,
Making ready for my business
In the night a feverish temptress,
Seeking nothing but a living.

Refractions from the brothel
Red and vicious, slashing, seething,
Filled the room with lust and wanton.
Demon voices laughing, hissing.
"Drop your money on the table.
Let us stain you with her body,
Lock your soul in mortal pleasures."

From the shadow just a whisper
Sad and poignant, rending, weeping
As he reached out toward me softly
And I saw his hands were bleeding.
Wrists and feet were torn and crimson.
Drops of blood upon the rubbish.
And he said, "I've bought you fully."

In my mind a faded yearning
Both ephemeral and yellowed
Of a steeple and a message
Of a girl bent at an altar
And a father's hands enfolded
While a mother's tears flowed freely
For the hopeful prayer that blossomed.

Then the voices from the brothel
Demon accents spat deriding,
"You're not worthy, you're not worthy."
And I turned in shame, in hiding

## Maxx's Well

Toward the fetter in the corner
With the filthy sheets and covers.
Toward that dark, corporeal prison.

There was movement in the chamber
And I feared that he was leaving.
But I felt him move in closer,
Felt his breath of life upon me.
It was on me, o're me, in me,
Swirling fresh and new and mighty.
And I cried out "Oh, please save me."

Shrieked the voices in the neon,
Red and beating from the brothel,
Screamed and howled in foul derision
As they glistened off the needles
And the remnants of my bondage.
But they failed to squelch the newness
In my heart, a gentle beating.

Then the shadow grew and strengthened,
Neon smashed with righteous thunder,
And his bloody hand, the window,
As the sky burst forth with rainfall.
Holy bathed and newly baptized,
Forsake all temporal riches
Prosper ceaseless, everlasting
Sheltered close, redeemed, forgiven.

# Section 2: The Descent

"Time takes it all whether you want it to or not, time takes it all. Time bares it away, and in the end, there is only darkness. Sometimes we find others in that darkness, and sometimes we lose them there again."

Stephen King

"One need not be a chamber to be haunted."

Emily Dickinson, The Complete Poems of Emily Dickinson

# Of Death and Miracles

I could sense that something was wrong.

The teal and white of my house felt as if they'd been dampened with cerulean and gray. I stepped onto the porch. The windows were dark. The knob seemed cold, the door heavy.

I pushed my way inside. My steps echoed on the entry tile.

My luggage sat by the front door; a note stuffed under the handle. I unfolded the paper. The words stung.

"Be gone before I get back. It's over."

I stumbled backward like I'd been punched in the gut. My shoulder struck the mirror, fracturing the glass and sending shards about the floor. A gasp escaped my mouth as my lungs constricted. I felt as if I might pass out.

I staggered down the hallway, my hand against the wall to keep my balance, my gait unsteady as if I'd aged sixty years in an instant.

"Johanna?" My voice was stretched thin like an overburdened rubber band.

I rushed into our bedroom. She wasn't there.

Our wedding picture was on the floor.

My throat burned; I tried to swallow. Heartache swelled within me. My mind flailed about in anger and frustration.

I hurried to the nursery, flipping on the light.

Empty.

The bed was draped with a pink Disney Princess comforter. Cinderella stood on the bureau. A collection of stuffed animals was stacked about the baseboard.

It was just as we'd left it after Chastity died.

I sat on the mattress in the same spot where I'd been less than two years prior.

Johanna had knelt on the floor with Chastity against her breast. We'd brought our daughter home to die. The cancer had already caused its damage. There's only so much a three-year-old body can withstand.

I ran my hand along her cheek, her skin paper thin and translucent. "Mommy and Daddy are here, honey."

Her eyes fluttered open, a distant glaze clouded them as if she'd already passed beyond our reach.

Johanna rocked against the bedside, tears streaming down her cheeks, prayers falling from her quivering mouth. "Hang on, baby." Her voice was a whisper. "God, please. Save her. Take me instead."

Chastity stirred. Faint words drifted from her lips. "Is it ok…" Her voice faltered. "…to go?"

Johanna lifted her, holding her close. "Stay with me. God can do a miracle."

I knew we were past miracles, past God. I reached to my daughter, my emaciated angel. She seemed in such pain. I took her hand, birdlike and frail. "Yes, Chastity, it's ok. You can go now."

For in instant there was a glimmer in her powder blue eyes. The corners of her mouth flickered upward. "I see angels." Then she was still.

Johanna wept. She curled onto the bed, wracked with sobs, the body of our only child tight against her.

I'd run my hand along her arm and tried to assuage her grief.

"You told her to go—" She gasped for air. "There could've been a miracle." Her eyes flashed cold beneath a sheen of tears. "You—" Her words were lost in a guttural moan.

I walked out and called 911.

We'd never spoken of that moment again.

Now I stood, a sense of loss flooded through me. I felt alone. Cut off. Hopeless.

Memories of my wife weeping in the night impaled me. I'd not gone to her. In two years, I never had.

I knew that I'd failed.

Guilt encircled me, an iron belt twisting tighter and tighter. It was hard to breathe. A physical pain pulsed through each nerve ending in my body. I dropped to my knees, my face falling onto Chastity's pillow. "No, no. Please. Not our marriage, too. Don't go. Don't go." I felt lost, cut off, alone. A hollowness grew cold and dark within me.

For the first time, I considered a life without the woman I'd married.

I couldn't stop trembling.

What God has joined together, let no man put asunder. That's what the preacher had said.

No man.

I looked to the ceiling and shook my fist. "I didn't do it, God." I was shouting. "I didn't want Chastity to go." My words stormed out. "She was sick. It's not my fault!"

Johanna thought it was. And that's what mattered. We'd never tried to get past it. Now we never would.

I left the nursery and headed for the front door.

No marriage could survive under the weight of such baggage. It was hopeless.

I picked up my luggage.

The sorrow in our relationship was deep, the wounds seemed mortal.

Could there still be a miracle?

No. I knew we were past miracles, past God. Our marriage had died years before alongside our daughter.

## Maxx's Well

I left through the front door and never looked back.

# El Cristo

The gun had gone off. It was an accident.

A medallion of El Cristo hung from the rearview mirror at the end of a silver chain. The dashboard splashed it with red light. Its polished surfaces reflected the desert moon. Manuel stared. It swung with every turn, each bump in the road. It was his only companion. He felt alone, in more ways than he cared to count.

El Cristo was watching him, he knew.

"Come on, come on!" He swore.

The Rio Grande, and escape, lay ahead. He checked behind, certain that the sky would soon be blazing with red and blue strobes. His foot was to the floor. The engine strained to maintain the pace. A sign blurred in the darkness. Fifteen more miles.

His heart raced; he could scarcely breathe. A cry jerked from his tightened throat.

He had robbed a church. The same church where his mother wept each day. She prayed without ceasing, always for him.

"I ask that El Cristo will humble you in this life, Manuel," she had once said, "so that you can live in the next. You and your gang think you're tough. But you're arrogant and cause nothing but pain. Niño, come pray with me."

He had pushed past her. "La Raza first, mi madre. El Cristo can wait."

When the gun fired, he had shrieked like a child and ran stumbling from the sanctuary. Arrogance had been stripped from him in a muzzle flash.

The tires kicked up gravel along the shoulder. He struggled to regain control. Branches from the sage brush slapped at the windshield like claws grasping for his throat. He swerved back onto the pavement, straddling the center line.

He had dumped the money box onto a table. There wasn't much from the poor congregation. He was searching for more when a hand touched his shoulder. He turned, startled, his muscles tensing. His finger squeezed the trigger. He hadn't meant to. The report was deafening, but not as jarring as the eyes that searched his own.

The exchange lasted no more than an instant. The instant seemed eternal and continued to replay in his mind.

What haunted him most was the sound of his mother's last word. "Niño?" She didn't seem angry, and there was no fear in her voice, no disappointment. Instead her tone was laced with confusion as if she were searching for a last puzzle piece that had somehow slipped away.

Then the bullet had pierced her face.

His eyes stung at the memory, his vision blurring with moisture. "Mi madre, mi madre, mi madre. Lo siento. Lamento mucho." The words choked him, burning as they spilled out. "I'm sorry. It was an accident."

Tears streamed down his cheeks. He swiped at his eyes, trying to shut off the torrent.

His face felt sticky.

He looked at his palm. It was smeared with blood, dark and clotted. He couldn't breathe. He rubbed his forehead, running his hand along his nose. More of the same, streaked and red. He screamed and began to claw at his face with shaking fingers, trying to scrape away his mother's gore.

But he was stained with it, both on his flesh and in his being.

He felt a blackness swallowing him, his soul being dragged into a depth he couldn't fathom. A weight pressed against his mind. "Mi madre! Why were you there? You weren't supposed to be there!"

She wept each day, always for him. "You cause nothing but pain. What will you do in the next life?"

He didn't hear the grating sound of metal shattering the wooden guardrail. The arroyo was one hundred feet deep, the embankment steep and rocky. His world became a tumbling cacophony. But all he could hear was his mother's confused voice, "Niño?" All he could see was El Cristo, flickering in the darkness and reaching for him.

And then there was nothing.

One arm was pinned. The steering wheel pressed into his ribs. Liquid, vile and hot, spilled from his mouth. The medallion of El Cristo swung before him, splashed red from his blood and that of his mother. Its polished surfaces reflected the flames coming through the engine compartment. Manuel stared. El Cristo was calling for him, he knew.

He closed his eyes. He saw himself covered with blood, the blood of El Cristo.

He stretched out his hand and grasped the medallion.

# Jennika

The stuffed teddy bear had a hole in the pink fur along its side. I'd bought it for my only daughter as a birthday gift. It seemed a lifetime ago. I ran my finger over the wound. Pieces of stray thread and white stuffing, ethereal in the clock-light, fell into the blackness of the bedroom.

3:45 AM. I couldn't remember when I'd last slept.

I sat on Jenny's bed, the blankets still smoothed and neat, the pillows fluffed and cold as they'd been for almost three days. Three days. My stomach knotted, and I felt a wave of nausea swell in my throat. I covered my mouth with shaking fingers, stifling a sob as my eyes began to spill.

It was no use. She was everywhere around me. I could feel her, hear her, smell her. I hugged the bear close and wept like a baby.

Pictures strobed through my mind like gunshots in a darkened room. Her torn sweater found behind the library. Drops of blood, spattered near the interstate. Her face, twisted and terrified, crying for help. Her bruised body writhing in pain.

Unthinkable visions that left my flesh as ice.

"Focus on hope—for her," the detective had told us. "Don't let those images in. They'll cripple you."

He was right. I fell and buried my face in the pillow, my body shaking uncontrollably. *This is my fault. I let her go. I should have stayed with her. I didn't even protect my most precious.*

A motion in the doorway caught my attention. The slight plastic-soled footsteps of a small girl with blonde ringlets scraped through the room. She was sucking her thumb, wearing one-piece jammies, pale blue eyes round and wide.

"Daddy?" Her voice was tremulous, unsure.

My heart skipped then pounded. I couldn't breathe. "Jennika?" I wiped my face and sat upright, my back rigid. "Honey, where have you been?" I reached for her. "Is it really you?"

She nodded unsteadily, hair bobbing across apple cheeks. A coarse blue light prickled about her, frigid, distant, threatening. "Daddy, I'm scared."

"Oh, what's the matter, sweetheart? Let me make it better." I motioned her near with open hands.

"Help me, Daddy."

"I will. I promise." I extended my reach as far as I could. "Let me cuddle you."

She spun about, staring out the doorway into the pitch of the house as her mouth gaped. She trembled, knees faltering. "D-daddy?"

A shadow lurched into the room, a pall of foreboding and sin.

I lunged forward, grasping, willing her to come. "I'm here! Daddy's here!" My words were choked and frantic. "Jenny!"

A last glimpse of her, arms stretched, fingers splayed, head bowed.

I couldn't watch and turned away...

...screaming, trying to catch my breath, but I couldn't draw in any air. I blinked, finding my face still buried in the pillow. The room was empty, vacant, hollow.

I was alone.

Raindrops began to ping on the tin roof. Creation wept.

I feared that my beloved was dead. The thought was more than I could bear.

"I'm so sorry, baby." I slumped over, elbows on my knees, hands covering my face.

"Focus on hope," the detective had told us.

"For what?' I'd asked. "That she be violated gently? Murdered quickly?" I pushed past him and stared out into a world racked with evil. A world that had taken my only child.

"Of course not." He placed his hand on my shoulder. "That she'll be returned home."

"Returned home?" I pounded my clenched fist on the sill. "She *is* my home!" My lungs burned and tightened, my eyes narrowing. "Why should I sacrifice my only child to such depravity?" My jaw was trembling. "She belongs here with me. Do you understand?"

"There is a will older and deeper than man's comprehension. A resolve that is beyond us. Jenny has a purpose in life, as do you. Above all else, trust in this."

I nodded. "Easy to believe, impossible to live when my daughter is at stake."

"Good will come."

The rain spattered above me. I picked up the bear once again and kissed it. I did have hope in things unseen. At that moment it was all I had.

The black horizon began to gray and soften. Dawn was beginning to push through the drizzle. A new hope? Or the end of all things?

I knew only that it was beyond my power to decide.

# Santaal and the Wooden Leg

## I

They stood together, she with no eyes and he with a wooden leg, as the shuttle flew away.

"We are fools, Fawlaan," he said. "The two of us. We are." He looked to the sky and the distant stars. "That ship carried your eyes and my leg. Yet here we remain!"

"What more can be made of it?" She took his arm, as she had grown accustomed. "Come. There is gathering to do."

"Bah, gathering what you cannot see and I cannot carry!"

She was the girl with a way of finding coal-spice. Others dug in vain using great machines that scarred the soil. Fawlaan would find it on the surface as if by magic, right in the open. Great nuggets of prized spice. Being sightless, this was a curiosity.

"God gave me eyes, Santaal," she once told him. "He just put them in my nose! I can smell things from a great distance."

He had smiled and patted her head. "Silly young girl," he said. "When you have as many years as me, you'll understand the difference."

He glanced up at the sky, toward the ship that was no longer there, toward the leg that he had found and then lost again. The small hand on his arm squeezed, and he smiled.

## II

His father had scolded him so many years before. "Santaal, don't run in the mines or you'll fall into the grinders and lose your legs! And where would be the good in that?" His father had been half right. When Santaal was eight, he had slipped and lost one leg to the machinery.

"See, I told you! What good will you come to now?" That was all his father would say.

The words stayed fresh for forty-five years.

## III

Santaal and Fawlaan first met at the clinic when the doctors visited. No, neither could be helped. What can be done at a clinic for the blind and lame?

"Have you considered," the doctor asked them, "traveling to Earth where they can replace what you have lost?"

Santaal had not imagined such a thing was even possible. "They can do this? Replace my leg? On Earth they have this ability?" He knocked on the wooden limb as if he were checking to see that it was still there. "I would consider such a trip!

Fawlaan only sat, playing with her ponytail. "What need is there for such a thing?"

Santaal gasped. "But for eyes! Surely this would be worth the journey, child! There is much to see in the world!"

"God has put great images in my mind." She raised her face to them. "He has shown me what the fragrance of the flowers look like, and I can see the sound of the wind in my hair! What more does one need than that?"

"But how do you live? How do you travel?"

"As to the living, there is coal-spice, and to the travel, with the help God provides at that moment."

"Bah! Where's the good in that?"

Again he saw her, that same evening after the doctor dismissed them. She waited for help in order to pass through the stream of trolleys and carts that clogged the thoroughfare. Her smile blossomed as the setting suns painted lavender across her cheeks, and he took to calling her Lilly.

"Greetings again, young Lilly," he had said.

"Santaal. I knew it was you."

"How did you know this?"

"The rhythm of your step on the walk, the scent of your cloak, and the aroma of vegetables you carry for your broth."

"Truly you see better than most!"

"And look," she extended her hand toward him. "Coal-spice, to add more flavor."

"Only if you'll join me in this humble meal. Here, let me help you to cross."

She placed her hand on his arm, and they set off. "Thank you. You are an excellent guide."

"Bah, I can barely walk, yet I excel as a guide?"

"God uses all things for good. Even slow walking."

He laughed as his father's words began to heal.

## IV

The shuttle was gone. They left the launch site together—he, her eyes, and she, his redemption.

"I have this thought in my head, Santaal," she said, "that it is a good thing you have a wooden leg."

"Yes," he agreed. "And to think a sightless girl has taught me to see this thing."

# The Inside Out Bellybutton
### By Veda Rue

T he overwhelming scent of bleach and Windex hovered over the kitchen like smoke even with the windows open. Soap stung the chapped skin crowning her nails as Raelyn scrubbed the cups, plates, and silverware floating in the sink under an icing of foam. Chunks of meals Raelyn couldn't remember making dotted the suds like dog poop in a field of snow.

The counter smashed against her fat stomach, and her back ached from bending the extra inches to reach the dishes. Her stomach burst through the gap between her threadbare leggings and her non-maternity camisole, now stretched so thin her swollen nipples nearly poked holes in the fabric.

But her bellybutton was worse. Raelyn had never thought twice about her bellybutton before the pregnancy, but now it looked like some sort of unnatural, misshapen growth. She always imaged the baby had accidentally pushed it too hard and turned it inside out.

Manasseh sauntered into the room, a dress draped over her elbow and a pair of sandals in her hands. "What about this one?"

Raelyn glanced over her shoulder at the strapless, teal sundress. It was longer than the average sundress, but Raelyn was sure it would fall above her knees now.

"It should be long enough, and it matches these flip flops." Manasseh laid the garment over one of the chairs at the table. "They won't constrict your feet like the boots."

Raelyn dunked an egg crusted frying pan into the sink, and water sloshed over the edge of the counter. It splashed over her already saturated shirt. She felt like a giant bib.

"Are you sure they go?" She asked.

"They're black flip flops." Manasseh said. "They will go with anything."

Sweat drizzled down her neck and shoulder blades. Raelyn could feel it soaking through her pants in a diamond over her tailbone. It must have been really attractive from behind. She imagined being pregnant was similar to being a ninety-year-old, arthritic woman. Every part of her body hurt and even the smallest chores made her exhausted. Now she knew why God or the universe or whatever else made it so old women couldn't give birth. At some point there's just no lower hill to go down.

"What if the weather is bad when they get here?" Raelyn asked.

Manasseh dropped the sandals on the seat of the chair. "The weather won't be bad."

"How do you know?"

Manasseh's voice sang from the hallway as she disappeared back into the bedroom. "Then you can wear the leather jacket you wore to the pumpkin patch last fall."

"Which jacket?"

It was hard to hear Manasseh over the clattering dishes. They slammed against the sides of the sink every time she moved the sponge back and forth. She didn't remember them making so much noise when she used to wash them.

"Do you not own any strapless bras anymore?" Manasseh called from the back room.

Raelyn looked at her sagging breasts. She hadn't worn a bra in close to a month. "Why do I need a strapless bra?"

Manasseh entered the kitchen again, this time with a leather jacket Raelyn had forgotten she owned. "Because it is a strapless dress. Have you thought about your hair yet?"

"What?"

"Your hair." Manasseh said. "How are you going to wear it?"

Raelyn shrugged and tried to remember how she had her hair now. Based on all the loose strands sticking to her forehead, it was most likely twisted up in a day-or-two-old bun. "Like this I guess."

"You're kidding."

Raelyn flung the sponge into the sink. It's hard to look good when there's a five-month-old baby wiggling around in her stomach whenever it damn well pleased.

"All I am worried about," Raelyn said, turning around, "is getting this ultrasound and getting them back on a plane before Sunday."

"Raelyn, that only gives them one day."

"An ultrasound doesn't take that long." Raelyn said.

Manasseh dropped the jacket over the dress then switched the two so the dress was on the top. She patted it, or maybe fluffed it. What the hell is the difference?

"You can wear one of my bras." Manasseh decided after a pause. "I've always been bigger than you."

Raelyn nodded her relenting agreement, eyes drifting from the clothes to the month's worth of groceries piled on the table. The two had been cleaning since Manasseh dropped Luca off at school, but the corners of the living room were still full of clutter—it had been there so long Raelyn didn't know what it was anymore—and the coffee table was covered in buckets of bleach and soaking stovetop.

The parents would arrive the next morning, and Raelyn still hadn't finished the dishes. Things never used to get this bad when Jaxson was around.

Raelyn gestured to the table before turning back to the sink. "Can you find a place for all that food?"

"Did you wash the inside of the pantry?"

Another chore to add to the list. Raelyn's cheeks flushed red with frustration and defense. "Why the hell would I do that?"

"What if they want some cereal?" Manasseh asked. "What if they go to get some and see stale crumbs in the cabinets?"

"So what if they do?" Raelyn snatched the sponge again, flinching from the water she managed to splash in her own face in the process. "Can you just put the food away?"

With the loud rustling of plastic, and Manasseh joined her at the counter, an armload of nacho cheese Doritos balanced under her chin. Those were Raelyn's favorites. After the accident, she could eat an entire bag in one sitting, which she should probably keep to herself if the parents asked about her diet.

Manasseh shoved the bags into an empty cupboard. Raelyn could tell her sister was watching her from the corner of her eye, and the next time Manasseh opened her mouth, her voice changed to that maternal, soothing voice, the way a chocolate milkshake might sound if it spoke to a girl tied up in menstrual knots.

"You should let them stay with you on Sunday."

Raelyn avoided the conversation. "Sundays are my rest days."

Manasseh flicked something—probably one of those stale crumbs, heaven forbid!—out of the cupboard. Now she wasn't making eye contact. Raelyn knew where this way going.

"Don't you rest the other days too?" Manasseh asked.

The action of scrubbing dishes suddenly didn't seem absorbing enough, so Raelyn opened the dishwasher and started loading some dirty dishes that weren't so bad.

"If this is about me getting a job or something, we've already had this conversation—"

"That's not what I meant."

Manasseh put a hand on Raelyn's shoulder, and Raelyn shook it off. She didn't have to turn around to know Manasseh's eyes were dipped in the teardrop drip. It was that understanding, comforting, confident, everything's-going-to-be-all-right look that Raelyn had witnessed being used to perfection whenever Luca had a scraped knee or a bad dream. They always fixed any of Luca's problems, a little kiss from mommy and anything was better.

They didn't work during the funeral though. Raelyn had a lot of bad dreams then. Manasseh had kissed and comforted her then. And they didn't make a single ounce of difference. The pain was always still there.

"Sunday's not a bad day." Manasseh said. "You've had a lot of Sundays to yourself now. Maybe you should start opening it up again."

Raelyn dropped dishes in the dishwasher as fast as she could. She dropped plates where the cups went and Tupperware where the pots where supposed to go. "I can keep to myself as long as I want."

"You probably shouldn't though."

Sometimes Raelyn still had the dreams. She would wake up in the night to see his stiff, purple body next to her in bed. She would look into his eyes, and they wouldn't look back. Then she would scream a few times and wake up for real.

Raelyn told Manasseh about it once, but she didn't mention it again this time.

Manasseh walked back to the table and returned carrying two boxes of peanut butter filled pretzels, the kind from Costco. Those had been Jaxson's favorite snacks, but though they always looked good on the store shelf, they never seemed appetizing after she bought them.

"We could put some of these out in that nice bowl from grandmother." Manasseh suggested, checking the expiration dates. "You know, the depression glass one?"

Raelyn shrugged. "Maybe."

Manasseh took it upon herself to rummage through other cupboards in search of the bowl. "I'm not sure if they will be able to get a returning flight that quickly. Besides, they are going to be tired."

Raelyn dug through the remaining dishes to gather all the silverware. She nicked her thumb on a black handled knife, and the soap made the cut sting.

"It's my house. If I say I only want them one night, then—"

"You put it up for adoption. It's their baby Raelyn." Manasseh interrupted. "They have a right to stay with it for longer than a day."

"It's not going anywhere." Raelyn said. "Hell, it's not even doing anything."

"It's their baby."

"And they'll get it when it comes out."

Manasseh closed the cupboard doors and gave up on her search. She walked back to the table, picked up a few things, and put them back down again. "It's been four months."

Raelyn blinked the sour pinch from the corners of her eyes and crammed more dishes in the overflowing dishwasher so Manasseh wouldn't see her face. "I know it's been four months."

"Then maybe you should let them stay." Manasseh grabbed the broom from its spot on the couch. "I'm going to finish the guest room."

When she left, Raelyn stopped loading the dishes. She poked her bellybutton hard, wishing it would pop back inside her the way it used to be. But it stuck straight out. It stuck out as she listened to Manasseh banging the broom against the baseboards. It stuck out as Raelyn removed the excess dishes from the dishwasher.

It stuck out.

Raelyn cupped her palm over it to make the throbbing stop.

But it was too late. Even when her bellybutton popped back in, it would never go back to the way it was before.

# Rhamadi

For a terrifying instant, there was no sound. A puff of smoke behind a low brick wall flipped a mental switch—then nothing—only the rending grate of my own breathing.

From the plume, an incoming RPG. The metal tip glinted orange, reflecting a sunset tinted with dust scorched in the Iraqi desert. At 170 meters, we had less than two seconds.

My world flickered and slowed like a nickelodeon movie that slipped off its reel.

I tracked the flight path, calculating its trajectory from the launch position beneath a silhouetted minaret to the point of our squad. The fatigue in my muscles evaporated, and I tensed, ready to dive into cover.

But I hesitated.

Danny was covering point.

*Danny.*

He'd run track with me in high school and kept on me about practice until we both made state finals senior year; he'd given up a full scholarship at UCLA to work his way through Fresno State with me; he'd held me for ten minutes when I proposed to his sister, tears of joy soaking my sweatshirt.

*Danny...*

He'd led me to Christ the day after my mother died of cervical cancer.

A vulture circled above the flaming maw of Rhamadi. The grenade streaked over the sand, a gray trail of burned propellant stretching behind like yarn pulled taught from a tangled skein. Its path was true, direct, deadly.

I couldn't, wouldn't, accept the inevitable.

I staggered toward him, running as if under water with a full pack. My movements encumbered, dull, despite the thunder in my chest. He hadn't seen, didn't know.

*Danny!*

He had a child, eight months old. Purity. Golden ringlets already. Her father's eyes, bright with laughter. He'd never met her. Only the pictures. Our deployment was ending in three weeks when my own daughter was due. We'd wanted to raise them as sisters.

I drew a breath, filling my lungs, and tried to shout a warning. But my throat constricted behind drawing lips, the lone sound of a muffled scream that dribbled through my mind like wet cotton.

Movements beside, Gunny was gesturing, fingers pointing as the squad began to disperse. They raised weapons, taking aim as they tumbled away...

...from Danny who turned, face twisted, mouth gaping.

*Valley of the shadow—valley of the shadow—valley of the shadow.* The words spit in machinegun rounds, cutting me as deeply as any wound—*of death.*

The cocoon of silence was breached by a rising growl, fierce and ominous. The rocket bore in, flaming red, a foreshadowing of the flesh it was about to consume.

"Danny!" I screamed, and the full tumult of chaos broke over me, Gunny barking orders, the clatter of armaments being readied, the press of breath as bodies fell to the dirt seeking shelter.

And Danny's eyes, wide, searching, staring at me.

I dropped my M-16 and hurtled toward him, my shoulder making impact with his chest in mid-leap. Concussive heat seared my back and legs as we toppled into a ditch.

Danny rolled my twitching frame off of him, shouting for a medic amid a scene that transfigured to black and white—and red. He stood by my boot, sodden with gore, in the center of the road while the crackle of return fire faded into whispers.

*The Lord is my shepherd—the Lord is my shepherd—the Lord is my shepherd.*

Darkness covered me as Danny knelt and held my hand.

# The Hieroglyphs

J effrey-Francis, he insisted we use his hyphenated name, bothered me. His wagging finger and religious tongue were a constant insult. I'd endured him as best I could. But at the convention, he'd gone too far. No forgiveness; I wanted slow revenge.

I held the anthropology chair at the University of Nevada. It was my duty to host the annual gathering of my colleagues. Jeffrey-Francis represented Aureate Christian where he was noted as having a weakness for ancient hieroglyphs.

Ten years I'd worked on my treatise of man. Ten years preparing to reshape my field. At the brink of success, he bettered me. Presented first, claiming Divine revelation. Revelation indeed! He'd stolen my research.

I'd found him in the lobby after hours. "Congratulations on your win." I said, my smile sincere despite the loathing in my breast.

"Bless you." He glanced to the floor and dipped his face but couldn't mask a prideful gleam. "God has rewarded me for unending work with widows and countless days of service at church."

I blanched at his tone. "Have you seen Barnard?"

He turned about, chin raised above a puffed chest. "He was ill. I think lunch didn't rest easy."

I'd dined with poor Barnard and knew this. "A shame. I need his opinion on some newly discovered hieroglyphs."

"Hieroglyphs?"

"An entire wall."

A swallow bobbed his throat. "Miracle! May I help?"

"No, no." I waved my hand at the milling crowd. "Stay and enjoy your well-deserved triumph. There'll be other finds."

His lips parted, tongue flicking. "It's my calling, my ministry. Barnard is sick." He clasped my arm. "Take me."

The corners of my mouth quivered. I leaned close, my voice conspiratorial. "Tell no one. There are thieves…"

Mt. Charleston is pocked with holes: silver mines, burial sites, and bottomless shafts. We tramped through sage, our lanterns illuminating the indistinguishable path.

I stopped and glanced back. "You told no one?"

He zipped his coat. "Virgin hieroglyphs. God may grant me another win with this find."

My jaw clenched. "Indeed."

I led him into the maw of the cave, the depth of the passage swallowing our feeble beams. The footfalls behind me stumbled and slowed. "Your claustrophobia," I said, turning. "I'd forgotten."

He was pale, pupils trembling, a labored wheeze in his throat. "We each bear a cross." He retrieved an inhaler from his pocket. "Asthma. The dust."

"And guilt, no doubt." I approached him. "I'm certain Barnard..."

He shoved past me. "Barnard doesn't know hieroglyphs from crayons."

I smirked.

Darkness constricted about us. Stalactites dripped wet and frigid like bleeding teeth. Swallowed by gloom, the only sound to reach my ears was the scraping of my companion's increasingly labored breaths.

Hesitating, I studied him. Jeffrey-Francis strangled his lantern beneath crossed arms like a child holding a teddy bear during a thunderstorm. Pathetic, feeble. I slumped against the boulders, tugging at my hair with uncertain fingers, questioning the plans I'd put into play.

"It gets tighter below. We'll have to crawl."

He shivered.

I touched him, doubt beginning to grip me. "No, I must take you out. To the hospital."

The fool pushed on. It was his choice, not mine.

Granite and quartz pressed tight about us. When the way could shrink no further, it narrowed still until an opening no larger than a ferret's nest stared like the eye of death.

I grabbed him, misgivings now fully ravaging my spirit. "Wait, this is meaningless, vanity. You've widows, church, service to God—"

"Let me be."

"You don't understand." I hung my head, conflicted. "There's nothing."

His mouth opened and closed.

"Friend, forgive me." I wept as guilt took hold. "Let's return."

He ground his teeth. "Liar. You want it all for yourself!"

"No!"

"God loves—" he squinted at the passage ahead. "—me." He wielded his sanctimony, a piercing spear.

"Is this obedience or lust?" My temples thundered and the malignance in my soul returned.

He looked away.

I released him.

Lying on his belly, he slithered through the cavity and into the pitch.

He stood, fingers tracing the ridges of the blank walls as I came in behind. A chain had been hidden in the tiny chamber, cleated to the rock. I locked it about his neck.

He turned, not comprehending. "The hieroglyphs?"

"Yes, a wall." Returning to the passageway, I left him.

From inside, a shriek and the rattling of chains, frenzied and incoherent.

I began to roll a boulder across the opening.

A noise, the steady sob of a tormented spirit, dripped along the floor. "A wall?"

Then silence.

The stone shifted into place.

"For the love of God!" His cry was severed as the passage disappeared.

"Or lack thereof."

# At 3:00 AM

### By Purity Snowe

I t isn't just the darkness...
At 3:00 AM, it's the resounding emptiness.
An errant creak in the basement,
the smell of stale alcohol in my sweat,
another faceless man in bed beside me.
I ache alone as shadows claw the window.
And there is no end, there is no end.

It isn't just the loneliness...
At 3:00 AM, it's the eternity till dawn.
Memories of a sordid past constrict about me,
Shameful choices that won't stay buried
beneath shallow parties, lethal drugs and empty sex.
I tremble, ashamed, as guilt condemns.
And there is no end, there is no end.

It isn't just the shame...
At 3:00 AM, it's the powerlessness.
The throbbing whispers of self-doubt,
the certainty that death is swallowing me,
the demonic laughter echoing from the distant borders of
awareness.
I weep in despair as flames consume.
And there is no end, there is no end.

## Maxx's Well

It isn't just the desperation...
At 3:00 AM, it's the ancient promise.
A pathway crooked and steep
leading up, away, through the desolate wilderness,
to a land of milk and honey.
I remember, and a flutter of hope tickles my breast.
And there is no end, there is no end.

# A Fitful Sky

"I-I think I love you. I know, it's crazy, makes no sense," Quin said, brow creased and shoulders hunched in an apologetic shrug. He motioned along the length of his frame. "I mean, there's not much to offer here."

Cossey touched fingers to her lips, eyes sheened with moisture. She placed her empty wine glass on the barrel-wood table next to his, the serenade of a sparrow falling gentle from the redwood trees surrounding the courtyard.

"I love you, too." She leaned against him, tracing his cheek with her nails. "More than I can say."

The sun flickered as clouds moved in. The broken sky smudged an overcast grey across the rich brown of her wide gaze, dimming the spark in her eyes and the heady promise of her words.

"But I can't. I shouldn't." She stiffened, shifting her stare past him, to the horizon and beyond, as if she could see an approaching storm.

He inched away from her across their shared wicker seat. He recognized she couldn't, and probably didn't, care about him, at least not how he hoped. It was the way of things. The natural order where the strong prospered, and guys like him, well, they never ended up with girls like Cossey.

"I understand," he conceded. "Of course not."

"No, it's not you. I do love you." She trembled. "It's Brett."

Brett. Quin grew up with him. Everybody in their little town did. But even if they all lived in a metropolis, Brett was the type people wanted to know, wanted to remember. Tall, educated, and well liked. He'd been beating Quin at everything their entire lives. Brett was preordained for grander accomplishments, and everyone knew it.

Quin slumped forward.

When Cossey's parents died, Brett's family took her in for the final years until graduation. Cossey and Brett were stars in their own private galaxy, inseparable. They performed the leading roles in school plays, sang duets in church choir, and lettered at track. They dated, as expected. Perfectly destined for each other.

"He'll never let me go."

"Yeah, I figured."

"He hates to lose."

"He does it so rarely." Quin pinched the ridge of his nose. "Kind of an acquired taste."

The corners of her mouth dipped as the afternoon darkened.

"Can't you just tell him it's over?"

"Brett? Seriously?" She shook her head. "No. It's not that easy."

"Why not?"

"You do remember we're engaged, right?" The wind rushed from across the grassy hills in a chilling gust, tugging at the strands of brunette hair looped behind her ears. "I'm on his list of expected achievements. Carved in stone."

"But if you're unhappy..." Quin hesitated, studying her.

She looked away.

"He does know you're unhappy, right?"

She glanced to the dirt beneath their settee.

Concern prickled the nape of his neck. He paused, feet and fingers suddenly cold.

The blush of her cheeks began to fade.

"Cossey, you do," he choked on the words, "you do want to leave him, right?"

She crossed her arms, pulling the seams of her wrap tightly against the deepening chill. "It's just that," her voice faded to a whisper. "He's all I've known. He's my whole identity, all I'm ever asked about. My friends, family." She sighed with a catching shiver. "He's been there, woven into everything, with me."

"But you were only kids."

"And these feelings now with you. I don't understand them. They're beautiful, but they seem wrong."

He straightened. "How so?"

"I mean, I'm engaged. Committed."

"You feel guilty? What we have kind of," he shrugged, "happened. It's organic. Is that so terrible?"

"The church, my friends, what would they say?"

"Maybe that we all get to choose our own path. Follow our own calling."

"Do we?" Finality tinged her words.

"Are you saying you're trapped?"

"I don't know. Or it might be familiar, comfortable."

Quin felt a weight begin to press on his mind as the edges of his consciousness frayed. "But you love me." He drew out the syllables in a slow lament.

"I-I," she stammered, shaking her head.

"Look, I don't blame you. I haven't amounted to anything, probably never will. I want you to be happy, and if that's with Brett, then I can't compete. I won't." He began to stand. "I should go. I'm so sorry."

"No, wait." She grasped his hand.

"You'll be better off without me."

"Stop it." Her voice became crisp. "I feel hurt when you talk that way." She drew him near again, softening her smile. "You are smart and strong, thoughtful and gentle." She kissed his cheek. "You have a beautiful soul."

He smirked, skeptical, even as reassuring warmth began swirling deep within as if he'd swallowed hot cocoa on a frigid winter morning.

"I'm telling the truth. And I love you."

Quin sat closer, their legs touching, the aroma of her lavender perfume an intoxicant. "And Brett?"

"I'm confused."

"Do you really love me? I want to believe, I do."

"Yes." She caressed his palm. "Yes, I do." She nuzzled his fingers. "It's just, maybe him, too, but in a different way. I mean, where would he go? What would he do? I don't want to hurt him. I don't want to be…" She stopped, speech strangled and murky.

"What? What is it?"

"Quin, I'm afraid."

"Of him?" He moved his arm around her shoulders, cuddling her against his chest.

"No, of being alone." She shuddered.

"I'm here."

"But are you? Here, I mean? For how long? Are you available to me? Forever?"

He flinched, almost imperceptibly, but not quite. A lifetime of doubts doesn't fade easily. But her voice was calming, her touch healing, her words strengthening.

"I could lose everything, everyone." Tears clung to her lashes.

Could he be there for her? A budding possibility stirred inside. "You won't."

"Alone, forever. I can't take that risk."

"No, no risk." His voice grew in confidence, the warmth returning to his spirit. "We will build a relationship, a life, together."

She didn't respond.

"I can be…" He swallowed. "I will be there. I do love you."

"Even if your family doesn't accept me?"

Quin tried to cuddle her, but she pulled away. "Shhh. How could they not? You're altogether lovely."

Cossey wrung her hands, fingers entwined like knotted yarn. "I wish I could believe that."

"You can. We can, together."

She leaned fully against him.

He refilled their glasses from the nearly empty bottle. "Cossey," he handed her the wine, a welcome spark of sun catching the golden liquid, igniting into a luminous explosion. For an instant, it seemed all things were possible. "What do you want?"

Cossey clasped the crystal stem between her thumb and fingers as the momentary hope was lost again to a fitful sky. Her countenance darkened. "I don't know. I'm so sorry. I want to, I do. But I—" A sob choked her quavering voice. "I just can't."

Quin turned away.

# A Fool's Hope

**H**ave you seen it? The night advancing in a long dark line. Breaking over your hurried defenses like an invading horde as your mind abandons the high ground and cringes alone in the shallow crags.

Have you seen it? Your reflection fading behind palls of seething smoke which claw your charred timbers and consume your disheveled foundation. The mirror cracks and shatters as you disappear in a swirl of torment.

Have you seen it? Your body bartering away your soul for a clutch of magic beans. Trading everything you thought you were for the futile chance to grasp everything you've ever wanted. But it's always only been a flawed and desperate fantasy.

Have you seen it? Advancing darkness, consuming fires, a fool's hope?

I have.

# Section 3: Outer Darkness

"Now this is the point. You fancy me mad. Madmen know nothing.
But you should have seen me. You should have seen how wisely I
proceeded..."

Edgar Allan Poe, The Tell-Tale Heart

"Stranger than you dreamt it
Can you even dare to look?
Or bear to think of me?
This loathsome gargoyle, who burns in hell
But secretly yearns for heaven
Secretly... secretly

Fear can turn to love—you'll learn to see
To find the man behind the monster
This repulsive carcass, who seems a beast
But secretly dreams of beauty
Secretly... secretly"

Andrew Lloyd-Webber, Stranger Than You Dreamt It

# The City Below

The winter sun fell through the sheer drapes, casting fleurettes on the dining room wall with the muted rays of evening. I arranged the table with four settings, Dad, Mom, Jimmy, and me, taking the chipped plate for myself though it usually went to my brother.

The air in the room felt thick.

Mom carried in the bowls of vegetables and potatoes. "Shana, bring the rolls, please," she prompted, straightening the silverware.

I didn't want to. I wasn't at all hungry.

Dad lit the dinner candles, asked the blessing, and scooped a serving of carrots. "Tonight I'll be finishing the bid on that downtown project." His face glowed with satisfaction.

The corner of Jimmy's mouth dipped, and his brow creased for an instant. He had to help with the materials list.

"Again? You work too much." Mom used her exasperated voice, but admiration sparkled across approving eyes.

"It's not work if you're having fun, right Jimmy?"

My older brother shrugged and poked at his salad.

"Ok, you guys, but not too late."

"Hey, one man's jail is another man's joy." Dad motioned for the pot roast. "I happen to love my job. So does my future partner over there."

Jimmy didn't look up. I knew why.

"Is that brown sugar in these veggies? Wonderful."

Mom blushed.

"Did you hear the Hopkins girl died Friday night?" Mom dabbed her chin with a napkin. "A deliberate overdose. Only 17."

I'd heard. She was in my calculus class.

Jimmy set his fork down.

"Is that why they missed church today?" Dad swallowed a mouthful of wine. "They live up in the estates. Well off. Makes no sense."

I pushed a cut of meat through a smudge of gravy and studied Jimmy. He stared past the window to the city lights beginning to flicker in the encroaching dim.

Dad reached across the table, snatched a roll, and glanced at me. "Remember when you and the Hopkins girl got stuck in the bounce house?"

I didn't.

"Don't forget, I made apple pie for dessert," Mom reminded. "Jimmy, weren't you talking with her after church last Sunday?"

He didn't seem to hear.

"Jimmy?"

"Michelle," Jimmy whispered.

Mom cocked her head.

"Her name was Michelle."

"Yes, of course. A lovely girl." Mom smiled.

"You never talked to her."

I had seen them kissing in the park when they thought nobody was around. I watched Michelle doodling hearts in her notebook during lectures. I overheard them making plans behind the sanctuary.

My stomach hurt.

Jimmy tossed his napkin. "I'm leaving."

"Not so fast. You hardly touched a single bite," Mom scolded.

Jimmy shook his head. "I earned enough credits to graduate, my finals are done, and I'm 18. I'm leaving home."

He said it. I'd hoped he wouldn't. I dropped my spoon, sending it careening to the floor.

Dad leaned over his plate. "What's this about?"

Jimmy raised his palms and gestured to the table, the paintings on the wall, and the construction truck in the driveway. "This is all you, not me."

"No, it is you," Dad said. "This house, our family, our business plans. This is your future. Your inheritance."

Jimmy grimaced. "I was just a kid. How could I make plans? I'd rather..."

"Relax," Dad interrupted. "You're still too young to be making these decisions. There's a lot you don't appreciate."

Jimmy's lips thinned.

"Think things through. You'll find yourself a girl, get married, settle down. Give it a little time."

Mom stood. "Who's ready for pie?"

Jimmy turned away. "Don't you understand? I had one."

"Before dinner?" Mom chided. "You ate a piece before dinner?"

"No, Mom, please."

"I was like you at your age. You see the world out there," Dad pointed to the city below, "and you want to run after it. But everything you need to be content is right here."

Jimmy combed determined fingers through his dark hair and paced the length of the room. "How can I explain when you don't listen? You taught me to speak, but you never learned to pay attention." His voice rose to a shout. "I'm an adult, damn it! How about treating me like one for a change?"

"You don't realize what you're saying."

"I had a girl. Michelle." Jimmy's voice cracked. "We were supposed to leave, be married. But her cruel parents didn't care. Just like you, they didn't listen! They said no, wouldn't let her be with me. So," he smudged his cheek with a balled fist, "she took her own life."

Mom gasped. "Oh honey, I didn't know."

"You don't know a lot of things, like what's important to me, what makes me happy." He turned toward the door. "And that's why I have to go away."

My eyes burned as heated tears began to spill. "Jimmy?"

He placed his hand on my shoulder. "I'm sorry, Shana."

# Good Sailing

By Curtis Layne

O f the things my aunt said before she died, I most remember that which came at the end, on that dry day when the curtains were full of light and she lay half up in the bed with the covers pushed down around her from the heat. She saw me at the door.

"What're you bringing in here?" she said.

I had just brought in her ice water and a few of the blue ices wrapped in paper towels to set before the fan, all this on a tray.

"Do you want your water?" I said. I left the tray on the dresser and brought her the glass.

She stared at me. "What're you bringing in here?"

"Have some water," I said. I tilted the glass close to her mouth, and she pulled forward to meet it, her lips tight and flaky. She didn't take more than a sip. A trickle. It would dry out halfway through her, I thought.

Her head fell back, and she pursed her lips a few times to get the cold out. Half up, leaned against the wall like she was, you almost thought she was in the middle of something and would get to her feet in a minute to finish. You almost thought she would sit forward and pick up this or that or blink and turn her head and stare at you.

My husband Dale and I had kept an eye on her all summer. She had come back from hospice with no more money from the house sale and nowhere else to go. I saw this as an opportunity. I was determined I would make everything right for her. I would make up for everything.

We set her up in the downstairs bedroom, and every day I brought her ice water and supplement drinks and tried to keep her comfortable. Now and then she said things. Most often she didn't.

On that last day, when Aunt May spoke, she spoke at an angle with her mouth upturned to the lit corner of the room above the window.

"I saw something get in," she said. "Today. I saw it."

I put the glass on her nightstand with all the other things we had put there. I sat on the chair. "In here?"

"I did," she replied. "I saw it pass the window twice. Then it came in."

"Want me to close the window?" I asked. I thought this was a bad idea, with the heat and all.

"No. No. It's got to stay open. I want to see what comes in to cut me down."

That was the first of the things she said that stuck with me. I was not alarmed by it on account of I knew it wasn't her so much as the medication that said it. And you can oblige a dying aunt that much, I figured. You can oblige her the right to say what's on her mind.

I sat beside her and rubbed her arm while the fan spun on the dresser top and she stared up at that lit corner. I figured I would listen until she had said all she wanted to say.

"It's not an accident," she said. "Would be wrong to treat it like one."

I tried to guess what she was talking about. "You mean, being sick?" I hoped it wasn't that. I wasn't ready to go back and forth about that.

"I mean it, yes. I mean all of this. Anything's an accident if you let it be." She pursed her lips. "But I won't."

I wondered if she wanted more water, but I didn't ask.

Aunt May blinked. "The woods. Look at the woods. No one planted the woods."

I followed her gaze up to the angle of sunlight in the corner. I thought maybe the room was too dark for her. Maybe I should have opened the drapes.

"But," she said, "if you want to think someone planted them, you can. You can think that. You wouldn't cut down a tree you thought belonged to someone."

"That's a good way to think of it, Aunt May," I said. "You should rest." I wanted her to stop talking. Every word out of her mouth came like a sack of wet flour, like something bulky and thick. She had to wrestle with each one. I doubted it was good for her.

Aunt May coughed and took a breath that rattled around in her bones. "We had a place in the woods up at Eel Rock," she continued. "The old house. This was before your father was born. Anyhow. The trees there were cold all year. You could touch them in the sun, press against them, and catch the cold seeping out."

I caught sight of her tongue between her lips and knew her mouth was dry. I lifted the glass of water, but she kept on.

"I saw elk lick them in the shade. There were herds of elk there. Your uncle John swore he saw a moose, though I guess a moose would've had to come a long way." She turned her head to face me. "Do you think it matters?"

"What?"

"The woods. What way they cut them down."

I chose my words. "I don't know."

She turned away again. "I guess we get to choose," she said. "I suspect we do. I always believed..."

She stopped and leaned forward. She looked around the room and blinked.

"What is it?" I asked.

"Oh," she said. She sounded confused. "Oh my. I thought I saw something in the room again."

This gave me a chill. I tried to spot the bug or crawler or whatever she had seen. I saw nothing. I laid the blame for it on the medication and settled in my chair. She had some roses set up on the sill, and the light came around them and made them like black hands or stick figures against the white drapes, all splayed out and open. I thought about the roses. I thought about all the ways we had made her comfortable.

Dale hadn't seen it the same way I had.

"She gets Social Security," he had said when I brought it up to him over breakfast in late spring. "That's more than you or I'll be able to say, you know."

"She can't live on that," I said. "Not with the medication." I couldn't believe him—that he would even make an issue of it.

We ate without saying anything. I knew he was thinking what I was thinking—that certain uncles and aunts and cousins and such would start to call each other on the phone again, maybe, if we did something like this. They might start to visit. This would be a great accomplishment.

Dale looked at me. "You're determined," he said.

"I'm determined."

He wiped his chin with his napkin and sat back. "We can make it work."

I sat with Aunt May most every day in the months that followed, and she said more on that last day than on any other. I think this is why it stuck with me. Her voice was unfamiliar, and in this way, it was unforgettable.

"The trees came right down to the bay," she said. "Humboldt Bay. That's a sailor's bay, you know. When your boat came up to the shore the trees would bend over you like praying hands." She licked her dry lips. "Do you pray?"

"Sometimes," I said. "Aunt May, you should rest. You've said a lot."

She blinked again, then closed her eyes. "Yes," she said. "I guess we get to choose."

Her head fell back. She inhaled, and again I thought it would crumble her into pieces. Each breath was a shaky, fragile thing. Her face had an ashy color, like old, thin snow.

I rubbed her arm. It felt cold. I thought I could feel the cold coming out of her.

"Aunt May," I said.

"Yes?"

"Nothing. Nothing, I guess."

"Oh." She laid her head back.

I got up and placed the blue ices in front of the fan. I tilted it so it blew into the corners of the room and not across her face. I wanted her to be comfortable.

When I turned to sit beside her again, her eyes were locked on the window. I looked. There was nothing there but a line of sunlight from around the drapes.

"Oh," she sighed. "It's in the room again." She closed her eyes.

"What is?" I asked. "What's in the room?"

She stared for a long minute. "Can't say," she said. Her head fell back against the pillow, and her eyes closed, but not in a peaceful way. Her brow furrowed.

"Aunt May? Are you all right?"

I'm not sure she heard me. She didn't answer my question, anyhow. She just mumbled one more thing, a final thing, and when she said it, her voice came out soft, almost not there.

"I don't know what it is," she said.

# On Hampshire Grade

My right eye throbbed and wouldn't open as an electric pain radiated through my jaw and sinus. I blinked grime from my left, squinting through the shattered windshield to the refracted beams of headlights. Particles of dust, caught in eddies of heated air from the stalled engine, circled about like miniature buzzards above dying prey. The dimly illuminated underbrush beyond grew thick and foreboding.

Had I been driving? I couldn't remember. Oh, yes, to Unger. No, wait. To Ridge. Home.

The seatbelts gouged my hips and shoulder. I groaned involuntarily when trying to right my body. Waves of vertigo spun me. I became disoriented as I realized I hung upside down. My car somehow flipped, and I found myself helpless in the West Virginia mountains.

The night sagged inky and dark. I'd left Martinsburg after midnight.

I struggled to reach the buckle but could scarcely move. Nausea gripped me as I noticed my right arm, grossly splayed, swollen, and bleeding.

I was trapped.

I gulped a mouthful of air, forcing back the wave of panic threatening to swamp my thoughts.

Help? No. I wouldn't be missed in Ridge—the house sat cold and vacant.

Had I been shopping? I recalled eating a salad, no, a ham sandwich, then filling the tank.

Gas. I filled the tank with gas.

I smelled fumes, dripping, leaking fumes. It was only a matter of time before...

"Oh God, no!" My breaths came rapid against grinding ribs. "Not like this. Not like this!"

I screamed, shrill and bestial until my lungs constricted, and I began spitting blood.

Nobody came. I remained alone.

Or did I?

An image flashed across my shredded memory. A face, young like Tommy's had been, turning toward me, washed by the bluish hues of a slouching autumn moon, eyes wide, mouth agape, hand raising in a futile attempt to stop...

Stop what?

...The car. My car. Speeding around a hairpin turn on Hampshire Grade.

"No. Not true," I scolded. But my vision shifted toward the circular impact on the windshield. I gasped.

I didn't see. There wasn't time.

"You hit a deer." My whispered voice pleaded. "Only a deer."

Did I?

The engine pinged and hissed as a tentacle of smoke began to escape through the wheel well.

"Get out!" My thoughts became frantic. "Get out of here!"

I swung my left arm to the buckle but froze. Those were the same words I'd shouted at Tommy. A mother's not supposed to talk that way to her son. Not when he's just graduated. Not when he's leaving home.

"Not when they're the last words you said to him." I trembled. It had been almost three years.

He'd died after a fall in the Blueridge Mountains, landing on a boulder, fracturing his spine. Alone. The coroner said it took days.

"Oh, Tommy," I sobbed. "You must have been so scared. And I wasn't there."

I pressed the button on the safety belt and fell, my head crashing against the roof of the car. My world darkened.

The image, the young face, flickered anew, moment by moment, frame by frame. Eyes, so terrified. Hood hanging loose over strands of blond hair. Rucksack slipping from his athletic shoulder. Hand raised, trying to push me away. Mouth gaping in a scream—a curdling, petrified shriek as if every evil thing in hell materialized and began charging toward him through the desolate night.

I'd spun the wheel, hit the brakes hard, tried to avoid him. But then came the sickening impact as the vehicle slid and flipped.

I willed my way back to consciousness, away from the frightened apparition. I started coughing again as the car roiled with acrid black smoke.

"No, no!" I cried. "Move! You won't die alone!"

I fumbled for the door latch and pushed. The metal scraped against gravel as I forced it open a few meager inches.

Flames licked about the floorboard above me.

I clawed my way through the opening as heat singed my flesh.

I stumbled to my feet, bent and dizzy. "You won't die alone. Not tonight. Dear God, please."

I staggered along the wayside toward where the first shards of glass lay scattered.

A crumpled rucksack sat near a gash in the underbrush where something had been hurtled in. I heard a weak moan in the darkness.

I held my breath and stepped through the broken hazelnut branches. "You won't die alone. I promise. I'm here."

# The Anniversary Gift

I

I fumbled about the mounds of papers and folders strewn across my desktop in search of the historical import trends from Southeast Asia over the prior fifty years. My eyes were parched from hours of research and felt as if each capillary pulsated in its own distinct rhythm. It had been a trying day. Orland had allowed me to use company time to finish my MBA thesis project, but I was struggling to make headway. My graduation had been delayed three times already. Orland had presented me with a private office, two doors down from his, in what was supposed to be a promotion to celebrate the long-awaited event. Instead, I was four days shy of having to suspend it for yet another semester. I wasn't going to allow that to happen.

"Jesse?" I was startled by the voice and looked up. Sandy smiled down at me, her teeth gleaming behind painted lips. "I knocked, but I guess you didn't hear me. Orland told me to throw you out of here on time today. You're already ten minutes late. Are you trying to get me in trouble, mister?" She had an infectious way of making every event be about her.

"What time is it?" I swiveled my head in search of my desk clock but realized it was buried beneath reams of market reports and old hamburger wrappers. My brain was rattled; there was no possible way it was quitting time already.

"It's now 4:11," she said, glancing at her watch in mock annoyance. "You've got to go!"

I cocked my head to the side and considered her news. Had I even taken a lunch break? How could that many hours have passed? I ran my hand across my face and back over my ear. Had I even finished one thing on my to-do list? I ground my teeth together as I rolled my head from side to side and groaned. I had wasted an entire day.

"Thanks, Sandy, I owe you one."

I stood and moved around the burnished walnut desk. My legs were stiff from a day of sitting and I bumped against a stack of folders sending them and their contents scattering across the carpet in a confused mess.

I knelt down to the jumble and began to straighten the pages back into their proper order. Sandy, too, stepped across the floor, removed her high-heeled shoes and squatted opposite me to help. I could feel my temples beginning to throb as I realized that two months' worth of organization was in total chaos.

"Each page has a header to match the folder it belongs in," I explained while examining a handful of documents. "Then each folder is divided by year and region. Make sense?"

I looked toward Sandy who was concentrating on a particular pile of paper. The skirt she was wearing, short even by college intern standards, had ridden far up her legs. Her thighs were firm and athletic, smooth and tanned. From my position I could not help but notice that she had chosen to wear cherry red panties, lacey and sheer. My eyes locked on the vision and my words faltered.

She seemed not to notice my inadvertent fascination. Instead, as she continued her straightening, each movement brought her private beauty more and more into view. I inched closer to her; mindless that I had placed my knee on top of the very papers I was to be picking up. I could feel the heat radiating from her and the cloud of lilacs and vanilla that emanated from her skin were like a narcotic to me. My pulse strengthened and sped as my neck beaded with sweat.

"Do you want me to do it?" she asked, her voice dangerous and near.

"Yes," I replied as my mind envisioned pressing her back onto the carpet. "Yes, that'd be great." I allowed my eyes to scan the rest of her form.

Sandy, however, remained busy at her work; evidently unaware of the impact her position had on me.

"You need to get out of here or Orland is going to kill me! I will do it, you just go!" Her eyes met mine, and she flashed an innocent smile. Then, swinging a folder at me, she swatted my arm as if shooing me toward the exit.

"Ok, ok, I'm going," I said, "no need to get physical." I retrieved my coat and was halfway out the door, my mind beginning to click through my calendar for the balance of the day, when I stopped cold. The reason that I needed to leave on time sprang to life in my brain. "Oh, that's just great."

"What's the matter?"

I looked back at Sandy, still gathering my papers, "Today is my anniversary. That is why I was supposed to leave on time." She stared at me, seeming to not understand my problem. "I worked right through lunch," I said. "I was supposed to go out and buy my wife a gift."

I pulled the watch from my pocket, checked the time, and swore. There was no way I would ever get to the store and home without ruining whatever Amber had planned.

"What are you going to do?"

My mind was blank. "I don't know. I guess just run to Sears and grab whatever I can find." I paused, calculating the damage I would do by showing up empty handed. "I've got to get something."

Sandy stood and approached me. "Wait. If you just run in and buy any old thing, you'll either end up with a vacuum cleaner or a negligee."

The choices seemed logical to me, but she laughed and rolled her eyes beneath the mascara on her lashes. "You goof," she said, "you don't want to buy her a lame gift, do you?"

I shrugged. "So, what do you, as a woman, suggest?"

Her face glowed with a pride that I hadn't yet seen, and she looked as if she was about to burst. It dawned on me that, at a mere twenty years of age, she might never have been addressed in public as a woman before. It seemed that she appreciated the acknowledgement. She raised her mouth into a captivating white smile and skittered barefoot across the carpet toward me.

"I have an idea. Does your wife wear perfume?"

I had to stop and think about the answer. "Yes," I paused, considering, "at least before the baby came."

I couldn't remember if Amber had worn perfume since Misty had been born over a year prior. My hand rubbed the back of my neck as I struggled to isolate a memory.

Sandy moved close in front of me, her body near. "Do you like my fragrance?"

I stood confused and paralyzed, as if a professor had just announced a pop quiz. I didn't move or respond but instead sensed my mouth going dry as I felt her tempting me.

"Can you smell it?" Her eyes were the lightest shade of blue I had seen, almost to the point of having no color at all. They were large and round and seemed to hold a wonder and excitement about things. They were looking at me. "Maybe it has worn off a little. Sniff my neck." She reached up and placed her hand on the back of my head and began to lower it toward her. "It's ok. I won't bite."

My hands moved to her hips out of reflex as my face descended to her ear. I could feel her nails, polished and smooth moving in small circles along the nape of my neck. She inched tighter to me as I inhaled her fragrance in a slow, deep draught. It swelled inside of me like a rising tide and I closed my eyes, wallowing in it.

I exhaled, aware of my breath hot against her neck. Her body shuddered between my hands. She stepped away, her smile a bit richer. "What do you think? Do you like it?"

"Uh, yea, sure," I was stammering for the second time in a few moments. "It's great." I wasn't sure where she was going with her demonstration, but the ride was more than intriguing.

She bounced on her toes and clapped her hands in front of her mouth. "I knew you would!" She bounded out of my office toward her desk a few cubicles away. "Wait right there." She vanished behind the maroon partitions before reappearing seconds later with a golden box in her hand. "It's called L'Extrait de Vanille et Lilas de Fleur. It's French! I have a brand-new bottle. Here!" She returned to my office, box proffered.

I was taken aback by her gesture. "I can't take your perfume. That's crazy."

"Seriously, Jesse, please." Her eyes were awash with sincerity as she pushed the box toward me with greater insistence. "My parents buy it for me all the time. And I haven't used this bottle at all. It's from Macy's."

I wasn't convinced. I wrestled with the basic concept of giving another woman's perfume to my wife on our anniversary. Something about it seemed dirty at the core. "I don't know..."

"You don't have time to argue," she insisted, taking my hand in hers and placing the box in it. "Now get out of here and have a good evening."

"Ok," I hesitated, "but I'll buy you a replacement."

I headed to the exit, feeling like I was strapped into a rollercoaster going up the first big hill, knowing a steep drop awaited. Sandy beamed and waved from my office as the elevator door closed.

## II

The apartment was quiet as I entered a darkness that I hadn't anticipated. The drapes were pulled, giving the impression of late night instead of early evening. I stepped in; my eyes wide in an effort to see as I edged my way around the unseen furniture. I flipped the switch and was surprised by the lack of results. A faint flickering caressed the walls; the source of the light was the dining area a few steps away. Following the glow, I found our table filled with a dozen candles, each with a finger of fire inviting me nearer, their luminance magnified by crystal, china, and silver we had received on our wedding day and only used on the rarest of occasions.

"Amber?" I called toward the blackened bedroom door.

There was no response, and it appeared that neither Amber nor Misty was home. I returned my attention to the table alight before me in search of a note or an explanation, but there was none.

The sound of a match being struck startled me from behind. I spun about; a new light was building from the sofa in the living room that I had just stumbled through, delicate hands clasping a flaming candlestick.

"I was wondering if you were going to make it home on time." Amber's voice was smooth and full, like hot rum and whipping cream. Her dark eyes, black in the dimness, reflected a smoldering radiance.

I had taken two steps toward her before I realized I was moving. I stopped and glanced once again to the bedroom, straining to hear any sounds.

"Is Misty asleep?" I asked, hoping that the answer was yes.

"Millicent's with Mom and Dad," she said, emphasizing our daughter's given name then waiting as if considering her words. Raising her eyebrows into a suggestive arc, she continued, "for the night."

Amber reclined on the sofa, the candle gracing her features and causing her skin to glow. Her hair spilled across her shoulders and neck in wisps of highlighted auburn, a vision of perfection. The shirt that she was wearing belonged to me and was draped about her, the buttons unfastened down to her navel. It appeared to be all that covered her.

I sat beside her, laying my coat on the coffee table and smoothing my hand across her rounded hips. She reached for me, running her fingers through my hair and pulling my head down to hers. I kissed her waiting lips, and she held me there.

"Happy sixth anniversary," she said as I moved my mouth to her neck and ear.

"It is, now that I am here with you," I whispered against her skin, and she giggled as my heated breath tickled her.

"I just want to make it special for you tonight."

"Mmmm, I won't complain. But why?" I moved my hand along her thighs, the hormones in my body making my speech heavy and slurred.

"I don't think I thank you enough for everything you do." Her hands moved along my shoulder blades, her fingers kneading into my tired muscles. "You are finishing up your degree plus working a full-time job all so I can stay home with the baby. I am very lucky to have you."

I kissed her shoulder in a light movement and mumbled, my voice barely audible, "I'm feeling fairly lucky, too, right about now."

"I think you deserve some gratitude." She arched her body and pressed herself against me. "So tonight, I plan on saying thanks," she circled her hips beneath my hand, and her voice became throaty, "a lot."

Closing her eyes, she inhaled and moved as if to kiss me once again. She froze in mid-motion, however, as her eyes roused themselves from their sultry distance. Her hands pushed me away and she scooted into a seated position. "You didn't, did you?"

My confusion was apparent, and she continued with little more than a quick breath. "I can smell it! It's all over you!" She looked at me once again with growing expectation. "Did you think you could hide it?" A sheen of doubt sprinkled itself about her, and her lips alternated between questioning and smiling.

The memory of Sandy's perfumed body pressed against me thundered across the horizon of my brain and I blushed. "Wha—what do you mean?" I turned my face from her as guilt percolated to the surface of my mind.

"Don't be embarrassed, just tell me! Did you buy me a little something?"

I reached to my coat and pulled the golden box of perfume, Sandy's perfume, from the pocket. She took it from me before I even had a chance to offer. She bounced like a schoolgirl on a trampoline as she opened it.

"Oh, Jesse, you did! You did! You shouldn't have! L'Extrait de Vanille et Lilas de Fleur! It even sounds perfect!" She opened the bottle as if she were handling a sacred relic and rubbed the applicator against her neck and wrists. "This is perfect, just perfect! This stuff costs a fortune! All my friends want it! They will be so jealous! What made you think of it? Oh, I love you!"

Her gaze moved from the bottle back to me once again, delight still sparking her motions. "I have something for you, too." Her eyes shifted to the shirt she wore. "But you'll have to unwrap it."

My breath caught in mid-inhalation as my fingers raced to her covering and began to wrestle with the buttons, but I was too eager to make them work. Instead, I grabbed each side of the garment and pulled, sending the recalcitrant plastic disks scattering about the room.

Amber laughed with delight at my zealousness and lifted her hips from beneath the remaining cloth. "I picked it out today, just for you!" She looked at me, lips parted and hungry. "You like it?"

My eyes locked onto the cherry-red cloth minimally covering her body. She had chosen panties made of sheer lace and now lay before me wearing nothing but. Amber pulled me to her and began to remove my shirt and tie. My nostrils filled with the aroma of lilac and vanilla, and the perversity of the situation struck me. She moved her nails in circles about the nape of my neck as our bodies joined and her breath rolled in complete contentment.

However, in my mind there was no satisfaction. I could see only eyes of the lightest shade of blue, to the point of having no color at all, and they were looking at me.

# Under the East River

I tasted blood that wasn't mine and found it to be like cocaine.

I became an addict.

The tunnel was black and smelled of mildew and rot. I had to drag the girl most of the distance. She wouldn't walk. My foot slipped into the gutter; mud sopped my shoes. I swore and shouldered open the rusted service door, pushing her inside.

She stumbled away from me until her back pressed against the opposite wall. The rats scurrying about her feet made her squirm to the corner.

"What? You don't like my place? Not as nice as your sorority?"

I threw the breaker, lighting the bulb. Her eyes were wide with panic behind strands of blond hair.

She whimpered, helpless and pathetic. She reeked of fear. I owned her.

I bolted the door.

The overhead pipes were slick and black with moisture from the East River above. I ducked beneath them and stepped toward her. She turned away and slid to the floor in a cowering crouch, her torn jeans pressed against her cleavage. I leaned over her and yanked the tape from her mouth.

She screamed.

I shook the tape in her face. "Do you want me to put this back on? Do you?" She blinked and tears spilled down her cheeks like a torrent. "I didn't think so. Just the same, we'll leave your hands bound until you settle down." I felt power swell within me. "I'm your whole world right now. Nobody comes here. Nobody can hear you."

"Don't hurt me. Please. Please. Don't hurt me..." Her voice faltered.

I laughed. "I wouldn't put money on that; but maybe if you begged."

She rolled her head from me, her expression twisted and trembling, blood dripping from her torn lips. She spoke in a muttered jumble. "Oh God, oh God, oh God."

"God?" I watched the rodents stare from the drain holes in the floor. "You really think God's going to come down here to save you?" I waved my hand toward the graffiti streaked walls. "This is my temple. You'd be better off praying to me."

Her eyes tracked my smallest movement. I was everything.

"What are you going to do with me?"

I stood over her and leaned down, grabbing the hair on both sides of her head. I lifted until her eyes were inches from mine. "I take whatever I want, and nobody can stop me." Flecks of my spittle peppered her face and mixed with her tears. "Are you afraid?"

She nodded in short spastic motions, her voice a constricted whisper. "Yes."

"Afraid to die?" I craved her broken submission.

"No. Not death." She inhaled and raised her chin.

Defiance? I opened my knife and held the blade to her throat. "Then what?"

She shuddered, her face pale and drained. "Just of what you'll do."

I slammed her against the wall and stepped away, kicking her legs as I moved. "Liar. Everyone's afraid to die."

She cried out on impact and crumpled in a heap. "No, I hope for more." Her breath was jagged and sharp. "There's more after this." She swallowed. "After you're done. There's more for me."

My fingers twitched, and I forced them through my hair. A fire raged in my gut; the pulse in my neck pounded. "You think I don't know what you're talking about? I know more than you. I've seen your churches. You all believe that God is so powerful, that everything works for good, that you get to go to heaven when you're dead." I spit on the ground by her face. "Then how do you explain me? Did God tell you to walk home alone tonight? Did he plan for you to be here?"

She seemed unsure, confused.

"Answer me!"

She sat herself back up. "It'll work for good."

"I'm not part of any plan. I make the plans." I was overcome with hatred toward the girl. "What possible good will come of this?"

She raised her eyes to mine and held them there, a new softness replaced the terror. "God loves you." She spoke the words as if her entire life existed simply to utter them at that moment in time.

I fell backward and crashed against the door. It felt like I had been hit.

My vision clouded then turned red. A grain of doubt took root. I pushed it aside and glared at the girl.

She closed her eyes and seemed at peace.

# The Prize

### By J. Gilligan

**N**ot long now. He could see the light at the end of the tunnel. His legs pounded through layers of ooze. Mud covered his body. His heart thundered, and not only from exertion.

The end was getting closer. Almost there.

His desperate footfalls failed to muffle the sounds of his pursuer. Or, perhaps, more than one. He, or they, were gaining, fast. Too fast.

He wished he had someone to help him, but they were gone. Killed, dragged off—or worse.

He was alone.

That's why his need to escape the maze and find the weapon was so strong. To save them. To save everybody.

Shouts, right behind him. Maybe one or two.

He could handle that. Maybe even three or four if he could wield the armament fast enough. But he had to get through first.

He pushed harder.

Only. A. Few. More. Steps.

He burst into the light.

Laying his hand on the prize, he turned to face his enemy.

And they were legion.

# A Letter from Dad

Cuddles:

I'm sorry baby girl. I know I kind of dropped a bombshell on the phone the other night. Who am I kidding? That was a nuclear detonation. Nobody ever wants a conversation like that, especially with their dad. Things kind of went south when we were talking. I didn't mean to make you cry, so I thought I'd try to do a better job of answering your questions here via email.

First, yes, I got a second and third and fourth opinion. I've spoken with the oncology teams at Johns Hopkins and Sloan Kettering. I'm still trying to get in down at the Mayo Clinic. Also, Dr. Hardaway sent my records to a friend of his out at Stanford. The best money can buy.

So far, they all agree it's inoperable. At the current rate of growth, we are looking at a few more months at best. With chemo and radiation, they think maybe we stretch that out to a year. But only if I'm extremely lucky. I'm the guy who has cancer, I'd say that's conclusive evidence that I don't attract good luck. They're still determining if I am stage three or four, but I have so many other markers, it really doesn't affect the prognosis. It's spreading so very fast. The first biopsy was inconclusive, so I am having a second one tomorrow. Plus, I'm sure there will be plenty of sticks, pokes, and prods after that. I'm really not sure of the point, though.

I'm sorry I've only got this one life to give you. I know your college graduation is coming. I'll be there, even if only in spirit.

Second, no, there is no need for you to come here. I can still get myself around fine, at least for the foreseeable future. They want me to have five rounds of chemo over the next 10 weeks. I'd have to spend a couple of nights in the hospital each time. But I don't think I'm going to do it. I have a couple months. Why spend it throwing up? I'm just going to keep working like usual. To know I'm still needed, that I still have some value.

I know my body will deteriorate. It's a physical certainty. I'm being eaten alive by this thing. You being here would not change that fact. Stay in school and graduate on time. Missing a semester will set you back years. With your Pfizer internship coming up this summer, there is no logical reason to derail things. I need you to be strong, to power through, even when it gets ugly for me.

Finally, no, I haven't told Katie or your mother. And I would rather not, at least not yet. Katie is your sister but you two are nothing alike. She is in no state to handle the news, assuming she would take my call. It would just be one more excuse to go on another drugged-out bender. We'd lose track of her for months again. If she resurfaced it would be long after I'm gone. Let me die with a clear conscience on that front. I don't want to be the reason she overdoses, or worse.

As for your mother, I don't know. Even after all this time, things are still so very tense. Maybe they are meant to be. I think about our life together, those years of marriage. We were a hot, passionate pair! But it all went so wrong. I'll never understand what happened. But I'm not interested in any of that awkward faux sympathy. When she served me with those papers, she pretty much made clear where she stands. So, no. I don't want to tell her or see her or talk to her. I don't want to be forced to endure her gloating as I slowly rot away. Please respect my wishes on this.

I just realized I will never meet any of my future grandkids should you ever find Mr. Wonderful and become a mother. How very sad! But you will be an awesome mommy one day!

My life has been a mess, no doubt. Much of it is my own fault, but some of it was dumped on me. Somehow out of all the crap that constantly buried me, you sprouted like a dazzling flower. There are so many bad things I didn't deserve. You, though, are an absolutely wonderful thing that I didn't deserve either. I think God, or the Universe, or Amazon, or whoever sent you into my life must have switched up the shipping label or something! You are definitely too good, too smart, and too beautiful to ever be a part of my life. That said, I'm so glad you are, even in these final days.

Love always.

~Dad

# The Breakup

"**I** can't take this anymore."

Jenny's clipped words hung like icicles in a January storm. Her slate eyes, narrowed to stiletto blades, slashed across the shadowed room.

"I want a—"

Ezra flinched. "Be careful," he interrupted, pointing a mulish finger at his wife. "Once you say something, it can never be unsaid."

"Careful? Me?" Jenny cinched her arms, tucking balled fists inside the long sleeves of her oversized cardigan. "You're the one who treats me like something you stepped in."

"That's such BS."

"Is it?" Her voice tightened and came in angry puffs. "You never talk to me, the two of us, alone. Like we used to."

Ezra waved his hands, gesturing to the living room. "I don't see anybody else here. And it sure sounds like we're talking."

Jenny's face darkened around thinning lips. "You know exactly what I mean."

He tossed the remote to the sofa. "I have no freaking idea."

"Don't go there. You can be such a prick." She brushed moisture from her cheeks.

Ezra's jaw clenched, and his shoulders squared. "What are you talking about? I was just standing here, and you walked in."

"That's right, I walked in. From a full day of work, a couple jobs—"

"I work hard, too. The granary is no office picnic."

"—walked in and all you can do is ask for a beer." Her voice caught as she swallowed a sob.

Ezra thrust his palms up in an exaggerated shrug, fingers curved like claws. "Are you serious right now? You said you'd pick some up on the way home."

"Well, I screwed up. Forgot, ok?"

"Perfect. The game's about to start, and I got nothing to enjoy with it again."

Jenny snatched a pillow from the chair and threw it. "It's not always about you, not about you!" Her tone became choked and taut, like a piano wire stretched to the breaking point. "I live here, too. This was supposed to be our life together, not me flitting around struggling to fill in the blanks of yours."

He pointed again, ominous and foreboding, framing his threatening glare. "I dropped out of college so you could finish your worthless degree. Don't tell me you're filling in my blanks."

"I never asked you to do that. You said you loved me, wanted to make my dreams come true."

"An English major, for God's sake. Now you're surprised the only jobs you can find are waiting tables and answering phones?"

"And writing!"

"Garbage."

Jenny's mouth gaped, a string of saliva stretching between her teeth. She stared. "I'm trying." Her nose began to run. "I'm trying to make something of myself."

"And me? I haul around 200-pound sacks of grain all day. For what? To be neglected in my own house?" He combed his fingers through dirty hair, muscles bulging beneath his t-shirt. "My job's hell, and I sure don't need this when I come home."

"If you'd bothered to ask, you'd know my day wasn't so peachy either."

"What, you broke a nail on the keyboard? Poor baby."

She pressed her fingertips into her temples. "I really hate you sometimes."

He turned to retrieve the remote. "Whatever."

"Mr. Anderson made a pass at me today in the supply room."

Ezra froze.

"Grabbed my waist and tried to kiss me."

He blinked, studying his wife. "We need that job. To cover rent and your student loans."

"You son of a—" she gasped. "You want me to sleep with him, too?"

"I just want to drink a beer in peace and watch the game without all this."

"Find your own beer, you pig. I'm not your personal barmaid."

"Don't get all sanctimonious on me. You worked in a bar. That's where we met, where you tried to seduce half the offensive line swishing your super tight sorority shorts."

Jenny rushed forward. "I hate you. I hate you!" She swung her hand, slapping Ezra, leaving a red welt under his two-day stubble.

He grasped her wrists, driving her down to the cushions. "I don't need this. I sure as hell don't need you." He stormed toward the door. "I'm going to O'Malley's to catch the game."

She sat, arms crossed, cheeks wet. "I can't take this anymore." Her words cracked and shattered, eyes swollen and resigned. "I want a divorce."

## The House on Bolgia Lane (Malebolge)
### By Purity Snowe

Dimly blinked the room in which she waited
Waited for a thing she never knew
Overwhelmed by memories she hated
Hated as the darkness in her grew
Until malignant whispers started calling
Promising the end to all her pain
Dante's eighth was all about her, falling
Falling in the house on Bolgia Lane

Fading colors shriveled as they perished
Perished for the want of being seen
Abandoned for the silhouettes she cherished
Cherished by a heart no longer clean
As shadowed suitors plotted her destruction
Forging links in her eternal chain
Virgil's dying words were her seduction
Seduction at the house on Bolgia Lane

Daylight faltered as the night contested
Contested to control what she perceived
Self-righteously indignant she protested
Protested, cursing every gift received
Goading laughter drove her on in madness
Each successive loss an evil gain
The three beasts multiplied her sadness
Sadness for the house on Bolgia Lane

# Maxx's Well

The fabric of the structure tore and shifted
Shifted to expose a path to Hell
Unmoored, with her anchor lost, she drifted
Drifted until through the rift she fell
Clutching hosts awoke with arms extended
Welcoming her to their foul domain
Malacoda grinned as she descended
Descended from the house on Bolgia Lane

The crags about the ninth pit seemed familiar
Familiar as her tepid point of view
Embracing fate, she knew the depths had filled her
Filled her with a need to disapprove
Too late she saw the demons cleave and sever
Sever her tormented bone and vein
The ghastly swordsman slashed as she forever
Forever lost the house on Bolgia Lane

# The Man at the End of the Warf

A man, stooped with age, tottered above unknown waters cold and deep
on creaking timbers of flaking periwinkle.
He cinched his threadbare sweatshirt, faint comfort against the swirling mist
which slithered about and seemingly through him.
Tendrils of grey matching his hair and wrap
causing him to appear translucent.

He lifted his eyes to the blanketed sun setting unseen beyond a horizon which wasn't there.
With trembling fingers, he reached out as if hoping, needing.
He bowed withered lips, abandoning his entreaty.
Shadows obscured the disenchanted wrinkles furrowing his shrunken visage.
His charcoal frame waivered, shrouded, separate, alone.
He removed his sweatshirt
and vanished.

# Section 4: The Ragged Edge

"But I am a worm and not a man.
I am scorned and despised by all!"

Psalms 22:6, New Living Translation

"The strongest trees are rooted in the dark places of the earth.
Darkness will be your cloak, your shield, your mother's milk. Darkness
will make you strong."

George R.R. Martin, A Dance with Dragons

# Scenes from my Window

Decades of grime encrust the corners and edges of the ancient windowpane, resembling the vignette frame of an 1860 black and white photograph. Charcoal clouds roil in layers above crumbling facades, like a furious watercolor of a whirlpool in a sea of India ink. Tired brownstones, sullied and weathered from a century of exhaust and road salt, reach pensive from the scarred sidewalk four stories below like beseeching fingers toward an unresponsive heaven. Hats, hoods, and umbrellas shuffle around soggy litter, urine stains, and sagging cardboard shanties of the homeless, vanishing behind melancholy doors and plate glass, ignoring the first scattered drops of icy rain. I shudder. A slender man in running shoes stumbles toward a final tenuous ray from the diminishing sun, which falls almost translucent against a graffiti streaked wall.

The staccato clatter of gunshots punctuates the threatening rumble of encroaching thunder, angry curses hurtled by rebellious man and a livid God. Red and blue strobes scar the bricks and plaster like spatters of blood from an as-yet-to-be-selected victim. I choke on the curdling uncertainty of who might be next. Traffic lights blink and flash in dots and dashes as if signaling a secret code, sending a message that is never understood, begging for a response that is never acknowledged. Members of the waning conflux stare through each other, lost in solitary images of thickening shadows and unfeeling hours. The skeletal man sinks to the pavement, knees sopped in a gutter spilling dirty brown water. He smears wet eyes with muddy palms.

# Maxx's Well

The stench of overflowing dumpsters and moldering excrement seeps through withered insulation in viscous, frigid undulations. Sheets of rain fall, uncaring, drenching both the just and the unjust, meting out haphazard retribution with wanton turmoil. Empty busses creep like drowning slugs, unfulfilled in their sodden tracking of disinclined passengers. Horns blare, crying into the void, hearing nothing. The remnant hunkers against stiffening gusts, trudging around darkened buildings and through moribund alleyways, they become silhouettes and ghosts, none looking back. The running man inches toward the horizon, searching the distance with weeping eyes in a desperate pursuit of the broken sky. I smudge my tearstained cheeks.

# The Cataclysm

By D. Eshara

I splashed water on my face and sighed deeply. My body felt run down and tired after everything that had been happening. The sink was full now. I turned off the water and drearily stared at my reflection. I took a deep breath and plunged my face in it. The water felt cool, nice and refreshing—much better than simply splashing my face. I stood up and grabbed the towel, running it over my eyes.

When I saw my reflection in the mirror, I was surprised by my pale skin and the dark rings around my eyes. It looked like I'd crawled out of my own grave. My hair was unkempt and dirty, and my beard was getting too long. I didn't have time to shave it. I shook my head and left the bathroom, dreading the meeting I was going to.

I pushed open the door and saw the long line of people waiting to use the restroom. We didn't have many down here.

As I walked past the soldiers, I noticed most of them were covered in scrapes, bruises, and bandages. We were not going to last. If we didn't get a reprieve soon, our defense would fall, and they would win.

I should have been at the meeting a few minutes ago.

I turned left at the hall junction. The underground facility felt claustrophobic, and the walls seemed to close in on me. Humans were never supposed to be underground for this long.

# Maxx's Well

The nauseating smell of necrotic flesh hit me before I approached the infirmary. I glanced in and closed my eyes in shame. So many soldiers were in here—most of them terminally injured or sick. The bodies were covered in blood and feces. Flies buzzed everywhere, and maggots clawed their way into the corpses. We simply didn't have the manpower left to help these poor souls or even move the dead bodies. And, unlike the great hero Tamie, I couldn't use healing magic. I just couldn't be of service to these people.

I heard shouting before I even reached the room. Tamethera and Zelda must be going at it. Again. I pushed the door open and closed it quickly behind me, tapping it and applying a sound-proofing enchantment before taking my place at the long oak table.

"If you hadn't shown up, everything would have been fine!" Tamethera shouted.

I gritted my teeth, knowing where this was going.

"You know that's bullshit! Even if I had stayed in the Tomb of Kings, you would have still been hit just as hard here!" Zelda retorted.

I let them argue. It was pretty funny watching two ancient robots going at it like this. An idea was playing in the back of my head, but I didn't want to acknowledge it yet. There had to be another way.

"Ladies, come on. Now isn't the time to argue," the Trellion sitting opposite me tried to interject.

"Shut up!" they both yelled at him.

This was really starting to annoy me.

"It's your fault!" Tamethera growled.

"That's it! If we are applying faults, it is yours, not mine! You were out there in the galaxy when the Coalizione first attacked! You had every chance to deal with it before they grew to this big of a threat! But did you? No! You did not!" Zelda reminded me of what I can only assume Tamie was like.

"Listen up, both of you!" I slammed my fist into the table, making a loud cracking sound and breaking it into three pieces. That shut them up. "If we keep arguing between each other like this, we will all be dead in a few hours! Can we please get back on topic?"

Zelda shot Tamethera a dirty look and held her hand out, an earth circle appearing on her palm. The table picked itself back up and put itself together. As the two continued to glare at each other, the Trellion looked at me hopelessly, and I shrugged. His species was the only one left that wasn't human. He was essentially a tall, humanoid being emitting a purple glow. They were extremely good at energy manipulation. Although not as strong as human magic, the Trellion could use it longer.

"Look, we only have two or three more days left to live. Are we really going to spend it arguing about who's at fault?" I asked.

"Well, what else do we have to talk about?" Tamethera asked, looking at me dead in my eyes with her arms crossed.

Her face always made me shiver. She had been designed to look like the great fallen hero Tamie, but Gretho had somehow screwed up. With what was left of her human-like skin, she looked like a mirrored version of Tamie, different hair and eye colors and a few other strange design choices. Half her face, and I can only assume half her body, was just her metallic skeleton and muscle fibers.

"You called this meeting." She said. "Why are we here?"

"I have an idea. I really didn't want to think about it, but we have no other choice," I said.

I held out my hand, palm up, and summoned the cataclysm circle. Its yellow and orange glow felt ominous every time I looked at it. This one wasn't like other circles. There were no runes for control or power. Instead, in the center of this circle, there were two fern-looking branches forming an X.

"Using the cataclysm? Are you sure? Even Tamie never used it," Zelda said.

I nodded.

"What other options do we have?"

"Are you kidding?" the Trellion stammered. "That spell will kill us all!"

"Yes, I understand it will, but we have to defend the Clock. If they figure out how to use it, they could rewind time in the universe and keep building themselves up until they are an unbeatable force, or they could kill us all before we even evolve. There are any number of things that could happen if they took control. We absolutely can't let that happen," I replied.

Stunned silence filled the room.

"Will this great cataclysm even work?" The Trellion asked.

I shrugged. "It is our only option. Our last big cannon. If our amplifier pushes the spell to the boundary of sol, the black hole will take care of the rest. How do I know? It was designed to assist us magicians in using magic. Zelda, I'm sure that Tamie told you about Crystal, right?"

She nodded.

"Let's do it then. We have to tell everyone," The Trellion said.

I nodded in agreement. "Tamethera, call an assembly. It's time we told the troops—"

A large shockwave shook the room, cutting me off and making me stumble.

"They're attacking again!" Zelda said.

She recovered a lot faster than I did since she was a combat robot.

"Tamethera, forget the assembly. Go gather the troops at the doors and activate our defenses. We need to push them back! Zelda, round up a group of twenty mages who know how to use the cataclysm and get to the amplifier room. We need to start this immediately!"

They ran off with their orders.

"I gotta say, Stone, you really are something else in terms of leadership," the Trellion said as he floated toward me. I had forgotten they don't walk.

I nodded. "Thanks, but we can't stay here either," I said as I walked over to the command console, pressing a few buttons and sending the alarms blaring throughout the facility. "We need to get to the front lines as well."

We left the room and sprinted through the knotted hallways until we got to the entrance. There were no longer doors, only a gaping hole to the outside. My troops were arriving quickly and getting into a defensive position, the gun wielding soldiers in the front and the mages in the back.

The first alien in the Coalizione scurried through the door, observing our defenses. One shot to the head and it went down. It howled as it died, and a cacophony of noises responded to the creatures dying howls.

A swarm of mismatched beings of all different shapes, sizes, and race rushed through the door, screaming. This was their normal tactic. They would initially rush the target and empty them of ammo. Once we were useless, the stronger and better armed soldiers came through, mowing down anything that moved.

It was my turn now.

I hovered in the air just above the defensive line. I only had a few seconds before they hit us. Taking a deep breath in concentration, I held out both my arms and shot two beams of shadow energy at the enemy. It cleaved through them easily, and I cleared the room fast. I aimed outside to see if I could hit anything else, maintaining it for about five more seconds before stopping.

I landed on the ground, and that was when they returned fire.

Waves of enemy bullets and lasers peppered the stronghold circles the mages put up as soon as my feet touched the ground. Dark energy barreled through the entrance and slammed into the strongholds. I froze for a second as five more dark energy attacks joined the first.

"Everyone duck!" I shouted as the strongholds cracked and shattered, sending bits of feathery matter fluttering around us.

The two mages who were maintaining the spells screamed in pain and fell to the ground. I looked back at the entrance, gathering more energy and taking a few steps forward as my soldiers got back up and took aim. Six figures walked into view, and I summoned a darkness sword, getting into a ready stance.

These aliens were different from the rest. They each had robotic limbs, old and crude looking, as if they got their implants centuries ago. One resembled a dragon and another had similar features to a fish here on earth.

Without hesitating, they jumped at me. Everything felt as if it was going in slow motion. The dragon summoned a huge ball of blue energy in her right hand while the fish darted around toward my back. The other four split up, some jumped into the air and others charged at me from the side.

I wouldn't be able to deal with them all at once.

The soldiers were emptying clip after clip, but it wasn't effective against these strange aliens. The bullets shattered against their magic shields. I gathered energy and slammed my foot onto the ground, expelling all my stored-up power in a simple yet effective repulse move.

The aliens lost their footing. I knew one was behind me, and I spun around, grabbing the flying body with one of my shadows before he had a chance to hit my soldiers. I pulled him close to me and swung my sword, cleaving the alien in two. I heard screams coming from behind me, and I spun around again, building energy for a shield.

Before I could cast it, the dragon's ball of energy slammed into my chest. I stumbled backward, gasping for breath, but before I could regain my balance, I felt a sharp pain in my right leg.

Crying out, I blindly swung my sword. The blow didn't hit, but the man who attacked me retreated. I stumbled to catch my footing, using my sword as a prop.

"Pull back!" Tamethera shouted. "Were compromised! Get to the amplifier room!"

The enemy soldiers streamed into the room, shooting anything that moved. The dragon threw another attack at me, but before it hit a stronghold circle appeared in front of me.

"Get moving!" Tamethera yelled at me.

I nodded my understanding as I followed my troops. Her circle disappeared as she started sprinting down the hall. I stumbled after her, using fire to cauterize my wound. The pain was unbearable, but if I stopped they would surely overtake me. I had to keep moving. As I half ran, half stumbled toward our amplifier, I glanced back. There had been several branches behind me, and the aliens had filled every one.

As I got closer to the amplifier room, I could hear the sounds of fighting already. Damn. I was too late. Some of the faster aliens had managed to get there before me.

I dispelled my sword and gathered power in my hand. I turned the final corner and took a quick look at the scene. There was a small group of about fifty Coalizione attacking the survivors. Thankfully, they were close enough that I could take them all down quickly. I dashed forward and attacked, my shadow springing from the ground and combining with the power in my right palm. It shot out like a bullet from a shotgun, splitting up and slicing through all fifty enemies.

I limped in as Zelda shut the door behind me.

"You're late Stone. We thought you were dead," she said.

"I'm sorry, but I could only go so fast with my leg as it is," I replied.

"What happened to your—"

"Never mind that," I interrupted. "How long until we can cast the spell?"

I looked around the room. I had never seen a scene like this before. Twenty mages had the cataclysm spell out and were channeling everything into the catalyst, which was in the center of the room. A strong wind pulled toward it, like a sucking vortex.

"Hopefully as soon as possible," Tamethera said. "If they attack again, we can't hold them."

She was right. There were only about three hundred of us left, and everyone looked battered and bruised.

"Only a few more minutes," Zelda said, glancing at me. "But are you sure about this?"

"Yes, I am. Besides, we don't have another choice, do we?" I pointed at the large yellow crystal in the middle of the room. "As soon as it's ready, cast it." I faced my soldiers. "I know we are tired, but nothing else enters this room. Do not let them cross this threshold!"

They picked themselves off the ground and started moving toward the door. But when I heard the howls of the aliens behind me, I realized it was too late.

"Get down!" Tamethera shouted as the door exploded inward.

The shards flew toward the catalyst, absorbing into the crystal. The all too familiar screams and yells of the Coalizione filled my ears as I hurled huge, red balls of pure energy at them. As the enemy swarmed into the room, their bullets were thrown off course by the wind around the catalyst, which had grown stronger since I arrived.

"Zelda, cast the spell!" I tried to yell over the noise. I didn't know if she heard me, so I looked back.

The crystal was moving, flying farther upward as energy swirled around it. The last thing I ever saw was the crystal expelling the energy outward. It slammed into every corner of the room and beyond, expanding outward in a violent surge, rendering every atom from all living creatures, friend and enemy alike, into dust.

# Cloud's Rest

**M**ountain hemlock trees grew along the trail like my memories… some new, others gnarled with time, and a few charred by painful fires.

Such was Yosemite for us.

We set out from Tenaya Lake early for the hike to Cloud's Rest. Jen always insisted we leave as the foredawn flared over the Sierras while families of deer lingered in meadows still moist with dew.

This year the grasses were brittle, and the deer were nowhere to be found.

The first time I met Jen was at 9,300 feet. I was picking my way along the narrow precipice, avoiding the 3,500 foot drop on either side. She brushed past me. All I can remember were her long tanned legs skipping from boulder to boulder, heedless of the potential slips.

It was a spectacular view.

One year later, I proposed at Cloud's Rest. Our feet hung over the edge, dangling above the Yosemite River half a mile below. The golden rays of sunset ignited a solitaire as I slipped an engagement ring onto her finger. The excitement in her eyes left me breathless.

We'd returned every year, except last year.

I was still in the hospital.

# Maxx's Well

Two years ago, I'd insisted Timmy join us. "Come on, Jen," I said. "He'll do ok."

"He's still a baby. What if he falls?"

I slipped my hand onto the small of her back and pulled her to me. "Not with a boulder hoppin' mom and a studly dad!"

She relented. "Ok, but you'll be carrying him, studly Dad."

In the end Timmy had done fine. A few extra snack breaks and a twenty-minute lesson on how to urinate behind a tree became cherished memories.

I knew this journey, our second as a family along the twisting trail, would be our last.

Dry heat from the valley whistled up the mountainside, filling the air with dust. I shifted Timmy's weight on my shoulders. "Sorry, Tiger. I know this isn't a postcard day." I moved my hand to Jen at my side. "But it'll have to do."

The trees thinned. Soon I could see a monstrous wedge of beige granite that jutted into the sky. Cloud's Rest. I stopped. Despite my exertions, I was terribly cold. My legs became weak, and I could no longer move. I sat with Timmy and Jen in the scant shade of a red fir.

I was ill prepared to handle the depth of pain that heaved inside of me.

I rose and approached the mountain, forcing myself forward despite my urge to run away. Beneath the shadow of the peak a boulder sat among emaciated weeds.

"Look at that, Jen. It's right where we left it."

Somehow, I didn't think it would be.

I reached into my pack and removed two flowers. I laid them at the base of the rock that almost killed me.

The last time I had seen the thing, I was screaming. It was crashing down the slope. It impacted my chest and threw me backward twenty feet. I landed, broken and bloodied in the gravel, as my mind became a gray haze.

I woke up in the hospital room where I would spend the next sixteen months of my life.

"Hey, you guys remember where you were when it happened?" I walked to the base of the stone incline. "You were right here, Tiger. Trying to toddle your way up. And Mom was busy trying to keep you safe." I had been watching them when the boulder fell. Maybe if I had been paying better attention...

I climbed along the ridge, my eyes blinking back tears. I paused where Jen had first brushed past me exactly nine years before. I smiled and placed my hand on her. I made my way to the summit, removed my backpack, and sat at the site of our betrothal. I dangled my feet into the emptiness...

...and emptiness consumed me.

"Well, this is it." I swallowed hard. "I'm sorry." I removed Timmy's box from my backpack and Jen's from my side-pouch. "I'm sorry that I didn't do a better job watching out for that boulder." My voice broke. "It was moving too fast to warn you. There was nothing I could do."

I opened the boxes and held them into space before me.

"You guys wait for me a little while. I'll see you on the other side."

I poured out their ashes, watching as they mingled and floated on the breezes of Cloud's Rest.

# Silence

The end of humanity began with the silent collision between estranged worlds. No scream was heard, no tear flowed, no blood spilled—all of that would come later in buckets.

I gulped the last of my Starbucks, setting the empty cup on Mindy's desk while at the same time slipping off my winter parka from over my suit and extending it to the girl who scurried from the coffee maker, steaming mug in hand.

"Mr. Johnson," Mindy's Dolce pumps clattered against the marble. "What—" She took my covering, replacing it with the fresh coffee.

I inhaled the warmth. "It's cold outside."

Her lips pursed beneath widening eyes. "You're not supposed to be here."

"Monday morning?" I checked my watch. "5:32?" I stared at the keeper of my calendar as she brushed my coat and hung it in a cedar lined hutch.

"The senate subcommittee?" She scowled. "Testimony on inter-dimensional research?"

I raised the mug to my lips and sipped. "Get me Senator—" Turning toward my office, I flipped through names in my mind.

"Griffin," Mindy reminded. "I put a call in while you were clearing security. You've been rescheduled to after lunch. The senator will call back." She stood straight, efficiency even in posture. "I've also phoned your wife. Latroya will pack your bag, the charcoal suit. A courier is on the way to your house now. It will be waiting at the airport." She squinted. "Two hours."

"Griffin, right." I rubbed my brow.

"Tisha says to fly safe, she loves you, and wants pizza when you get home." The phone on her desk chirped. "The senator. I'll transfer him."

I pressed the blinking button on the speakerphone as the heavy office door swung closed. "Bill," stepping around the mahogany desktop I sat, leaning forward on the leather chair. "How's your family?"

"They're good, Thomas. Thank you. My granddaughter is turning twelve. She has a big party planned back in Tennessee. I'm hoping to wrap up these hearings on time." His voice lingered, the last word stretched into multiple syllables, accusatory, concerned.

I flushed, "Having a bit of trouble getting air born. Thanks for rescheduling."

Outside my window, a bird hopped among pine branches dusted with frost and the remnants of persistent snow. The earliest signs of spring, songbirds. Change seemed inevitable.

"Listen," the Senator's voice lowered, "Stevens has lined up some tough experts against you. I've read the advanced reports." He swallowed, a dry, crackling sound. "Is what they say true? You're creating an inter-dimensional rift? Shouldn't we know what's on the other side before..."

# Maxx's Well

I glanced at the elevator across the office. It led to a research facility nearly a mile below the surface gouged out of solid granite. A bunker sheathed behind multiple containment fields, powered by a dozen nuclear reactors, and housing the world's only neutronium accelerator. It was my revolutionary masterpiece—my portal.

I waved a dismissive hand and leaned back against the headrest. "A billion dollars of scientific grants," I listened to the sparrows chirping, "and now you get cold feet?"

"But I never thought you'd get this far…"

The office door wrenched open. Mindy fidgeted, face pale, hand trembling as she pointed to the computer screen behind me.

My back stiffened. "I'll be there in a few hours, Senator." I studied her. "We'll, um, do lunch." I pressed the button, disconnecting the call.

"It's the lab. Something's—wrong." She backed away, bumping against the wall, and tripping on the chair.

My monitor flashed the surveillance images from near the accelerator housing. A red light swiveled there, pulsing like an arterial wound through an expanding cloud of hyper-energized vapor.

"What?" I bolted up, leaning closer.

From beneath me, a nauseating pulse, a silent contraction that could be neither heard nor felt—at least not through the physical senses.

A foreboding silence engulfed the office, the birds, and beyond—as if creation knew something had slipped out of alignment and blamed— me.

For an eternal instant, all was still.

I stumbled, pressing the intercom. "Security, what's going on down there? Security!"

The phone crackled, "Breach in outer containment." The voice coughed, gasped.

I ran my hand through my hair, tugging. Impossible. The containment walls were 15 feet thick reinforced concrete. Nothing in this world could breach that. "Say again—"

Commotion screeched through the speaker. Garbled shouts mixed with gunshots. "Get out! Get—"

The elevator door trembled as the lights flickered and died.

Silence.

I realized I wasn't breathing.

# In Madison

**M**y cell sputtered and vibrated, the screen illuminating the darkness in the house, that house. My childhood house. Vacant now, all these years.

I stumbled across the parlor to reach it, to answer.

"Ashley?" Mama's voice was thin and sallow, like watery grits with too little butter. "Where are you?"

"It's storming, hard, and I walked miles. I'm soaked." That sounded stupid. I hated the slipping feeling in my mind. "Of course, I'm wet if I was in the rain."

"Walked?" She questioned. "Where? You're only 15."

I searched the dimness, my pale blue fingers clutching the phone. I twisted about, surrounded by ancient charcoal walls...

...walls that expanded and contracted as if made of balloons. Breathing, living, balloons all about me, panting and gasping over the back of my neck.

"Sugar?"

"I'm," my words seemed engulfed by the tempest pounding against leaking shingles. "Home, Mama." I shouted. "I'm, I'm home."

"I am, too. Here at the kitchen table."

"No, not there. This house. It's angry." I shuddered. "Angry at me."

Mama didn't respond.

"I broke a window."

"Ashley, what are you saying?"

She knew. How could she not? I grasped matted strands of hair and yanked. "I told you! I'm back home."

From the stairwell, the spectral face of a young boy, perhaps four years old, peered through the gloom. I became ensnared by the sensation of looking into a mirror, brown hair, round eyes, and Papa's pointed chin. But not a mirror of the present. Rather one of a decade past, clouded by whispers and doctors and medications.

I reached an unsteady hand toward him.

He placed a finger on his lips. "Shhh! It's a secret." The whisper of his voice became lost in the moans of the structure and the scratching of wild honeysuckle in the seething wind.

I struggled to understand.

The squeak of a chair grated through the phone followed by heavy footfalls along a neatly polished wooden floor. Our floor, the one in Birmingham.

"I'm coming, Sugar." Mama's voice quivered.

She couldn't. Not where I was.

Her breath began to labor as she ascended the steps to my bedroom door. I could almost feel her willing me to be there.

But I wasn't.

She pushed into my room.

# Maxx's Well

I pressed the phone to my mouth. "I had to go."

"Are you," she swallowed, "in Georgia again?"

The floorboards started to sway, prodding me toward the staircase across the darkened parlor.

"In Madison. And you know why."

"They're hallucinations," Mama protested. "Since you were a little girl."

"Are they?"

I sprawled beside the dusty bannister as the walls swelled against me and the risers began to shake. The child climbed, beckoning me to follow, ghostly feet translucent above the rotting wood.

Mama clattered through my drawers 200 miles away. "Your medicine. Dr. Steinman's prescription is full. You stopped taking your Seroquel? It calms your spells."

The innocent calliope of childlike laughter circled from a nursery on the landing. I glanced in. Two siblings giggled, playing.

"It's," I tilted my head, uncertain. "Mama, it's me. As a baby. And the boy from my dreams. He's, he's my—"

Outside the storm screamed through the birch trees as lightening flashed.

The shutters blew open, exposing broken glass as flashes strobed across the torrential night. On the wall, a skeletal shadow loomed, creeping toward the children with each successive bolt.

It raised boney fingers, reaching, threatening.

"No," I cried. "Run!"

And I did. The young me. She turned and hurried to the closet.

The boy only smiled and waved...

...as a gnarled hand shoved him out the window amidst a deafening clap of thunder.

The room spun. Dizzied, I fell back against the breathing, bulging closet wall as the building groaned anew. I slammed the door, shaking like it was 40 below.

"Hush," my young self reassured. "It wasn't your fault."

"What are you saying?"

She blinked at my confusion as the house twisted and moaned.

"Not my fault?"

"No."

"That boy, the little boy—who? Who?"

"We know, you and I. You feel him."

"A brother? But I don't have—don't have—"

"Of course, we do."

Lightning struck, shaking the structure like a rag doll. The building buckled and pitched in the screaming maelstrom.

"And the shadow?" I screamed. "It was me? I pushed him?"

She nodded, her movement slight with concern.

The winds roiled, goading me like satanic laughter.

"No!"

"It's true."

"Not possible!"

"I was there. Forgive us, forgive yourself." She kissed me, fading.

The closet door opened.

I blinked away the light in the room. My room. My bedroom in Birmingham. "Mama?"

She knelt, holding me close. "It's over now, just in your mind. Dreams, visions is all."

"Or memories?" I trembled. "Did I have a brother?"

She stiffened.

"I-I killed him?"

A tear tracked her rounded face. "Oh, Sugar—" Mama placed her hands on my cheeks, staring directly into my eyes. "You best stop thinking like that. Cause you nothing but grief. Some things are best left in the past."

I looked away, weeping.

# Separation

T he glass between them was a quarter inch thick. Her husband sat on the other side of the visitation booth wearing an orange jumpsuit, a prisoner number on his chest. His face appeared blotched and puffy from recent injuries. Jana lifted the handset of the phone. Her jagged breath caught in the mouthpiece, rasping through the device back into her own ear.

"Honey," she choked on the words, "are you ok?"

Robert tried to force a reassuring smile, but his thin lips tightened, and his eyes retreated noticeably.

"Did someone hurt you? Attack you?" She felt a thickness in her mouth, the same as when watching Schindler's List for the first time as a little girl. "Did you tell somebody?" She looked around. "A guard or maybe the warden?"

"No, no," he shrugged. "It's fine."

Jana placed her palm against the window. It seemed artificial, cold, and institutional, like the lid of an overused trash bin. She was surprised it didn't feel like glass at all, maybe instead it was some sort of acrylic. That explained why he appeared distorted, as if in a funhouse mirror.

Robert reciprocated, his hand a reflection of her own.

"Honey, I..." her voice cracked as a sheen of tears flooded her eyes and began spilling from the corners. "I..." She tried to calm herself, leaning near to him. "I've talked to a bondsman. We can use the house as collateral. I'm going to get you out of there."

He shook his head. "No."

"I did. We can do this, bring you home."

"We can't risk the house."

"Yes. We have to." Her face contorted anew as she scanned his beaten visage. "You can't stay in—"

"Listen," he slumped on the stool. "The house is for you and the baby. You can't be on the streets when I'm in here."

"We'll fight this."

"Listen to me—"

"We'll win. You'll be free."

"Jana, listen," his voice became tense.

"We've got to. We've got to! For Bobby's sake if not mine."

"Please, stop," he begged. "For just a minute."

She felt her eyes open wide with distress beneath her creased brow. She tried to breathe.

"I drank too much, failed the breathalyzer. I missed the turn and hit those kids."

"But it was an accident."

"Tell that to the parents." He looked to the tabletop in shame. "I told the attorney to accept whatever plea deal the DA offers. He thinks seven to ten, out in five."

"You don't lock people up for an accident."

"If I go to trial and lose, I'll be facing 15 or more if the DA wants to push two counts of vehicular manslaughter with a DUI enhancement."

She brought her hand to her mouth.

"I need to know you're safe with a roof over your head. You can borrow against the equity if things get tight. See things through."

"I can't—"

"Yes. Go to the bank."

She shook her head as if trying to ward off a clutch of demons in the shadows. "I can quit school. Get my old job back. I can—"

"You're too close to graduating. One more year of classes then you can get your dream job," he said. "Don't throw that away. Not because of this, because of my stupid mistake."

"I won't," she sobbed, "just leave you here. Like this." She motioned again to his injuries.

"I killed two kids. I deserve a lot worse."

"No."

"You don't understand. I see their faces in my mind. Constantly. That moment in the headlights, their terrified expressions." He sobbed. "They're in my dreams."

"You're good. A good man."

"Not anymore."

"You're wrong."

"I can't let this ruin your life, Bobby's life as well." He started to push away from the counter. "Move on. For everyone's sake. Live your life. Don't wait for me. I may not survive this."

The words hit her like a hammer. "What are you saying? Robert?"

A buzzer sounded, signaling their time was through as the line went dead. Jana replaced the receiver into its cradle, weeping as Robert was cuffed and escorted by two guards through a slatted steel door.

She stood, uncertain, then stumbled toward the exit.

# Turneffe Island

I woke to the sound of a child's voice calling from the edge of my subconscious mind. My body was beaded with sweat. It was too hot to sleep.

The Caribbean breeze stirred about the cabana through open patio doors. I stood and let it encircle me, cooling my flesh. I slipped into a lace robe to cover my near-nakedness and stepped onto the deck. A waning moon reflected across the waters as torches flickered among the coconut palms. I inhaled the freshness and listened to the collared plovers warbling in the marshes.

We had come to Turneffe Island to celebrate our fifth anniversary. I had come to escape; I prayed for deliverance.

I glanced behind me. Paul slept; his face bathed by the red digits of the alarm clock. It was 2:48 AM. We had spent the day snorkeling among fish as brilliant as a kaleidoscope display. When darkness forced us to shore, we sipped pina-coladas around a bonfire. Local fishermen recounted the legend of El Monstruo del Océano, the monster that stalked victims along the waterline and snatched babies from the grasp of helpless mothers.

I had shuddered in my husband's arms.

"I'm here," he whispered in my ear, "Nothing can harm you." He kissed my neck.

I wished I could believe him. Monsters tended to seek me out and stay around.

A movement caught my attention. A small child scampered through the darkness toward the waves.

My mind sensed a growing danger. I was uneasy. "Stop," I called.

The child turned and stared at me, then motioned for me to follow.

I looked about for the parents. Nobody else was there.

The child laughed. "Hurry, come on!" The figure turned and bounded to the waterline.

"Wait!" I ran, my wrap flowing behind, luminous in the moonlight. My heart began to pound, and my breath tightened.

The child was ankle deep and splashing, wearing a flowered swimsuit. She was a girl of about eight. She studied me, strands of blond hair falling across her wide eyes. Laughter slipped from her mouth, playful and carefree. "This way!"

She moved deeper into the waves then stopped and smiled.

I recognized her smile. It was Billy's smile.

I was suddenly cold.

I had told Paul about all of my old boyfriends, my nothing romances, my infatuations. But I had never told him about Billy.

She giggled. "Today's going to be my birthday." She bounced on her toes. "I get to go, and you're invited, too."

My mouth formed words, but no sound came out. My knees weakened. "Your father, where's your father?"

"My birthday, my birthday, my birthday." She danced in a circle in the waves.

"Shelby?" My throat burned as I spoke. My therapist had warned me to not give her a name. I was told I needed to let go.

She winked.

The ocean began to swell behind the small figure. A wave larger than the others moved toward the shore. But it was more than a wave. It was solid. There was a shape submerged in the brine.

I felt a sudden urge to protect the girl before me. I rushed into the water.

She followed my gaze and turned to look at the approaching mound. She didn't move.

"Shelby, come with me. Hurry."

She shook her head, her jaw set and firm.

Billy used to get the same expression. He was stubborn and determined. I was too young to resist. He made me do things that I'd never told anyone about.

The shape in the water drew near. It was darkness. A blot in a midnight sky. It seemed to absorb every goodness, leaving emptiness in its wake. El Monstruo del Océano. It rose up, towering above us. It reached out and seized the girl.

I grabbed her hand. "No!" I screamed at the creature and tugged against its strength.

Shelby didn't struggle.

"I can't lose you, Shelby. Don't let it take you."

"It's my birthday. I finally get to go. It's taking me home." There was relief in her voice.

"No. I need you here!" My eyes spilled tears as I fought the demon. "I'm sorry I didn't carry you. Please don't leave!"

The creature increased its pull, and Shelby began to slip from my fingers.

"It's time for you to let go now, Mommy. See you in heaven?"

I lost my grip. Shelby's face beamed as she disappeared below the waves. I sank to my knees in the surf and wept.

# The Coming Darkness

The roiling black cloud churned across the horizon, like a tumultuous maelstrom of desiccated embers, filth, and splinters of broken obsidian. It obliterated the peaks and clawed ruthlessly through the valleys, inching ever closer, calling to him. Night when it should have been midday. Cold when there should have been warmth. Despondency when there should have been hope.

Jamie looked back to the shanty, now distant in the fading illumination, its dingy, slatted timbers almost lost among the branches of withered shrubbery. The icy wind gouged across his ears, and he thought he could still hear her, the young girl cowering in the closet behind mounds of unwashed linens.

"They're watching," she had whispered, voice tremulous as her rounded, skittish eyes darted from shadow to shadow.

He knelt before her. "Who, Sweetness?" He took her hand in his. "Who's watching you?"

She placed a finger over her pursed lips.

Jamie leaned near, softening his tone. "Who?"

"Please. Don't let them."

His skin prickled at the desperation in her words. "Let them what?" He swallowed. "Do they hurt you?"

She pointed to heavy drapes over a spattered window. "The darkness is coming. Did you see?" She pressed herself deeper into the corner. "They're trying to lock me away."

Jamie hadn't seen as much as sensed something in the enclosing sky. He'd been wandering in the night, seemingly for ages, chancing on the small cabin in the failing starlight. He heard the helpless calls of the child, almost unrecognizable among the baleful yipping of coyotes scavenging nearby. There'd been no answer at the door, no life in the room when he entered, nobody at all—until he opened the closet.

"I can help you," he reassured. "Are you alone?"

Her mouth gaped into a horrified mask.

"But out here, nowhere near a town. In this godless wilderness. Who would bring you here?" He studied her. "Your parents, maybe?"

Her eyes pooled, damp lashes flickering down into a gloomy blink. She shook her head in a slow, despondent motion.

"I'm sorry." He touched her shoulder. "No family." He motioned his head toward the dirty window. "I feel alone out there a lot of times. No meaning. No reason to be. I know it hurts."

"They don't want me out. They want me buried."

"Buried?"

"Forever. Lost. Forgotten."

Jamie straightened, the tendons in his jaw clenching. The image of innocence in peril seared his mind. "Then come away. You'll always be safe with me."

For an instant she'd brightened. The faintest glint of yearning darted across her eyes before vanishing once again as clouds overtook her thoughts. "I can't go out. They'll be angry."

"But if you stay..."

"They watch. They see. They find me." She wept. "I have to stay. There's no choice. I'm trapped."

"We can make it. I promise. Don't sacrifice your own happiness for them. If we leave now, we could..."

"Did you notice it? The darkness? It's coming. I'm so afraid."

"You don't need to be. I'm here."

She gasped, shrinking low into the gloom until all he could make out were her wide, panicked eyes, desperate behind curled strands of dark hair. "No. No! Run!"

The boards of the dilapidated structure popped, the rusted hinges on the front door groaning as they swung open. Two darkened figures skulked inside.

Jamie stood and quietly closed the closet, facing the new arrivals.

"I know why you're here," a male voice growled. "You can't take her."

"I read her thoughts," the second shape, a female, warned. "I'm always watching."

Jamie stepped forward. "What's going on here? Who are you people?"

They cackled in a deranged, foreboding cadence. "Keepers of the night, you might say," said the man.

"Extinguishers of light," the woman corrected. "But it's not your concern."

Jamie clenched his hands. "And the girl?"

The shadowed man surged into Jamie's face. "She's mine," he raged. "Not yours. Get out!"

"I don't understand," Jamie argued. "Why the girl? She's got nothing to do with shadows and darkness. She's obviously terrified. What's her role in all this?"

The woman laughed once again. "You fool. Don't you grasp anything? She is the light."

"What do you mean? You're going to—" Jamie blanched at the image. "—to kill her?"

"Extinguish, put out, hide away forever, kill. Choose the word you want. She can't run loose. She's light."

"But not for long," added the man, so close now Jamie felt rancid breath against his skin.

"She wants to go. Why force her to stay? Let me take her."

"And miss out on all this fun?" The man waived his arm around the charcoal dimness filled with patchy obscurities and concealed recesses. "Never."

The young girl's voice echoed through Jamie's mind anew. "Help me! I'm so afraid! Don't let them do this!"

"I'm not leaving here without her."

"Are you so sure?" The woman raised her palms, spilling rivulets of ink that puddled on the dirty floorboards, forming what appeared to be bottomless pits of despair. "I'm the mistress of shadow. I command the darkness. I extinguish all hope with my breath." She inhaled and blew out a stagnant graphite steam which filled the room and swallowed any remnant of light. "When I speak, the mists obey my every syllable." She waved to the gloom. "Remove him."

Silhouetted wraiths sprang from nowhere and grasped Jamie's arms, binding him with webs that seemed as if they were spun in the depths of hell. They wrestled black cords around his throat, twisting them as his lungs began to fail. He struggled, striking out against mere shadows as they forced him toward the open door.

"No!" He choked. "I'm taking her."

"You want to play the hero?" the man sneered. "Sometimes heroes lose, especially here. She belongs to me. She's beyond your reach."

The ropes around Jamie's neck tightened until his mind flickered out as the demeaning sounds of ridicule reverberated about him...

...and everything vanished in the darkness.

He regained consciousness in the scrub brush, a weak dawn fighting helplessly against the thickening sky. Jamie stood exhausted, powerless, and confused. He stumbled, struggling to regain his bearings, to force the remaining haze from his awareness.

The shadows spilling ever nearer beckoned him come to rejoin the night. It all seemed so simple. Wandering lost in the abyss with no purpose was his destiny.

"Please, please help me," the girl had cried.

"Extinguishers of light," the woman said. "And she's the light."

His mind sank, lost, worthless, as the encroaching miasma swirled and looped morose tentacles about his feet and ankles. Hopefulness and courage seeped from his grasp.

"Sometimes heroes lose," he remembered. "Especially here." He waded into the inky blackness, alone. "But stories aren't supposed to end like this."

In the distance the child screamed.

He turned toward the remote cabin as a dying light sputtered in the window. "Wait," he awoke. "I'm coming!"

# At a Pay Phone in the Fog

### By Curtis Layne

A cold silence settled in as the rattling of the truck's engine disappeared into the fog, and Noel was alone. She tried to tell herself that he would come back for her, that no sane man could abandon his daughter twelve miles out into the countryside, but it didn't make her feel any better. Ivan was hardly a sane man.

She shivered; her body numb beneath the thin shirt that clung to her back. The air was oppressive, cold. So very cold. She slumped to the ground beneath the pay phone, huddling there, her clothes already soaked with mist. The phone was no more than a rusted hulk of metal, but Ivan told her it still worked. He was expecting her to call and apologize for what she'd done, but she wasn't sorry. Not yet anyway.

She didn't even know why she'd done it.

Noel shuddered, bit her lip. She couldn't call the police; if Ivan found out, he would kill her. He said so. And help had never come before— not when her mother had run away, not when Ivan had locked Noel in her room for three days during one of Kimi's track tournaments. Nobody knew, nobody cared. Noel was just another girl at a pay phone in the fog.

She felt her chest tightening, the asthma settling in. The air was so cold; it hurt to breathe. She squeezed her eyes shut, buried her face in her sleeves, and tried to pretend she was back on Tyson's ranch riding the horses. She loved horses, and she was good at pretending. But none of it was real.

She was so cold.

Shaking, she got to her feet and began to follow the road, opposite the direction Ivan had taken. Even the walking was hard on her lungs. Kimi would have had no trouble at all—she was an athlete, a star, and Ivan was proud of her, the older of his two daughters. He had always liked Kimi more. Noel had never been good enough.

Maybe that was why she'd done it—to show Ivan that she was more than what he tried to make her be, more than a shy girl who was sick all the time.

She trudged on, further up the darkening road. Something loomed in the stagnant mist ahead of her—an old barn, like the one where Tyson kept his horses. The rotted doors gave way to a dripping hollowness within where the fog hung in the fading light that slanted between the rafters. Nothing moved as she stepped inside. All around her, years of decay held their breath.

And her own refused to come. She tried to inhale; a sharp pain cut through her chest—her lungs constricted; she couldn't breathe...

She found herself on the floor, not sure how she got there. Her chest ached. She lifted her head to breathe, and her gaze fell on something that protruded from one of the empty cattle stalls.

A dead horse.

Noel didn't move, just laid there staring at the thing. Its fleshless face grinned back at her, not far from her own in the moldering straw and weeds. Right there, at the end of the barn. A dead horse. It had decomposed to the point of being inseparable from the ground beneath it. There was grass growing on its back; its teeth jutted from the soil like gravestones.

Noel crept forward on her stomach, wanting a closer look. It was a large horse, possibly a Clydesdale, although she couldn't be sure. Long dead either way. The thing was a cemetery unto itself, and Noel wondered why it had been left to die.

Perhaps it had gotten injured somehow, had been unable to keep up with the others. Perhaps it had been born sick. No doubt there had been a better animal available, a healthier, faster one.

But Noel doubted that the horse had tried to kill its sister.

She stood, left the barn, made her way back to the pay phone. Slipping her only quarter into the slot, she dialed Ivan's number. The other line rang eight times before he answered.

"Ivan," Noel said, softly, "I want to come home."

"You think I'm going to let you come back after what you did?" He laughed. She could hear the truck's engine rumbling in the background. He was still driving. "You're stuck out there, kid."

She said, "I'm sorry," but the phone clicked dead in reply.

# But Inside

**m**e, sewn together from fragments of a stolen past...

but inside
battered ruins crumble beneath the siege of your relentless
indifference, and I wince behind eyes dry with years of neglect.
You crush me, desolate, nonexistent—as
I hide in a memory of swaddle, powder, and warmth to
prolong the fallacy of what I pretend to be

but inside
old wounds seep crimson, gouged with barbed grousing and apathetic
unconcern, coldness, ice, and I falter behind a practiced smile.
You shred me, thoughtless, dispassionate—as
I huddle beneath the fading memory of mother's unconditional eyes,
grasping at a failing image of who I'd hoped to be

but inside
the edges of sanity curl and split in the graying night;
ashen chalk and bitter smoke shadow cheeks drawn with whispered
sorrow.
You starve me, thieving, keeping—as
I hunger to suckle on the memory of a sheltered infancy buried
within the person that I once prayed to be...

there is no chance to again find my lost sanctuary of innocence.

# Section 5: The Gates of Hell

"Darkness does not leave us as easily as we would hope."

Margaret Stohl

"When you spend so long trapped in darkness, you find that the darkness begins to stare back."

Sarah J. Maas, A Court of Mist and Fury

# Constance

The waves taunted gray and black in a twilight that flickered away into nothingness. What remained of the fallen sun choked in a smoky memory of fading crimson, the last whimper of a promise stolen.

A small hand grasped my finger, damp, slick, then slipped away.

I spun. A sob knotted my raw throat and tore from me. My foot caught on the protrusions of a half-buried stone, and I fell as a heron wailed distant, forlorn, in the enveloping gloom.

In the wet sand, only solitary footprints.

An empty bottle dropped from my grasp, dribbling the remnants of bourbon into the splotchy froth that marked the limits of the tide.

A weight pressed me lower, deeper. My spirit sank beneath an ocean of sorrow. I couldn't breathe. I no longer cared.

My vision clouded, the sand beneath me becoming fluid, unsteady. The cacophony of waves softened and ebbed until I could distinguish a single murmur, a whisper.

"Daddy?" She was distant, lost among the swells. "Daddy, I'm scared."

The sensation again, a worried grip squeezing my finger. I looked about, my heart thundering. "It's ok, baby girl." I said to no one, a memory. "I've got you."

"Can we go back to the fire and cook schmallows?" Her eyes had been dewy, wide in the surf, searching my face. My four-year-old daughter. My angel.

Charcoal water had licked about her thighs, greedy, hungry, as flecks of amber and cerulean fled across the heavens. Night rose with a vengeance as we stood with shells at our toes and behind us plovers scampered across the cooling silt. We waited, hoping for dolphins.

"You bet. Cuddled and warm, roasting marshies. You and me." I smiled, but glancing down past blond tresses, my blood ran cold.

Her expression. She knew. Right then, even before. She knew.

Her pallid cheeks had become mottled as if a shadow hovered near. She trembled and inched toward me. "Can we go?"

From beneath us, a surge rose and towered above her ringlets. It knocked me backward, and in that desperate moment, I felt her grip tighten about my fingers—a squeeze, nothing more.

Then she slipped away.

My muscles had seized, and my jaw dropped open for an eternal instant as the wave slithered—taking my daughter with it.

"Wh-where are you?" I'd choked, not believing.

No reply.

# Maxx's Well

"Constance?" Louder, screaming. "Constance?"

I thrashed, groping blindly beneath the surface. How long could she—
Had it been a minute? More? I flailed, running after the receding
beast, searching, feeling, as darkness swallowed me.

They'd found her near the jetty after dawn.

I blinked, bowing my head. If only—but there were no more ifs.

The breeze stiffened, pushing the empty bottle across the shore and
topping the crest of the rising waves. Swirls of froth motioned to me
from the depths, calling, promising. "We can take you to her. Come.
Let your grief have meaning."

And I wanted to go, to become lost in a morose thickness, to be
swallowed by shadow.

My baby girl, lost, the murk having stolen her from me. Now I, too,
trapped in the depths of my despair.

I lifted my face to the seducing brine, eyes brimming.

"Daddy?" Her frail voice picked at the frayed edges of my mind.
"Daddy, I'm scared."

I smudged tears from the stubble on my chin. "Constance?"

I stood, retrieving the bottle as the wind whipped about me and the
waves clawed at my legs.

"Your daughter," the waves mocked, "we took her from you, she's
ours."

"No." I clenched my jaw, the muscles in my neck distending. I raised my fist into the driving spray and shouted. "No!" My voice rose and echoed, battling the roar of the sea. "You can't. She was just a little girl!"

"Then come! Come and find her. Take her back!"

I sobbed. The emptiness in my heart bled for her, my baby, my Constance. A dark weight enveloped what miniscule strength I held.

"Daddy?"

I threw the bottle, shattering it against the rocks and stumbled into the inky blackness.

# Suicide at Hawthorn Tower

He was on the seventeenth floor. It was after working hours. He turned the doorknob. It was unlocked.

Bob had walked past that office every day for twenty-four years. It had always been locked; the contents sealed away from him like so many other things. He knew something was behind that door. Something that made the floors tremble and the walls shake late at night when he was there alone.

He was an account representative in the Hawthorn Towers. Not a senior account representative or an executive. Those positions were given to younger people with ivy league diplomas. Kids who laughed at the old man that sat at the desk between the ancient fax machine and the unused copier.

Only Cynthia seemed to care, and she had gone away.

But it didn't matter anymore because, on that night, the doorknob turned. It turned in Bob's hand, not for some pubescent college graduate or unrealized romance.

There were times when the building shook so powerfully around him that he had to hold onto his desk to keep from falling out of his chair. In those moments he would hear noises echoing through his mind. Sounds, like voices from another dimension, calling to him, pleading for him to join them. Join them where, he did not know. They were an other-worldly, alien chorus.

He pushed against the door, and it swung open. He stepped inside.

The room was empty, the carpet new. The walls seemed recently painted in ecru and gold. The smell of formaldehyde and mineral oil burned his nose.

Then he saw it. The window. It shimmered and pulsed. The moonlight twisted through it, glinting a bluish hue. It was ethereal.

It was open.

His mind struggled with the sight. It seemed familiar. He'd read of similar things in his science fiction magazines on those nights when he'd already seen everything on TV. He swallowed. It had to be. What else could explain what he was seeing? An interstellar portal.

No wonder they kept the door locked.

But it wasn't locked on that night. The knob had turned in his hand. They planned on him finding the portal. The voices wanted him.

It was as if they'd sent a message. To him. Bob. Twenty-four years as an account representative. The voices were calling him.

All he had to do was answer.

What would the ivy leaguers have to say about that?

Would Cynthia mourn him after he'd left on a journey to another world?

He stepped to the portal as a radiant light coated his skin. He waited. He always waited. He'd waited for most of his life, and what had it ever gotten him?

"He who hesitates—" Was that his voice speaking? "He who hesitates loses."

He'd lost Cynthia.

Hers had been the desk in the corner, covered with frames and flowers. "We should try to get together sometime," she'd said.

He knew that getting together was like a date and that dating led to marriage. But he'd waited. Then one day her desk was empty. That had been 15 years prior.

He wasn't going to wait anymore.

He reached his hand through the extraterrestrial threshold. It felt cool on the other side—not like the office building that closed in about him for twenty-four years.

He removed a picture of Cynthia from his wallet. It was crinkled and matted. He had taken it from her desk long ago. She was smiling in the arms of another man. They both seemed so happy.

Bob held it close to his cheek, his breath caught short. If he could be any man, he'd want to be the man smiling with Cynthia, captured forever in a photograph. He wanted the voices waiting for him on the other side to know that.

He took one last look about him, the empty office, the door that had always been locked, and the life that he was leaving behind. He'd miss none of it. Fulfillment could only be found beyond. Were it any different, he was sure that Cynthia, or someone, would have told him.

Finding the portal had given him hope, the only hope he'd ever known.

The walls about him began to vibrate. His heart leapt. The floors beneath his feet trembled, excitement built in his breast. He clutched the photo in his hand. It was his ticket to salvation, his passport to a new world.

He heard the voices calling to him from the recesses of his mind. "There's nothing for you there. Join us. Join us."

He ran toward the portal and leapt through.

# Pretend

"Listen," Rita paused and pointed to the corrugated roof, "It's starting to rain, I think. Hear?" She placed a hand on her baby's leg and tickled in rhythm, "Drip, drop, drip, drop, drip, drip, drop."

Kalei kicked her legs and laughed, the flecks of powder blue in her eyes reflecting the light from the woodstove. She rolled to her side and cooed.

Rita bent low, her face inches from the four-month-old, and began again. "Drip, drop, drip, drop, drip, drip, drop." This time kissing wisps of blonde hair from her daughter's round cheeks and forehead between syllables.

Kalei gurgled, lifted unsteady hands, and grabbed her mother's ears.

"That's why mommy stopped wearing earrings. Yes, it is!" She nuzzled. "Yes, it is!"

She sat up, breaking free from the delicate grip, and smoothed the wrinkles from the floral blanket spread on the floor. She turned to the pile of crayons and scratch paper on the Little Tykes table in the corner.

"Jazzy, will you bring Mommy her iPhone, please?"

Jasmine glanced across the room and lifted pudgy fingers, gripping a twice broken Crayola. "What colow dis one?"

"Purple. Can you please bring me the phone?"

"All gone wed." Her lower lip extended as she slowly stood and picked up the iPhone from the table.

"I'll help you find red in a minute, ok?" She straightened the bow on the two-year-old's ponytails. "Can you please help watch Kalei while Mommy checks for messages?"

Cell reception in the shadow of Mt. Baker, Washington was virtually nonexistent even on the best days. The signal from the Bellingham towers was blocked by ridges, valleys, and forests. Jake said the booster he'd installed picked up the feed from Mt. Sumas to the north, which followed the Nooksack River Valley. When all went well, and it rarely did, three bars.

Rita sighed. Things hadn't gone well—howling winds hurtling pinecones and limbs at the cabin, roiling clouds when the forecast had called for sun, and now unexpected rain. Of course, being huddled inside the bunker made reception even worse. She checked the touch screen—flickering between one and none even on tiptoes near the lone window. Not enough to attempt a call. Barely enough for the occasional burst of texts. She drummed her fingers on the metal walls.

They'd decided together to buy the old hunting cabin in the forests well east of Mosquito Lake. Mrs. Tremble had sold them an easement across her timberland following the abandoned logging road. She'd turned down many an offer before, but Jake had a way with people. The abundant wildlife made the solitude worthwhile, but the distance from civilization made landlines for either phone or power an impossibility.

Gusts howled about the structure, shaking the walls and making noises like a funeral of inconsolable ghosts. She crossed her arms and glanced about as if making certain the room was still in one piece, glad she'd moved the family to the relative safety of the bunker when the first branch had thundered through the bedroom window. There'd been more crashes since she'd sealed the metal door.

She thumbed through her received text messages, making certain she hadn't missed a new addition. Still only four, all from Jake in Bellingham.

Jake. 9:15 AM. Massive waves and water here. Am ok but much damage. Tried call but ur reception down? Don't worry.

Jake. 9:22 AM. Most of city flooded. Am safe. Be careful. Love you.

Jake. 9:34 AM. My God. Unbelievable destruction. Let me know u & girls ok.

Jake. 9:47 AM. Strong winds now. Driving difficult. R U safe? Trees may come down. Wait in bunker till I get home.

All the messages were received at 10:09 during a moment of stronger signal. Over 90 minutes had passed since. Nothing.

She typed a new message and hit send. "Still here. We r all safe. Come home." It moved to her outbox where it sat with her previous efforts, waiting for enough signal to transmit. She shook the phone, slapping it against her hand. "Come on! Do something!"

"Mommy mad?" Jasmine stared with wide eyes.

Rita turned, "No, Jazzy. Mommy's not mad." She forced a smile.

"Phone a bad giwl?" Her voice was tighter, tainted with doubt.

"Of course not, sweetie. It's just with all the wind and now rain the phone signal isn't working again, so we can't talk to Daddy."

Jasmine crossed her arms and creased her brow. "Phone get timeout, Mommy."

"Silly!" Rita flicked her daughter's hair. "Should I put it in the corner?" She stopped and looked up toward the window. It was in the junction of the northern and western walls high up near the seam. Her hand moved to her chin. "I wonder. If I could put it up in that corner, maybe…"

The room known as the bunker wasn't in reality a bunker at all. It was a 20-foot steel shipping container hooked to the house just off the kitchen and mostly buried under the hill sloping up away from the cabin. At over 2 tons, Jake had nearly burned out the truck motor hauling it up the mountain and into place. Its primary purpose was to serve as a panic room should predators, either the four legged or two-legged variety, break in while Jake was away.

They'd installed a woodstove for warmth, two triple-screened and louvered apertures for safety ventilation, a half bath, and, in the one unburied corner of the metal room, a small triple paned window for light. It was only a foot or so square, but still, it might provide some level of reception.

She stretched on tiptoes, not even close to reaching the glass some nine feet above the floor. Rita was barely 5'5" when she was wearing three-inch heels, which she wasn't. "How would you keep it there, anyway, Einstein?" she muttered to herself. "Nails? Glue? Helium balloon?" She looked about, spotting a clear plastic dispenser on the table. "No, tape."

Kalei sneezed.

Rita turned, smiling. "Gracious! What was that?" She lifted the squirming infant and turned in a circle, surveying the room. "Daddy took his ladder. Yes, he did." She rocked as she walked to the far end of the chamber, shifting Kalei to her shoulder. "Jazzy, let's play a game."

Jasmine ran to catch-up. "What game, Mommy?"

"Well, Daddy took his ladder and Mommy needs to climb up to that window," she began to pull storage boxes from their stacks, "so we need to find something big and heavy I can stand on."

Jasmine sucked her fingers and stared.

Rita laid Kalei near her sister. "You two start looking over here." She opened the first container, maternity clothes and Jake's old fatigues. Another: photo albums, old CDs, and stuffed animals from her teen years.

Jasmine reached in, pulled out a plush pony, and hugged it.

"That was Mommy's from before I met Daddy." Rita smiled at the image of her and her daughter's childhoods overlapping. Along the wall, partially buried under sleeping bags and used camping gear, a row of oversized number 10 cans caught her attention. "Hey, check this out girls," she pulled a heavy container of peaches out, "these might work."

Jake kept the bunker stocked with the big cans from Costco in case they were ever snowed in over winter. Fruit, beans, ketchup, and most anything else needed to survive for a few weeks with no outside help.

Beyond the shelter, a gust and a jarring crack. Close. Followed by the crashing of a huge limb, perhaps an entire tree. The ground shook with deafening splinters.

Rita's hands jerked to her mouth, an inadvertent gasp escaping, eyes wide.

The girls began to cry.

She wiped her cheeks and knelt, scooping Kalei into shaking arms. "Wow, what a big boom, huh?"

Jasmine pressed close, grasping her mother's blouse in both fists.

"There, there," she comforted. "Hush, hush. It will be ok. A little scare, that's all. Just enough to make us jump. But it's all better now."

Rita began to hum a nursery tune, soothing, soft, gentle. She felt Jasmine's knotted fists loosen, the baby begin to relax. They swayed together.

"I tell you what," she kissed her daughters' hair, "let's move some of those cans and put them under the window. I bet we'll get a message from Daddy. Or maybe even a call."

Jasmine nodded but grasped her mother's hand. Kalei fussed and kicked.

"It will be a new game." She led her daughters to the food supply. "This time we get to build, see?" Rita used her foot to lay the cans on their sides then roll them toward the window. "Now, look what I found, Jazzy. "She reached into her diaper bag. "Graham crackers! Because you were such a good helper. And the binky for Kalei because Mommy really needs both hands right now."

Four stacks, two cans high served as a base on which she placed the legs of the Little Tykes table. Two more cans on the table in case she still needed an extra boost.

"Here goes nothing."

Phone in one hand and tape in the other she stepped first onto the undersized chair and then onto the unsteady plastic surface.

"I'm really tall, aren't I girls?" She waved to her daughters. "Mommy's a giant!"

Rita pressed against the wall and lifted her head toward the window. Too short. Even with toes extended. Reaching up, she placed the phone against the glass and used the tape to secure it.

"If a signal comes, this is the best way to catch it." She glanced back down and smiled. "I'll bet Daddy's sent some love for you! Your daddy is wonderful like that!"

Sliding the extra cans across the table she placed her feet on them and pushed up. Her eyes cleared the sill. She gasped, branches, splinters, and pine needles were everywhere. The giant Douglas fir at the end of the clearing, the one they'd thought was twelve hundred years old, the one with the 40-foot circumference trunk, the one that was over 200 feet tall had come down. It had landed on everything; the cabin included and flattened it all. Debris swirled and pelted the glass, driven by horrendous gusts. Rita gaped, stare frozen, mouth opening and closing.

"Be strong," she thought. "Your daughters need you." She cleared her throat and stepped away. "Well, uh," she bit her cheek, "sure is stormy." A forced smile stretched moist cheeks. "But we're in here. We're safe. Everything's going to be fine." She climbed down, her eyes glancing back over her shoulder at the window and the taped cell phone searching fruitlessly for signal.

Jasmine stood, pale eyes troubled, "Mommy, whewe doggy?" Cracker crumbs spilled from her shirt to the floor. Rufus usually licked up her messes.

He'd had been on his morning patrol in the forest when the winds began. He hadn't come when called into the shelter.

"Oh," Rita thought of the downed tree and flattened cabin. Could a dog have been able to survive that? "He's out." She paused. "Probably chasing his squirrel friends."

Jasmine scowled.

"He's fine. I'm sure of it. Probably running and playing in the rain." She rubbed the toddler's back. "Remember how much he loves the mud?"

"Doggy scawed?"

"Maybe a little. But Rufus is a big brave doggy. He knows it will be ok. So, he will try hard not to be scared today. Ok? Now, how about we do some coloring together? Kalei, too. Just us girls. I'll help you find the red crayon."

The window vibrated and chirped; a text message received.

Rita stumbled back and caught a sob in her throat. Scrambling to the chair she climbed, reached to the phone, and yanked it from its mount.

Her hands trembled. "Please, Jake, please, please, please…" She fumbled with the touch screen as she opened the message box. 7 new texts.

Jake. 10:11 AM. Still no call? R u ok? Go to bunker. Seal door. I'm coming.

Mom. 10:18 AM. Tsunami! Are you and family safe? You're out of sig range? Call me.

Mom. 10:29 AM. News says wave hitting down to So Cal. Huge disaster. Bring girls and Jake home to the ranch till things clear.

Jake. 10:33 AM. Sick dizzy. Head hurts. Kiss the girls. I love you.

Mom. 10:45 AM. Rita, baby, call. I can't get through. News says terrorist gas attack. Thousands dead. Be safe. Call.

Mom. 11:09 AM. If you're getting these know I love you so much. And your precious family.

Mom. 11:20 AM. Poison gas, honey. Seal the windows and vents. Don't breathe it.

Rita cried aloud. "Jake!" She leaned against the wall and began dialing his number. "Come on. Come on!" The call dropped and failed. "No. No. No." Her body shook, and she squeezed her eyes shut.

She re-read the messages. "God, what is happening out there?" Her thumbs pecked across the tiny screen, "We're in bunker. Falling trees crushed house. So scared." She sent it to Jake and her mother, holding the phone up to the glass. "Please answer."

The phone rang.

The screen showed a picture of her mother. "Mom? What's going on?"

"Oh baby, you're alive!" the voice crackled and skipped. "I was so worried. The girls? Jake?"

"The girls are with me." Her voice broke. "Jake was in town. Bellingham. He sent messages, but—" she looked down to her daughters. "Oh Mom…"

"…you're breaking up, the signal is poor. Do you hear me?"

"I hear you. I'm here. Mom?" She stretched toward the window, willing a better connection.

"Rita, the news says there's poison gas. Can you hear me? Baby, seal the doors and windows. Don't let the gas in. Are you there? Rita?"

The connection faltered.

"Gas? What are you talking about?" She shook the phone. "Mom? What gas? The wind will blow it away, right? Mom?"

The call failed.

She squinted out at the trees, thrashing in the tempest. "Blow it away," she thought, "or bring it right to you." She stepped up onto the can, peering once again over the sill. "But how will you know?" She stared, needing clues, a sign, something.

A dark shape hurtled against the window, black and brown fur obscuring the world in a sickening thud.

Rita jumped and nearly fell.

The form writhed into the clearing, frothing and clawing. Rufus. His eyes were bulging and tinted red. He fell, struggling to regain his feet. Dragging his hind quarters back toward the shelter. He vomited and cried, falling onto his side in a convulsive fit.

Rita screamed, reflexive and guttural. It echoed about the metal confines.

The children began to wail.

She twisted away from the sight, back against the wall, arms and fingers splayed. "My God, my God!" She jumped from the tabletop, falling to the floor. She crawled to her daughters and held them. "My babies. Oh God."

Jasmine sobbed, nose running. "Mommy..."

Rita kissed the girls, "No, no. This can't be." She fought the tears singeing her eyes and forced a slow breath. "Wait." She stood, "wait." She searched the length of the walls. "Where are you?"

With its door sealed, the air in a shipping container would become stale and rancid unless ventilation is installed. Jake had insisted on two vents, one on each wall, about 7 feet off the floor. They were designed to funnel bad air out and bring in fresh waves of oxygen.

Or poison gas.

Her jaw set, eyes narrow. "We can do this."

She ran to Jasmine's art shelf, pushing paper, stickers, and paint bottles onto the floor before grabbing an old margarine container. She pulled off the warped lid, retrieving the thick moist mass from inside.

"Go, hurry..."

She'd prepared an oversized batch of homemade Play Dough the day prior. Jasmine always seemed to eat more than she molded.

Rita sprinted the length of the chamber, flattening the mixture as she ran. The vents were about 8 inch by 4 inch metal rectangles. Louvers controlled the flow of air but couldn't stop it completely. She took a deep breath and threw herself against the wall. Reaching up she closed the louvers, pressing the grape flavored dough into every crevasse. Without breathing, she repeated the process on the second vent.

She stumbled away, brushing her body with doughy hands, stomping, and twisting as if she were covered with spiders.

"Off, off—" Her voice sputtered reflexively. "Go—away!"

She turned toward the sound of crying, inhaled deeply, and gathered her daughters into the far corner. "We're fine. We're fine. It's going to be ok."

Kalei fussed and kicked.

"I know, I know," Rita soothed, "you need to be changed and eat, right?" She opened the diaper bag and pulled out a dry diaper and wipes.

The fire in the woodstove popped.

She stroked the round head nestled against her breast, the fundamental act of sustenance settling her pulse. Jasmine cuddled close as well, eating a sandwich of peanut butter and homemade blackberry jelly.

"Eat, little ones," she whispered. "Eat well."

The stove was a high efficiency, clean burning model. Jake chose it specifically because of the airtight seal in the chamber to help prevent smoke and carbon monoxide from seeping into the house. To allow for maximum safety, both the intake and outflow were ducted to the outside. Fire, like people, needed oxygen to survive. Without it, asphyxiation and death.

A small cloud of poisonous gas would be dispersed in the wind, wouldn't it? But what if it wasn't a small cloud? What if it stretched for miles? It might take hours to dissipate. Or more. She eyed the Play Dough seals, the window, the seam along the door. How long could they possibly work? A few minutes? A few hours? Or were they leaking already?

Rita watched as the flames flickered from red to dark orange to sickly yellow. It was starving, dying.

"Stay alive. Fight." Beads of sweat peppered her brow as she willed the fire back. "What are you breathing? What's out there? How much more? How much?" She closed her eyes and prayed. "Not now. Not my family. Not like Rufus. I won't let you."

Jasmine had a tendency toward bronchial infections, which could leave her coughing for hour after tortuous hour. The doctor had eventually prescribed cough syrup laced with codeine, not a strong enough dose to harm a young body but just enough potency to relax the bronchial airways and let the toddler sleep. The bottle was locked away in the medicine box on the upper shelf near the door.

With both girls fed and changed, Rita took it out.

"Jazzy, will you bring me the pillow? I think we'll take a little nap after such a big lunch." She pulled together blankets and sleeping bags, making a soft mattress. "I know I could use a rest."

Jasmine, with pillow in tow, walked across the shelter. "Not tiwed, Mommy."

"Sometimes we lay down even when we aren't tired, princess. We'll just have to pretend." She placed the pillows with the others. "But first let's take our medicine, ok? We don't want to start coughing."

Jasmine sucked her fingers and sat on the makeshift bed.

Rita laid Kalei on the blankets. She leaned over and kissed her. "You first, little one." She squeezed a quarter teaspoon into unsuspecting cheeks, followed by a second. "I know, I know. You've never tasted this before. It will be ok."

Kalei kicked, fussed, and choked on a swallow. She began to cry.

"Now your turn, Jazzy." She poured two teaspoons into the dispenser. "Just like always."

Jasmine held her mother's hand as the fluid spilled down her throat.

"Such a big girl. Good job." She helped Jasmine lay beside her sister. "Help Kalei settle down." She raised the bottle to her mouth and took a long swallow before locking it away once again. "We'll all sleep for a while."

Outside the wind and rain churned past the tiny window. The stove flames receded, remaining only in the creases of the charred log.

"Sounds like it may never end." Rita curled up next to her children, pulling a unicorn blanket over them all. "Shhh, don't cry. Soon a dream will sweep you away." She smoothed their hair. "Close your eyes now. We can be together in dreamland. Daddy will be there, too. And Rufus. You'll see. It's a happy place."

Kalei quieted, breaths soft, her eyes closing.

Jasmine sucked her fingers and rolled onto her side, lashes flickering.

"It will be all right. No need to stay awake. Hush now."

Jasmine closed her eyes and nestled under the covers.

"Don't be scared. No need to bother." The room dimmed and blurred. Rita felt her vision slipping away. "Oh God. Oh God." She reached out her arm and held her children.

In the woodstove, the fire went out.

# The Door Ahead

I reached. The knob, doorknob, moved. My fingers scratched the wall, breaking already chipped and splintered nails.

My breath caught in ragged gulps. "Jimmy no. Jimmy, no..."

The knob seemed to float, drifting upward into an ever-thickening gloom. It glinted, reflecting flames in the scuffed and grimy finish—like gemstones choked in mud. Diamonds—like the one Jimmy promised...

Falling. My head hit the floor. I covered my face. "I-I'm sorry, I didn't mean to." Tears pulled at my already swollen cheek.

The dishes in the kitchen. The sink, spattered. I needed them cleaned. He hated dirty dishes. My belly clinched. If he finds them...

"Jesus loves me, this I know..." The words were deep in my throat, hidden, from a childhood long stained and misused.

I twisted the knob, crawling to the hall.

My hand hit glass, a gasp ripped through me as shards sliced my palm. The broken frame, the picture, shattered on the floor beneath the scar on the wall.

"No..."

I hadn't cleaned after he threw it.

The photo shook in my trembling grasp. Disneyland. Beaming by the Matterhorn. Jimmy had been so kind. Bought me a Tinkerbell necklace.

"Oh, Jimmy..." I traced his form, perfect eyes, the smile that was never there anymore.

He'd thrown it, the frame, the picture, our memories—at me. I slumped against the wainscot, kissing the image of Jimmy as my shoulders curled.

I ran bloody fingers over knotted hair. He liked me pretty for him. It was my fault. I hadn't brushed, no make-up. He was home early. I should've been ready in case.

"Stupid girl. Stupid! Stupid!"

I hit my forehead with my palm again, again, again.

"They are precious..." I bit my lip. "They are precious..." The words spit and caught. "Not true, can't be."

Smoke curled from the bedroom, a condemning serpent.

"I'll try harder. Next time. My hair and the vacuuming."

He'd hit me—as usual. His beer wasn't cold enough. I never remembered when to put it into the fridge. But he hadn't seen the dirty clothes, heaped by the washer.

His mother was an army wife. Laundry every day. Folded, stacked.

I closed my eyes, pressing them against my knees, swaying, shuddering. So wrong. Images of a steeple, a white dress, a castle in the clouds flickered as if from an antique projector. Promises. Lies.

Fool's gold.

I'd tasted the whiskey on his lips and tongue. "Jimmy, no." I'd pushed. "Jimmy, no." He was stronger. Drunk—even drunk—especially drunk.

"Ungrateful," his voice was a growl, dark, evil; his words a slime of malevolence. "I'll take what's mine anytime I feel like it." He laughed. "Pathetic."

I couldn't. I didn't want to. Not again. Snarled hair, swollen cheek, and tears burning, ever burning, tormenting. Hell inside...

...suffocating me, ME, every day.

He'd passed out, finished, drool slick about the harsh stubble of his chin. The whiskey spilled, pouring from the bottle, drenching him, the sheets.

My dress had been torn. I looked bad. I'd stumbled, straightening my disheveled clothing over wobbling legs. Sore, tired—isolated. I'd reached for the sewing box.

Must be pretty for him.

I lifted the plastic lid.

The stink of stale sweat and flowing alcohol had twisted with anger and fear.

Somehow I knew there was supposed to be more, yet hope had died.

On the tray, thread, needle, scissors...

...matches.

Nausea crippled me. He was going to see the laundry.

I'd lit one...

...and fled.

The smoke detector screamed from the hallway ceiling above.

The picture fell from my hands, lost in the growing maelstrom of fire and ash.

"Jimmy, I'm sorry..."

Sirens drew near.

I clawed the wall and stood. "They are precious in his sight." I faltered in the thickening gloom. "Precious in his sight," I coughed.

Could it still be true?

The door, ahead.

# Worm Grunting

### By Veda Rue

### I

A bleary morning sun peaked through the gaps in the trees and yawned out a puff of cold wind that made Braylee's cheeks sting. He scanned through the blanket of soggy leaves covering the forest floor, searching, searching, searching for—

There!

He plunged his fingers into the damp soil, chasing the wiggling butt of a pink earthworm.

He missed.

"That's not how we catch them." Parent said, pulling Braylee's hands back out of the mud. "Good try, though."

Braylee rubbed his palms together, smearing mud over his skin and the cuffs of his too-big-for-him jacket. It was Parent's jacket. They let Braylee borrow it since he outgrew his old one.

"I almost had it."

Crouching down next to him, Parent slung their backpack on the ground and pulled out a thick wooden stake. They tossed it to Braylee.

"We hunting vampires? Braylee asked.

Parent laughed. "Not vampires. These are for the worms!"

"To smack them with?"

"It's called a staub." Parent said. "You have to stab it in the ground. Try it."

Braylee poked the tip of his staub into the dirt and, sitting up on his knees, pushed it several inches down. When he leaned back, Parent gave it one last push and a quick wiggle to make sure it was secure.

"Ok, now we need our..." Parent dug around in the backpack some more and pulled out a thin sheet of metal, "iron."

Braylee frowned. "That doesn't look like an iron."

"It's a different type of iron."

Parent dropped it in Braylee's hands and, Braylee thought, it was heavier than it looked.

"You use this iron to scrape the top of the staub." Parent plucked the iron back out of Braylee's grasp like it weighed nothing. "Like this."

Parent rubbed the iron over the staub, and Braylee's hands immediately flew to his ears. The sound it made was long and screechy, and it bounced all the leaves and twigs off the ground around it like popping popcorn.

Parent sat back on their heels. "Loud huh?"

Braylee kept his fingers plastered over his ears and nodded.

"Well," Parent said, "rubbing the iron over the staub creates vibrations that shoot down into the ground. The earth worms think those vibrations are moles coming to eat them, so they pop up out of the dirt to get away. After that, all you have to do is grab them."

Parent tossed a tin can into Braylee's lap. "Your job is catching them once they pop up. Ready?"

Braylee reluctantly moved his hands away from his ears and cupped them around the edges of the can. "Yeah."

"You gotta be fast."

"Ok."

"Here I go!"

Parent rubbed the metal iron back and forth over the staub.

Skrrrt.

Skrrrt.

Skrrrt.

The sound bounced off the trees and echoed back louder. After a few short moments, earthworm heads poked out of the dirt and flopped up onto the coating of leaves. Braylee jumped to his feet and scooped up one worm, two worm, three worm until he accidentally stepped on one and pulled at the same time and—

Pop.

—It ripped in half.

Braylee's eyes glued to the half of the worm in his hand, inching along his palm. It was still... he lifted up his foot and saw the other half flopping back and forth underneath it.

Alive?

Dropping the ripped worm back on the ground, Braylee yelped and bolted to Parent's side. Ducking behind their shoulder, he pointed at the living, dead thing, stuttering over his words.

Parent seemed to already know what happened. They always knew.

"It's ok." They said. "Worms have five hearts. You didn't hurt it. You just makes two new worms."

"Really?"

"Yup. It's completely natural."

Braylee glanced back to where he left the worm—or worms, but he couldn't pick them out of the other worms squiggling in the soil.

"Don't worry." Parent gave his shoulder a pat. "It happens all the time."

Braylee curled his shaking fingers around the can.

"Really?"

Parent laughed. "Yes. Now you better get picking, or these worms are going to get away."

Braylee stepped back out from behind Parent, checking the ground before placing each foot. He gently, carefully, slowly grabbed another worm as Parent started skrrrting again.

II

The backyard shed was were the worms lived.

Rows and rows of fish aquariums stacked from the floor to the ceiling along every wall, each one full of exactly 100 worms. Most of the floor space was taken up by a wobbly table, and the only light came from a single bulb that dangled from the ceiling. It flickered a lot, and the color wasn't right, so it painted everything a dull shade of orange.

Braylee perched on top of the shed table, the can of earthworms balanced between his crisscrossed legs. The worms slipped and slithered inside their tin can, tangled together in a slimy knot, and Braylee watched the ones on top poke their skinny heads in the air.

Were they watching him back?

Did they have eyes?

He leaned so close to the can the bobbing worms nearly poke his nose, but he didn't see any eyes on those faceless faces.

Braylee reached in and plucked one of the worms out of the knot. It dangled and flicked back and forth like the tip of a cat's tail. Braylee dropped it in the empty tank next to him.

One.

He grabbed a second, feeling the slimy flesh squish between his fingers, and flicked it into the tank as well.

Two.

The next worm was long, almost as long as his lower arm. It was like two worms stuck together.

Three.

Braylee kept picking and counting. He pinched the head of the twenty-seventh worm between two fingers then reached around with his other hand and grabbed the bottom. A quick, sharp tug and—pop. Braylee stared at the two, wriggling worms in his hands.

Both still alive.

Both still moving.

He tossed both ends into the tank and reached for the next worm (was this the twenty-eighth or twenty-ninth?).

Pop.

Two new worms.

They squirmed around in his fingers like they didn't even notice they had been ripped apart. But it must hurt, right? Thinking about it made Braylee's insides flop like a giant beach wave. A hard lump formed at the bottom of his throat, and Braylee flung the worms in the tank and wiped his sticky hands on the knees of his pants.

Just keep counting.

Thirty. Thirty-one. Thirty-two. Thirty-three.

When a worm gets ripped in half, is it still the same worm?

Braylee hesitated, hand hovering over the can as the thought flashed across his mind. Do they still act like the same worm? Or do they each go off and do their own things? He risked a glance back at the tank, but he couldn't find the ripped-in-half worms in the growing pile. Did they stick themselves back together? Could they do that?

A shiver ran down his spine, and Braylee started counting faster.

Forty-five. Forty-six. Forty-seven.

What would two halves of the same worm do when they saw each other?

Fifty-two. Fifty-three. Fifty-four.

Do they recognize each other?

Sixty-eight. Sixty-nine. Seventy.

Do they pretend they're an entirely different worm?

Seventy-six. Seventy-seven. Seventy-eight.

Can they even tell?

Braylee dropped the last worm into the tank. Ninety-three. Not enough for a batch. He chewed his bottom lip and studied the little pink bodies. It didn't hurt them... It's completely natural... He reached back into the tank.

Pop.

Pop.

Pop.

Pop.

Pop.

Pop.

Pop.

III

Braylee propped his chin on the edge of the table, watching the worm he had carefully picked from the perfect batch of 100 inch around in front of his nose. He had managed to drag one of the kitchen chairs out the back door when the shouting started. Now he scooted it so close to the table it smashed his ribs.

The worm turned toward the edge of the table, and Braylee blew it back the other way.

He wondered how long it would last. When the next farmer came along and bought this worm, would it get pecked in half by a bird? Would a rock fall on it and cut it in half? Would the farmer cut it in half?

Braylee blew on it again. Then a second time, making it roll three rolls like a log.

Does every worm end up ripped in half? Surely not all of them. Surely not.

The latch on the shed door whined as it lifted, and Braylee lunched across the table, scooping the worm up into the palm of his hands. He twirled around in the kitchen chair as Parent poked their head through the door.

"Brayl—what's that chair doing out—oh never mind." Parent stepped the rest of the way inside and closed the door with a click behind them. "Braylee, we want to talk—well, explain something to you. Can we do that?"

The worm poked its head against Braylee's fingers, and he clasped his hands tighter.

Parent crouched in front of Braylee, resting a hand on the tip of his knee. "We love you. We always will. You know that right?"

Braylee shrugged.

"We do." Parent assured. "But we don't love ourselves anymore. Not like we used to."

The skin at the top of Parent's head split apart in a tiny tear, right in the part of their hair. Braylee's stomach churned as a thin line of blood bubbled out, and his eyes glued to the red as it drooled down the tip of their nose.

The worm tossed and turned in his hands.

"It's ok." Parent said.

The tear opened into a crevice, making the sides of Parent's head flop over like wilted rose petals.

"We still love you."

A cold chill swept down the back of Braylee's neck as the rip split between Parent's eyes and down the middle of their toothy smile, strings of brain, snot, blood, and spit stretching between the two faces.

Braylee leapt from the chair and scurried behind it, clutching the worm to his chest. It twisted so violently in his hands it made his fingers tremble.

Parent didn't stop smiling. "What's wrong?"

One of Parent's arms reached forward, tearing the neck and shoulder away from the other. A wave of chunky blood hit the floor with a splat, speckling the aquariums of worms with red dots. Braylee flinched and stumbled back into the towering rows of tanks.

"We'll still see you. Everyday."

The two halves spoke at the same time with the same voice. Braylee could see the two sides of tongue flick against two sets of teeth through the gaping holes. He wanted to get out, but the door was over there behind... behind. So he scrambled around the table instead.

Both smiles poked down in a frown at the same moment.

"You seem upset." Parent said.

One of the legs stepped toward Braylee, ripping the rest of the body clean in half. Braylee's breath caught in his throat, and he ducked underneath the table, the worm in his hands snapping hard against his skin. The two halves of Parent balanced, swaying, on one foot each.

"Just take a deep breath." One knee bent, and half a face peered under the roof of the table. The mouth peeked into a smile again. "It'll be ok."

Braylee wanted to close his eyes, but they were stuck open. Stuck seeing the bent half open and close its hand as it started singing.

"Open shut them. Open shut them. Give a little clap, clap, clap."

The standing half started hopping in the puddles of blood, waving its hand in time with the tune.

"Open shut them. Open shut them. Put them in your lap, lap, lap."

Splish splashes of blood drummed against the tanks, making the glass shatter and spilling tangled masses of worms to the floor.

The bent half wiggled their fingers like spider legs. "Creep them crawl them."

"Creep them crawl them right up to your chin, chin, chin." The standing half jumped around the piles of worms, and more tanks exploded, raining hundreds of worms over Braylee's huddled shoulders.

He ducked his head under his arms as worms stuck to his hair and slipped down the back of his shirt. The worm in his hands pressed against his fingers, making them throb in rhythm with his racing heartbeat.

"Open up your little mouth..." Parent sang.

The worms slithered down his forehead and over his eyelids until all he could see was slimy brown segments. The thump of Parent's hopping drummed in his ears.

"But do not let the worms get in!"

Dozens of worm heads slipped between Braylee's lips, and he finally screamed.

# The Carnival

P aling Blvd. was deserted, the congestion of daytime long since cleared. Amy stood on the sidewalk beneath a moonless sky. Across the street was darkness. A vacant space where the carnival had been. It was gone. She'd missed it.

She crossed mid-block, footfalls echoing on the asphalt as her vision struggled in the failing light. Empty popcorn bags rustled beyond the open gate as shadowy rats foraged among candy-apple cores and half eaten hotdogs. Startled, a yelp wrenched her throat. She glanced behind, eyes wet, toward a sputtering porch lamp.

*I'm never going back.*

The grounds were cloaked in pitch. Cropped grass had been trampled to dry nubs that crackled as she walked. Disappointment swept through her in waves. No Ferris-wheel or carousel, no rollercoaster or game booths, no clowns. Nothing...

...except in the distance, a solitary shimmer. Near where the arcade once stood, a single beacon.

She followed it.

The shape of a structure emerged from the murk like the bow of a freighter in fog, looming over her. The front was festooned as a giant face with huge painted eyes about the windows. A large gaudy clown's mouth stretched the full breadth and served as the entry. Bulbs flickered beneath the thick lips, neon teeth.

Amy shuddered. There was nothing but emptiness around her. Alone. She stood alone amongst the nothing. Nothing except this one place. This single source of hope.

She turned the knob and went inside.

"Hello?" A hall filled with mirrors contorted her form as she inched forward. The door swung shut.

Ahead, a scraping clamor echoed beyond view.

A silhouette stumbled into the room, tall and wide, blackened by an ominous glow. "Chicago." A man's voice muttered. "Everyone laughed in Chicago."

Amy pressed against a grinning canvas, her heart pounding.

The figure turned, gasping, teeth bared. His face was painted white, crimson dots on his cheeks, eyes arched high with blue makeup, and a leering maw drawn to reach his ears. "Who—get out!" He snarled, words slurred. "We're closed."

Her knees went slack. "I missed the carnival and..."

Tendrils of smoke slithered along the floor.

The clown lurched near, lifting a revolver. The burnished steel glinted sharp and black.

Amy fought for air, cold enveloping her, a scream tearing from reflexive depths.

The tendons in his neck flexed as he thrust the weapon forward. "Shut up! You hear? Shut up!"

She bit her lip, swallowing barbed and painful sobs.

His eyes darted between the increasing glow and the cringing girl. "What are you doing here?" His breath was fetid, laced with alcohol.

Amy spoke, but no words came. She struggled. "I-I only wanted to join the carnival. Run away with it to—"

He pushed her to the floor. "Idiot brat!"

Her back bumped against a balloon mural, and she lifted her jaw. "I'm-I'm sixteen."

Smoke thickened as the room began to seethe in yellow and orange. "Punk kid." He ran his fingers through billowing hair then pointed to the spreading flames and laughed.

Her chin trembled. "No, no." She shook her head. "I want—"

"Want?" He coughed. "You want the carnival?" He clawed at the make-up on his face. "You came for this?" Dark streaks scarred his façade. "This stuff isn't the carnival." He brandished the gun in the rising tumult. "This is."

"I don't believe you!"

"The carnival destroys. Breaks you." His voice cracked. "I was funny in Chicago. Funny. But they don't care—used me." He placed the muzzle to his temple. "Red in tooth and claw." His wide eyes blinked. "The carnival is death."

Amy stood. "No! You're wrong. There's laughter, excitement! Nobody tells you what to do! Parents don't fight! The carnival makes people happy!" She reached to him, fingers grasping. "Please, I want to go away with you."

Black smoke twisted about the clown's feet. "Can't you understand?" A tear traced the curve of his cheek. "It's all a lie. The carnival won't help you."

An explosion shook the building, and heat erupted into the room. Flames leapt to the ceiling, swirling, hungry. Amy stumbled toward the door but stopped and turned.

The clown hadn't moved.

He trembled, sad and slow beneath his makeup. "If you're not happy before you get here, don't bother."

"Then what hope is there in life?"

He shrugged as the hem of his costume ignited. "There is none." A shot detonated. His body fell.

Amy staggered out, landing in the stubbled grass as the building collapsed. "None. There is none." She turned to the wreckage in search of the gun.

# The Old Grey Goose

Her fingers, Lettie could move them, and her arms, at least a little. But pressure, such an awful weight, felt unbearable on her hips and legs, she couldn't move anything else. She scratched her nails into the—the what? Slatted farmhouse floors? No. That wasn't right. It should have been carpet. Her carpet. Apartment 1961, Ossury Towers, South. It was indeed carpeting, but it was thick with grime, jagged shards, and debris.

Lettie struggled to open her eyes, only to realize they were already wide. Blind? No. She had the perfect vision of a 24-year-old flight attendant, at least earlier, before. But the room, her living room, was as dark as midnight. She wasn't certain. Her mind slipped into believing she was at the ranch outside Omaha. Her childhood bedroom? No. That was gone when her father passed so many years before.

She struggled to stay in the present, the now. Around her, the crashing, the snapping like the trunks of birch trees splintering in a tornado, that was real. That was happening. The last thing she saw was her shelves falling from her apartment walls, spilling picture frames, mementos, and her grandmother's antique china. Fragments scattering, joining the thundering rumble as the building lurched violently back and forth.

Earthquake. She had no memory of it. Just the plunge, a collapsing from above and below, and then—blackness.

She tried to lift herself, pressing against the floor. A searing pain tore through her and a cry filled the darkness. It came from her, reflexive, animalistic, and piercing as she felt crushed bone fragments grinding together.

Trapped. Unable to move.

She flailed as panic swallowed her mind, arms and hands thrashing as she simultaneously pushed away and tried to grab everything within reach. But there wasn't much beyond sharp edges, slicing points, and crumbled chunks of—what? The ceiling? Was it the ceiling that had come down? On her? She felt along her body to her waist and hips. Heavy timbers pinned her down, like an insect beneath a careless shoe. She felt pinched and small, misshapen and twisted, the unbearable weight holding her prone. It would take a dozen rescuers to lift an entire ceiling and pull her free. At least a dozen, once they arrived on the 19th floor of the Ossury Towers, South.

Towers. There was a reason for the name.

Lettie's ceiling was hers, but it was also the floor of the 20th level. Abigail Rhody lived there, directly above. At 85 years old, everyone who knew her affectionately called her Aunt Rhody. All the neighbors in Ossury loved her. Especially Lettie, who considered Aunt Rhody the mama she never really had. And above Aunt Rhody's home perched the 21st floor. And the 22nd. There were 48 stories total. Each level with dozens of units. Each unit with families. People like Aunt Rhody. Children. Friends. Had it all come down? Bringing them with it? Was the entire building lying across her back? Was she buried alive under an incalculable pile of rubble and bodies? Alone with corpses? Cutoff in the dark?

It was then Lettie screamed. With every ounce of strength, she hurtled her terrified voice out to the edges of the sarcophagus in which she was entombed until her lungs could draw no more air and her head spun with dizziness.

The only reply was the eerie groan as the wreck of her building continued to compact and the faint drip, drip, dripping from somewhere in the deep.

Nausea gripped her. Silence and icicles smothered her mind. She lost consciousness, buried in the wreckage of her crumbled world.

Time became an irrelevant construct. She regained awareness but could not tell if only a minute had passed or if it was hours, perhaps days.

She knew only two things.

The first was the tattered remnants of an ominous dream. Faceless men in black robes clutched at her hair and arms, dragging her down, down along a steep descent into an endless pit. Despite her struggles, she could not break free. It was death coming for her, she knew. That certainty forced her to the ragged edges of sanity.

The second was the continuous dripping in the darkness, a steady rhythm that penetrated her every thought as if it were the heartbeat of her deathly new reality. She found her senses unnaturally focused on the sound. It was captivating, the final thread between her and the world outside. A broken pipe or leaky fixture trickling down around the sandwiched floors, through Aunt Rhody's apartment and into hers. Somewhere just beyond reach in the shadows.

Lettie began to note the dryness in her mouth and the thirst crackling in her throat. She stretched her arms and finger toward the muddy splashes, but her crushed body could not accommodate the effort.

Pain ravaged her anew with each movement as a horrid frustration choked her spirit.

Lettie's memory echoed, retrieving the scent of Aunt Rhody's powder, the comforting words she'd whisper during times of trouble, the steadying presence she provided when everything went wrong.

Lettie simultaneously wished Aunt Rhody was there to help and glad the octogenarian had talked of spending the day at the beach with her great-grandson.

Lettie would have given anything at that moment for a reassuring smile, a gentle touch, and a warm, "Things will turn out, Sweetheart. They always do."

Except maybe they wouldn't this time. She just didn't know.

In her troubled weakness, Lettie may have fainted anew, but she wasn't sure. How could she be when fully aware and completely gone looked and felt the exact same? Once she regained her faculties, she began counting the drops, steady as a metronome, but sluggish, she thought. Not so much like water but rather muddier and thicker.

Lettie lurched as something brushed against her finger. It was a fleeting sensation, and she first thought she imagined it. Perhaps a spasm or a twitch in a rapidly declining body. But, no, she was certain it was real. She inched her hand farther out, searching, feeling, for anything beyond the detritus on her floor.

And she found it. Thin, leathery, like a tiny rope—but alive. It twitched between her fingers and yanked away with a hissing screech followed promptly by the cutting bite of razor-sharp teeth. A rat. It had to be. And it was trapped in the chamber with her defenseless face, throat, and wide, wide eyes. Delicate, tasty eyes. She'd heard what city rats did to those when given the chance. She screamed and covered her head with her arms, waiting, listening.

But the rodent didn't attack. Instead it sounded as if it was scuffling about the drip, drip, drip; drinking it's fill of the pool of muddy water.

She could hear its lips smacking in the dark.

Then the scratching of tiny claws.

The rapid inhalations of a snout scenting its way through darkness...

...toward her.

Lettie felt its whiskers against her forearm and wrist, its tongue tasting her palm, moving toward her face. They were wet from the dripping. Wet from the feasting. She could feel the coolness of the moisture on her dry skin. Trying to grab the creature, she lunged as best she could, but it quickly skittered away.

Lettie became consumed by thirst, shoving her damp hand and arm to her mouth, desperately trying to capture any of the errant fluid left by the creature.

There wasn't much relief. But what she found wasn't water. It smelled like moldering iron, similar to the waste tanks at the abattoir where her father took the fatted hogs each fall. And there were chunks and specks, soft enough to squish with her eager tongue but thick enough to hold shape. Blood. It was blood, congealing in the darkness...

...and Lettie relished it, taking every smudge into her mouth.

Quickly, she felt about and grasped a splinter of wood. She reached with it into the void in the direction she'd heard the rat satiating itself. She scooped in the sludgy resistance, coating her tool, then licking it clean. Again and again she repeated the exercise.

Until her stomach began to turn and she began to wonder who could possibly be drip, drip, dripping blood onto the living room carpet.

Her thoughts succumbed to panic, and she felt the faceless men returning, their skeletal fingers clawing at her hair and limbs.

"No," she mumbled.

She'd lost her father and never knew her mama. In her life she'd only ever been truly accepted by the elderly woman on the 20th floor.

"No, no. You were going to the beach."

The apartment right above her. Where the occupant would have fallen when the quake struck, fallen if her family plans had been changed at the last minute.

"No! It can't be!" She fought anew against her constraints as she wretched.

The wreckage of the building shook anew, gripped in an aftershock. A thunderous rumble emanated from below as the impact of concrete blocks and steel girders resonated all about her.

Lettie screamed, "No! No! Aunt Rhody!"

The floor in front of her collapsed, and for a moment a shaft of light from outside cut through the billowing cloud of dust. Lettie could see she was still high, very high. Suspended and dangling nearly 100 feet up above a chasm of smoke and budding flames. From above her and object fell, hanging up in the debris, pausing there for an interminable moment. The wounded body of Aunt Rhody, pale and bruised, cut and bleeding, she hung in space like a Christmas goose in a butcher's window, her limp hand resting on Lettie's arm.

Lettie looked at her face. The woman she loved. The mother she never had. Her caregiver and guardian. Lettie searched the eyes that remained open, that should have been dead, but were not. Stained with tears, they blinked.

In that instant Aunt Rhody groaned and fell, slipping through Lettie's grasping, blood slicked fingers.

"No!" Lettie's scream was at once both horrified and hopeless. She stretched, reaching, flailing, trying—but all she caught was emptiness. She was alone, trapped, suspended as the momentary light faltered and died.

# The Corner

I didn't want to travel, preferring the familiarity of my own country, my own home, my own walls. Yet travel we did, to the dismal hills south of São Paulo, to a decrepit shanty, which Airbnb had assured was a vacation estate where a couple might relax and renew. Since renewal was urgently needed, so tenuous had our relationship become of late after my diagnosis at the institution, and the price of only $10 per night fit even my beleaguered mill salary, Krystal and I left the comforts of Detroit to find our peace. But instead, we found a tin roof with no ceiling, ancient lanterns a poor substitute for electric lights, windows—absent glass—with only slatted shutters, and a feral cat who refused to leave. Krystal insisted it was charmingly rustic.

The sounds, the smells, the trees, even the disgusting crawling awful pests—especially those—were all so different and strange, adding uncertainties that my jagged psyche could scarcely manage. I understood within an instant things were not going to end well.

No doubt you, like the doctors at Northville Regional Psychiatric Hospital, will think I'm crazy, that something slipped in my mind, and I'd have trouble refuting the claim. But it started almost immediately on our arrival. Wild birds, a virtual cacophony, screeched frenetically as our confused driver—who confirmed with us three times if we were at the correct address, his eyes darting between me and the structure—pulled away. I only saw their distant silhouettes shadowed against the cloudy evening sky partially concealed among the tops of the sprawling mangrove trees that populate the Atlantic Forest. They churned in panic, I could tell, shrieking warnings about strange invaders and impending doom. I wondered if their hysteria was focused on us or someone—something—else. Of course, Krystal scoffed in that way she does when dismissing my errant thoughts, telling me they sounded pretty and that I worried too much.

But she would soon learn who was right. We both would.

The miserable cat, gray and mottled, crouched on the only usable surface in the entire shack as I pushed open the door, shoulders and arms overloaded with too many bags and cases of beauty products. It hissed at me as I struggled to unload my cargo, swiping exposed claws toward my face. It hated me, I sensed it, and I can assure you the feeling was instantaneously mutual. I did well to avoid a wicked scratch while heaving the luggage forward, sending the creature scurrying for safety...

...which it found in Krystal's arms. She scooped up and cuddled the animal as if it were the child I'd never been able to provide her, cooing and kissing the smelly thing. For no apparent reason, she took to calling it Blinky.

Being the level two inventory technician at the mill gave me experience at unloading our supplies and setting them up in the kitchen and bathroom. I'd been promoted to level two several years earlier by the assistant to the vice president of operations due to my keen eye and astute senses. I see and hear things others can't. It's my gift, although Krystal was a skeptic. Either way, her doubts didn't keep her from sitting on the threadbare sofa with stinky Blinky directing my every move—just the way Mr. Jackson did in warehouse five at the mill before his accident.

It was in the bedroom as I was smoothing the sheets and hanging our clothing that I first heard it. Careful and secretive it was, scantly noticeable beneath the sound of the first drops of rain, which had begun pinging off the corrugated roof. But I noticed it, though Krystal did not. A scratching, like a single tooth of a tiny metal pocket comb being scraped and tapped along the aged plaster of the wall. An infinitesimal chhhhhh-tick, chhhhhh-tick, chhhhhh-tick. I tilted my head, eyes rounded, searching, listening, tracking. It was there, and as I zeroed in, I could tell—from the upper corner of the room, the corner above the bed, my side of the bed. In the corner above where my head would be during the darkness of the night, when my eyes would be useless and my ears would compensate by hearing every form of brush and whisper, when my mind would recognize every demon and death watch, in that corner was a dark and horrid gash, the insides of which I did not see. But seeing wasn't needed because I already comprehended, somehow in my unconscious, I already realized, and my special ability reaffirmed, from such a wound comes no good thing.

Krystal laughed. Not out loud, but inside she mocked my concerns when I raised them—when I pointed out the splintered corner and described the scratching, scratching, scratching.

I'd not known the depths of her malcontent until that moment. She claimed to see nothing, no hole, no damaged plaster, no spilling gloom.

Nervous—very, very dreadfully nervous—I was when she, my supposed love, she insisted we sleep.

"Imagining things," she said. "Better in the morning," she taunted. "Take your pills," she berated. All the while ignoring the infernal chhhhhh-tick, chhhhhh-tick, chhhhhh-tick from the hole in the wall.

# Maxx's Well

But it was all I heard as I latched the shutters, extinguished the lantern, and lay my fevered head on the pillow, Krystal and Blinky beside me and the grave image from my childhood of my father's ever disappointed scowl recurring in my memories.

And that is when the storm came, bringing gusts and torrents and terror.

I slept not even the briefest, briefest of moments. At least I don't believe I did. When the shadows of the room converge with the darkness in the mind, how can you tell if your eyes are open or closed? But after what felt like hours, no, not hours—hours don't do the sensation justice—not hours, days. After what felt like days lost in blackness, my acuteness dragged my senses to the corner above me, to that gaping maw from which my torment spilled through derisive scraping, the devilish clawing of what I did not know.

"Get hold of yourself, son," my long-deceased father scolded, as he so often did—his voice among the drumming as the drops, like pellets, savaged the structure.

How I could see it, I don't understand. Again, you must remember my ability to perceive things others do not. But it was there, a complete absence of all goodness and light, a wound in the universe, and from it emerged a leg, long and spindly. A leg like an insect, but hinged, hideously hinged, so I recognized in an instant it was a spider. But not just any. The ever-growing length of the appendage was proof of the arachnid's enormous size. The microscopic claws on the edges of its foot slipped along the shadowed plaster, chhhhhh, before gripping with the sickening tick. A second leg emerged, chhhhhh-tick. Followed by a third, chhhhhh-tick. And another, and another, chhhhhh-tick, chhhhhh-tick! Until at last the fangs, those deathly, unnerving fangs on the head of the beast—because it was not insect, no small pest, it was hulking and powerful, and most certainly deadly. The head of the beast protruded ever so purposefully, wicked fangs deliberate, moving from side to side as if flexing or searching for nearby prey.

And I couldn't move, I couldn't move! I lay frozen, the terror in me like cement, completely incapacitating my body...

...as the torso of the monstrosity squeezed itself free through the opening, and it clung fully to the wall directly above me in my helpless state.

I—couldn't—breathe.

The room was black, entirely cast in shadows. The spider, if that is indeed what it was, seemed to be part of the pitch, an extension of the evil I'd sensed in and around me since our arrival. With each move it made. Every step, every step, chhhhhh-tick, chhhhhh-tick, chhhhhh-tick, the darkness reverberated as if all of night were a fatal web and I'd become thoroughly entangled.

It moved toward me, unswervingly toward me, fangs now firm and pointed at me, at my throat, my jugular. It knew! I could tell it knew the neck was my greatest vulnerability, the place where venom might be injected most efficiently so the poison would paralyze me quickly. And then? My horrified mind fled, unable to grasp it. The slow feasting? The consumption of my haggard flesh over the course of weeks? As I lay bound, conscious, and still living in a webbed sarcophagus?

I had no time for such considerations, however. Because as it descended, trailing murky string behind it. As it drew near, I saw for the first time its eyes. Eight spherical orbs scattered about the massive skull. They were red, they glowed, as if a fire burned inside each one, and they were staring at me...

...except they weren't. Because, as I was transfixed by my encroaching doom, as I watched death sweep lower and lower still, as what little hope I carried evaporated into nothing, I saw those weren't eyes at all. They weren't eyes because the leviathan wasn't constructed of flesh and blood, at least not most of it. Somehow the legs, the head, and the eager fangs appeared to be machine, fabricated by who, or what, I could not fathom. And those eyes, those blood red eyes, were cameras or sensors or infrared scanners or some other form of malfeasance. All this, the minute mechanical features, were attached to that very real, very much living, bulbous and sloshing body.

The thing—because I didn't know if it was an animal or a robot, it was neither, yet both—the thing began crouching for a final jump from the wall mere inches above my head. The spindly metal legs gathering themselves, the dagger fangs raised and dripping with poison, the filament of web adhered to the plaster.

I had no breath in me. None. I'd not drawn the smallest gasp since I'd first seen the brute emerging from its hellish lair. But I screamed none-the-less, not with words or tone or volume, but rather my overwrought mind was consumed by a cry of mortal terror. It echoed between memories of my scowling father, the mill, Mr. Jackson, and Northville Regional Psychiatric Hospital, consuming what little rational space I had left. As I lost any grasp of reality, my muscles began to twitch, my body began to spasm, as I accepted my sealed fate.

It jumped. A black creature in a black room on a black, black night.

But my seizure must have been too much. Extended claws struck my face. Again, and again, drawing blood. That infernal cat in her hatred for me had become incensed I'd woken her with my excessive shaking. Blinky prepared to strike me anew, but in that moment of forced clarity, as the shadow demon flew through the air, I spun away, legs tangled into the sheets, swinging my right arm blindly, striking the solid, metal, mechanical weight unseen above me. As I fell to the floor, my head smashing into the shutters, causing them to fly open into the force of the storm. Blinky arched and hissed, triumphant in her defense of the bed...

...until the spider landed on her back, fangs puncturing her neck over and over. The cat flung itself forward, more out of reflex, careening off the nightstand and onto the floorboards at my feet. The fiend dug steel claws into the fur of her shoulders and held tight as Blinky thrashed, mewling through the foam beginning to form around her mouth, fighting for her life against that, that thing.

In a moment it was over. I sat dumbfounded, trembling, and numb, blood and rainwater flowing down my scalp to my chest and legs. The ogre set about its work, exuding a dark, sticky web, wrapping the body as if in wet tissue paper as she still twitched with awareness.

It then began to climb. Chhhhhh-tick. Its prey feebly struggling. Chhhhhh-tick. Up the wall still painted with inky shadows. Chhhhhh-tick. Slowly, slowly. Chhhhhh-tick. Blinky in tow. Chhhhhh-tick. Smudging froth and feline urine as they ascended. Chhhhhh-tick. Up, up, up to the fissure in the corner. Chhhhhh-tick. Where they disappeared, mechanical legs, glowing eyes, murderous fangs, dying cat, and all.

Only then did I find my breath. Only then did sound escape my mouth. All the desperation and confusion and horror that churned within me burst forward in gasping cries. My eyes were wide, trembling fingers pointing to the portal, my screams, fevered.

Krystal sprang up in the bed, searching the night, calling out "What is it? What's going on?"

I pulled myself up, the windowsill, my desperately needed support; my nails digging into the rain drenched wood until I suffered splinters gouging my fingers and palm. So unsteady was I that my knees buckled, and I nearly fell again.

"You're scaring me," she cried. "Tell me!"

I raised my hand, the hand flowing with blood from my wounds, the hand that had deflected the heavy weight of the monster onto Blinky, and pointed anew—to the corner, that brutal corner where the passageway to hades belched its evil contents into this unprepared world. But I formed no coherent words, just garbled grunts and ramblings.

Krystal looked up. "I told you. Nothing is there. It's all in your mind."

I shook, shook, my head—spittle from my lips mingling with horrorstruck tears—protesting her foolishness.

She inched across the bed toward me. "Baby? Are you—ok? Your medications?"

But I wasn't ok. Not at all was I ok. And no amount of medication would erase what I'd seen, what I'd witnessed. No drug in the world would seal the gash in the corner above my bed, above me, that place through which death itself passes to hunt among the living. And it wasn't done, it wasn't done. I sensed there was more, more...

Chhhhhh-tick.

Behind me, lightning flashed, and a screech of wind savaged the room while thunder shook the earth.

Krystal reached out, "You're frightening me."

My mouth gaped as the spindly legs reappeared in the corner...

...Chhhhhh-tick.

The fangs, those dagger fangs.

"Please, come back to bed."

But I couldn't, couldn't, not as long as...

...Chhhhhh-tick.

The eyes red and searching.

It crouched, making ready.

Krystal didn't move, questioning.

The storm dislodged our building, tearing away the tin roof in the onslaught.

The evil being jumped, swinging down like a boulder.

Lightening split a tree just beyond the casement, the force of the impact compelling me forward.

I hurtled myself at Krystal just as the thing landed on her shoulder, claws digging into her flesh.

"Noooo!" I shrieked epithets, all the rage within me harnessed in my assault.

The spider punctured her neck in a mortal blow, injecting poison, withdrawing and repeating the damage over and over again.

Krystal screamed, hysterical, recognizing all too late that death was upon her.

I seized the creature, pulling with all my might, but I couldn't break its grasp. I clawed and tore at Krystal's neck, struggling, struggling to free her until her blood mingled with my own in a hideous flow of mortality, staining the mattress beneath us.

Krystal looked at me—at me—so confused. Not understanding—as if I were the cause of her demise...

...until her twitching body went limp and the devil began binding her with its unwholesome web.

I turned away...

...unable to stop it...

...crumbling to the floor as...

...Chhhhhh-tick...

...Krystal...

...Chhhhhh-tick...

...my Krystal...

...Chhhhhh-tick...

...was dragged up, up the wall...

...Chhhhhh-tick...

...and through the gates of Hell.

# The Pit

The door was unlocked; the latch had been broken since we were kids. Things like burglary—and murder—didn't happen here. The wailing of frogs from the creek bed warned me to stop, but I couldn't. Lo was inside, trapped. And Doogs wasn't going to just let her go.

At one time he'd been my best friend—the kid across the street, small town buddies—until he became fascinated with fire, knives, and pain. Something had changed inside of him. He camped over when we were ten. At midnight, he tossed a kerosene lantern under the chicken coop and laughed at the shrieks as the blaze spread. The stench of charred feathers and burning flesh stained me. My parents never allowed him back.

The door warped and stuck against the frame when I twisted the knob. I pressed with the toe of my Nikes, lifting the handle, trying to move it without a sound. It inched open with a deep, resounding growl. The house popped and groaned in the changing pressure, an evil presence in the depth of night.

Like the thing that had taken hold of Doogs.

I stepped inside, listening for movement, any sign I'd been heard. The air was damp, heavy with mildew and rot, like the crypts down near the marsh. It pressed about me, accentuating the silence that throbbed in my ears.

O. W. Maxx

Doogs had been expelled from Vidalia High after fighting with two varsity football players. In less than a minute, he'd flattened the quarterback's nose and torn three teeth from the receiver's mouth. I'd never seen a face tainted with such dark delight as his was at that moment.

Light prickled through the warn insulation surrounding the basement door. My heart thundered. He was down there. Down there with Lo. Doing God knows what. God. Had He ever entered here? I leaned against the wall and rubbed a hand over my face, praying for help. The building seemed to tremble in agitation at my whispered words.

The basement. I'd seen the sort of things he did in there.

Rev. Parcels daughter, Tammy, strayed too deep. I found her tied to a rusted kitchen chair, pink welts beneath the rope binding her wrists and ankles. Doogs stroked her thigh, eyes smug and twisted. He swore it was all in fun.

The reverend banished him from church. Said he was demon possessed. Forbade the congregation to go near.

Maybe we should have anyway.

I stepped over the empty paint cans and broken bottles strewn about the stairs. A single bulb glowed at the bottom, around the corner, out of view. The shadowed refractions left the steps in a muddy haze, and I clutched the railing. Something struck my ankle. I gasped. A rat thrashed near a half-eaten box of poison, its eyes burning red as death approached. I stumbled, nearly falling the remainder of the way.

The slow scraping sound of a shovel blade in earth came from the depths of the chamber.

I tried to swallow, but my mouth was dry, my throat constricted. The bulb twisted and spun at the end of a cracked wire. It flickered, sputtering as condensation collected and dripped. Shadows swayed, arcing and curling, tentacles of darkness grasping at me.

Across the room, pocked shoulders hefted scoops of dirt toward a shallow pit carved into the floor. Doogs hadn't seen me, didn't know I was there. His eyes were wild, grotesquely splayed over a face pallid with madness.

"Doogs?" My words were hollow, sodden with shock.

He spun, swinging the shovel blindly. The spastic light heightened the twitching of his eyelids. "What—why are you here?" The voice was beastly, unfamiliar.

I edged forward, hands extended. "Lo's missing, buddy. She with you?"

He looked to the pit. Darkness swelled and receded from the depth like Satanic breaths. "We were just playing. I-I—" A mask of anger seized him; his teeth bared as saliva spilled down his chin. "She deserved it! You all do!"

His unearthly rage overwhelmed me. My eyes closed, seeking strength. "Tell me where Lo is."

He wavered. "It's not my fault! She shouldn't—none of you—I was alone with it inside me." He clawed his face with filthy nails. "What'd you think would happen?"

"You're not alone anymore. Jesus." I moved to him, placed my hand on his arm. "Where?"

His expression was skeletal, lost. "Help me..."

In the pit, fingers protruded from black soil.

I retched. "Oh God."

## My Breath Fails Me

Darkness, seething, batters the walls.
I'm alone.
Claws—the window cracking.
I never wanted it this way.
Inside—no!
My breath fails me...

# Section 6: Canto – Judecca

"I've seen the dark before, but not like this.
This is cold, this is empty, this is numb.
The life I knew is over, the lights are out.
Hello, darkness, I'm ready to succumb."

Kristen Bell, The Next Right Thing

You know you are close to the end when you can no longer find peace within the darkness.

Pride Ed

# The Dust

By Curtis Layne

I

Night had fallen over the Arizona desert. An old rusted van bouncing over stones and potholes as it careened down a dusty dirt road provided the only source of sound or movement.

At the wheel of this dilapidated vehicle sat a girl by the name of Stacie Chausika. Being sixteen years of age and having just earned her driver's license the day before, she and four of her friends embarked on a "midnight drive" after an all-evening party at Stacie's house. It was this excursion that found them out in the desert, traveling along an unpaved street.

"Hey, could somebody toss me another Coke?" Stacie asked, keeping her eyes on the road ahead and one hand on the steering wheel.

"Sure," came the reply from the back seat where a short, spike-haired kid named Mike sat with a half-used 12-pack box of sodas by his feet. He pulled a can of Coke out and handed it to Katy, the 15-year-old girl sitting next to him. She took the Coke and dropped it into Stacie's free hand.

"Thanks," Stacie said, popping open the lid to the can.

The soda inside foamed and bubbled out of the container all over Stacie's hand and arm.

An uproar of laughter came from the back seat. Another of the partygoers, a young man by the name of Jon, teased.

"It's amazing what a bumpy car ride does to a can of Coke, isn't it?"

This invariably brought more merriment from the van's other passengers. Stacie, who had not entirely enjoyed the episode, happily appeased her wounded pride by dumping the can of soda down the front of Jon's shirt. The group met this action with quite an applause, not the least of which came from Travis Eldwin, the young man who occupied the front passenger seat. He remained silent for most of the drive but now didn't hesitate to join in the laughter.

Stacie tossed the empty Coke can away and glanced across the car at Travis. He was seventeen, good-looking, and one of Stacie's closest friends. Usually quiet and a bit melancholic, Travis had been credited with an almost unemotional sense of calm. He rarely became excited, and nothing seemed to catch him off his guard. Though seldom seen without a smile, it was a scarce occasion that he ever joined in a good laugh. This fact made Stacie turn her head toward him in curiosity.

"Enjoying yourself, Travis?" she wondered, looking back toward the road.

"As much as a guy in my situation could," Travis replied. "But I'm just wondering, where are we going?"

"Down the road to perdition?" Jon quipped from the back seat. Katy gave him a shove.

"Hey, we're running out of Cokes," said Mike, tossing an empty can behind him and popping open another one.

"I haven't even gotten any yet," Katy added. "Is there anywhere we can stop and get more?"

"Now that you mention it, we're running low on gas as well," Stacie said, eyeing a flickering sign in the distance. "I think there's a gas station coming up."

II

Only minutes later the aging van came to a rumbling stop in front of a small gas station and food mart. Katy, Jon, and Mike immediately jumped out and headed for the little grocery shop.

Travis stepped out and studied the structure. "This building has got to be 100 years old, at least. Like out of an old movie." He looked at Stacie then began pumping gas.

Stacie sat for a moment in the driver's seat then opened the door and hopped to the ground. "Everything out here is a relic, I suppose." The night air eddied lukewarm with a soft breeze that reeked of oil and car exhaust—that combination of smells common to all gas stations. "Not much changes."

Now that the excitement had died down momentarily, Stacie realized how sore her arms were. It was hard work, she decided, driving for hours on an unpaved road in the middle of the night, especially in a decrepit vehicle that had the power steering of a wheelbarrow.

She massaged her shoulders for a few seconds then took to swinging her arms back and forth to loosen her stiff joints.

"So, where're y'all headed, Princess?"

Stacie whirled around, startled by the strange voice. Sitting on an ancient bench near the food mart, not four yards from her, perched a bearded, wispy haired man. His clothes were stained and tattered, and he wore short, prickly whiskers. The man must have been at least as old as the battered slats on which he sat. That would have put him near eighty, if not more. He looked as though he had been sitting in the same place for decades.

"Sorry if I startled you, Princess," the man assured. "The name's Amos." He slowed his drawl to a snails pace, his whiskered face parting in a wide smile. "I kin see I'm scarin' you, little girl. Don't you worry, I means no harm. Jest thought I shud warn ya's all."

"Warn me about what?" Stacie questioned, not without a hint of nervousness in her voice. She wasn't sure exactly what to make of the peculiar man.

"Well, seems 's yer headin' west down this heer road, c'rect?"

"Yeah," Stacie said, confused. "We—I mean, my friends and I are out for a drive. I just got my driver's license yesterday."

"All well 'n good as I always says, but still," he scratched his hairy chin and paused for a moment, lost in thought. "Th' only thing down this road is an old 'aunted ghost town. Now I knows you young folks is always out for thrills 'n chills, but if I was you, Princess, I'd turn 'round and head home now. No use visitin' 'aunted places, I always says." He chuckled. It was a dry, rasping sound. "Especially not *this* ghost town! Heh!" He laughed again, though it sounded more like someone being strangled, Stacie thought.

"What's so bad about this ghost town?" Stacie asked.

Amos spat on the pavement. "Rumor has it thet a long time ago, some twelve or thirteen miners—can't recollect 'xactly how many—were diggin' a big hole quite a ways down this road. Well, they evenchally came upon a big open space in the rock, like a bubble trapped under th' ground. A cavern as they calls it." The man cleared his throat as if in deep thought. "Anyhow, this 'ntire cave was full of dust, and I means real heavy dust, too. It covered the cavern floor 'bout six inches thick, it did."

Suddenly the old man's face seemed to tighten up, and he stared off into space as though watching a string of horrifying pictures playing in his mind. His voice grew softer. "It stalked the miners one by one and swallowed them alive. It was the dust. It lived; it devoured each one of them! There—there were dead things—dead things, everywhere! Horrible dead things in the dust!"

Amos stopped talking and took a breath. He seemed to calm, and his face once again broke into a smile. "Th's ain't frightnin' you, is it Princess?"

Stacie didn't respond. The old man chuckled.

"Anyhow, some big idiot company went in there an' built a huge grocery store right over th' old mine shaft," Amos went on. "The townsfolk tried to stop 'em, of course, 'cause the villagers knew that the mine shaft was haunted, but the company wouldn't listen. Rumor is now that the dust haunts that supermarket and the rest of the town with it." He stared into an unseen distance, his voice becoming lost. "You see, the dust had lain dormant for thousands of years before those miners woke it from its slumber. It should not be woken again. So, you jest remember this, little girl: no matter what happens, don't stop in that town. Jest drive straight through it. If you can avoid it, don't go there at all."

Stacie nodded her head without speaking. She wasn't sure she believed what this man said to her, and she was in no way going to cut her midnight drive short.

Katy, Jon, and Mike appeared outside the door of the food mart, each carrying a huge pack of soda. Stacie felt glad for an excuse to get away from the old man. She walked over to the van and joined her friends. Travis finished pumping gas and returned to sitting quietly in the passenger seat. Jon, Mike, and Katy, all laughing and talking, resumed their places on the back. Stacie paused while climbing into the driver's seat; the things that Amos had said running through her mind.

Stacie glanced back to the bench where Amos had been sitting. He was gone, most likely into the little food mart. She hesitated for several seconds, holding the van key a few inches from the ignition slot. Finally, she pushed it in and twisted. The old vehicle started with an echoing clank. Stacie noticed Travis glance at her from the passenger seat. In that single look, Stacie realized that he had heard every word Amos had said. For a brief second, she thought about turning around and heading home.

But then Travis would think she was afraid of something that quite likely didn't even exist. *She* didn't believe all the things Amos told her, so what was she so worried about?

Stacie pushed her foot down on the gas petal, and the van lurched forward.

III

Stacie still sat behind the wheel of the old van a half-hour later. She hadn't seen anything that even remotely resembled a ghost town, so she was beginning to feel a little less tense, figuring it seemed rather safe to say that Amos had perhaps gotten his facts a little mixed up. Katy had fallen asleep, and Travis passed the time by refereeing an arm-wrestling competition that raged between Jon and Mike. Stacie still held the monotonous and ironically difficult job of driving, but she didn't mind too much, considering that four cans of Coke had supercharged her nerves. She tried to relax and let her thoughts drift.

But the one thing that kept running through her imagination was an image of Amos, sitting on an old bench, his face pale, his eyes wide, as he whispered the words, *"It stalked the miners one by one, and swallowed them alive. It was the dust. It lived; it devoured each one of them! There—there were dead things—dead things, everywhere! Horrible dead things in the dust!"*

Stacie's thoughts consumed her; she no longer remained aware of the world around her. All she could see before her was the grotesque picture Amos had described. Her body grew ice cold, but beads of sweat ran down her face. She began to tremble. Why, she wondered, did she feel so scared? There could realistically be absolutely no truth to Amos' words. What, then, prompted this malignant sixth sense that lurked so dark and foreboding in the back of her mind?

"You ok Stacie?" Travis questioned.

Stacie became aware of her surroundings again. She had completely let go of the steering wheel—not that it really mattered as they were driving on a flat plain—and Travis's hand rested on her arm. He leaned in looking at her; his eyes were filled with concern.

Stacie turned her head toward him and nodded a reply to his question then looked back toward the moonlit road in front of her.

What she saw then caused her breath to leave her in a short gasp.

There on the horizon, dimly illuminated by the ghostly shimmer of a pale moon, were rows of ramshackle houses, bordered by overgrown farmland and dead gardens. Everything moldered in a state of utter disrepair. An old, tattered scarecrow stood, swaying in the breeze in an ancient patch of cornfield, its empty, lifeless face gazing mournfully toward the road. A timeworn waterwheel creaked and groaned weakly as it was sluggishly turned by a small trickle of water from a dying stream. A low stone wall, overgrown with leafless vines, bordered the road on one side; beyond it stood a dark, empty house. The entire scene hung stagnant in an eerie, silent hostility.

"The ghost town!" Stacie muttered hoarsely, almost inaudibly.

Why she didn't stop and turn around then, she didn't know. Something, some malevolent will that was not her own, caused her to keep driving forward.

Old, dilapidated houses rolled by as the vehicle continued down the road. It presented a chilling picture, this dismal, abandoned village. The entire town bathed in a faint, ashen moonlight that seemed to make the silent buildings waver in a ghostly color.

Out of nowhere, however, something seemed to rise up and block out the light of the moon. It didn't take Stacie long to realize the meaning. It was a huge, black, warehouse-sized building—the supermarket that Amos had described.

"Hey, cool, where are we?" Katy inquired from the back seat.

Stacie didn't bother to answer. *"Ok,"* she thought, *"so Amos was right, at least about the supermarket and the ghost town. Then—then he could be right about the dust and the miners, too..."*

"Woah, Stacie, your van's making weird noises," Mike interjected, pointing toward the hood.

Stacie listened for a few seconds to the churn of the ancient vehicle's engine. Sure enough, she could hear a new sound: a loud, incessant rattle.

"So what?" Katy said. "It's an old van, right?"

"Yeah, Mike," Jon piled on. "Personally, I'd be much more worried if this piece of junk *stopped* making strange noises."

But Stacie *was* worried. What could be wrong with her van?

As if on cue, a sickening *clank* erupted from the vehicle's engine. Steam began pouring from under the van's hood. Stacie slammed on the brakes. But, being new to the driving experience, she underestimated how quickly the vehicle would stop. Stacie's head banged against the steering wheel as the van came to a lurching halt—right in front of the old supermarket.

Everything became silent.

Stacie sighed and slumped back in her seat, letting her arms fall to her sides. She listened as Mike, Jon, and Katy uttered cries of dismay and began chattering worriedly about how they were going to get home. She gingerly touched her forehead with her hand. The vinyl-wrapped steering wheel had gashed her right temple, and it hurt like crazy— but that was the least of her problems.

Her van had broken down, in the middle of the night, a three-hour drive from home. To make matters worse, it all happened in the center of an apparently haunted ghost town. Stacie pulled her knees up to her chin and looked around at the eerie, chilling stillness surrounding the motionless vehicle. Her eyes stopped on the sinister shape of the grocery store that loomed not more than fifty yards from where she sat. It stood dark and shadowy in the dim light of the moon and filled her with such a sense of dread that, for a moment, she couldn't divert her eyes from it.

She heard the van door open, and she spun around in her seat. Jon and Mike had already clambered out of the vehicle, and Katy was about to follow.

"Where're you going?" Stacie demanded.

"To fix the van," Jon countered. "Seeing as how you've managed to get us stuck in the middle of the desert."

Katy hopped to the ground, and Jon slammed the door closed. Stacie turned and looked at Travis, wondering if he was going to leave as well. Travis glanced at Stacie.

"Are you all right?" he worried.

"Yeah," Stacie replied.

Her forehead throbbed.

Travis nodded, then opened his door and stepped to the ground. Stacie didn't want to abandon the security of the vehicle, but she knew she needed to help her friends get the van running again; so, reluctantly, she opened the driver's side door and climbed out.

Jon, Mike, Travis, and Katy already had the van's hood open and were inspecting the engine when Stacie got around to the front of the vehicle. Katy stood shining a flashlight onto the exposed motor where Travis was messing around with a bundle of tubes and wires of some sort. After a few seconds, he stopped and wiped his greasy hands on his pants.

"It looks like the problem," he said, "is with the radiator. We're probably going to need some tools in order to fix it."

"I think there's a crowbar in the back of the van," Jon mentioned. "That might help."

He left to get it. Katy clicked off the flashlight and walked over to Mike, who waited some ways away. The two began talking in hushed tones. Travis left the van's hood open and sat down on the little rock wall that ran along the side of the road. Stacie sat down next to him.

"Travis," she mouthed so as not to be overheard, "did you hear what that old man at the gas station said—about this ghost town?"

Travis glanced at her and sighed. 'Yeah, I did."

"Well, do you—do you *believe* what he said?"

"No, not really."

Stacie nodded, looking away.

Travis asked, "*You* don't believe him, do you?"

"Well, no, I don't," Stacie said, shaking her head.

Travis didn't say anything. The silence seemed to close in on them, and Stacie gave a little involuntary shiver. The night was growing cold.

Katy walked over to them. "Hey," she said, "Mike and I were thinking there might be some tools or something in that big store there."

She pointed toward the supermarket.

Jon approached, holding a crowbar. "Good idea, Katy," he said.

Stacie saw Travis glance at her. She definitely didn't want to go into the store, but she wasn't going to back out of an adventure in front of her friends, either. Travis didn't believe what Amos had said, so why should she?

She took a deep breath, stood up, and said, "All right. Let's go."

## IV

The doors at the front of the store swung open and closed, like a gaping mouth, revealing the tomblike darkness inside. Mike and Katy were leading the way into the building; Travis and Stacie followed just behind them, and Jon brought up the rear.

From the moment Stacie set foot in the supermarket, she wondered whether she had made a mistake; for the floor was nearly six inches thick with dust—as were the shelves and the food and virtually everything else within the building.

*"Oh, get over it,"* she told herself. *"This store has been here for so long; the dust is probably natural."* She tried to push her fear aside and kept walking with her friends.

The interior of the supermarket posed an even more chilling spectacle than the outside. Shadowy aisles, each faintly illuminated with a pale light that seemed to come from nowhere, opened like eerie caverns between rows of musty shelves. Everything blanketed thick with dust and cobwebs, some of which stretched completely across the aisles and from the floor to the ceiling. Every step that the friends took made a small cloud of dust rise.

"Ok, let's get our job done and get out," Travis said. "Mike, this was your idea. You get to go look for tools."

"Right," Mike mumbled. He took the flashlight from Katy and began walking down the first aisle. "You guys wait here; I'll be back in a minute."

Stacie watched as Mike disappeared into the darkness, until all that remained of him was a wavering flashlight beam.

Travis, brushing the dust and cobwebs off one of the cash registers, spoke up. "I wonder if there's any money left in this thing."

"Let's break into it and find out," Katy suggested, joining Travis at the checkout counter. "Where's that crowbar, Jon?"

There was no reply. Katy looked around, confused. "Where is he?"

That got Stacie's attention. She turned away from watching the glow of Mike's flashlight beam and glanced over where her friends were standing. Jon seemed to not be among them.

"Jon?" Stacie called.

Silence.

"Jon?" she called again, louder and more frantic this time. She walked a little way down the first aisle, peering into the darkness, trying to spot her friend.

Was that what had happened to Jon? Had the dust devoured him like it had the miners all those years before? Stacie shuddered. What if Amos had been right after all?

She heard a soft thump from behind the shelf at her right. Stacie whirled around. A shadow seemed to stir for a split second—then nothing moved.

Stacie stammered with a tightened voice, "J-Jon?"

Something grabbed her from behind. She uttered a sharp scream and pulled away, spinning around to face the thing.

It was Jon. He stood laughing as only a prankster like him could laugh.

"Stacie, you scare *so* easy!" he teased.

Stacie began to turn red with embarrassment as she realized the trick that her friend had played. "I wasn't scared," she said indignantly. "You just startled me, is all."

Jon just kept laughing as he walked to where Travis and Katy were standing. He handed Katy the crowbar.

"That was *not* funny, Jon," she snapped, taking the tool from him. "You had us all worried."

"Kind of the point," Jon said.

Stacie crossed her arms over her chest and stalked away, further down the aisle. There, she sat down and slumped against a row of shelves, glaring at the dusty floor. Jon made a fool out of her, and *he* thought it was incredibly funny. Oh well, whatever. She wasn't going to let it happen again.

Stacie continued to stare at the floor. Then she picked up some dust and examined it closely. It didn't look like any dust she had ever seen before. It *felt* strange as well. Its consistency was that of flour, similar more to powder than to actual house dust.

Then, as she held the dust in her hand and let it slowly slip through her fingers, she thought she heard a faint whisper rising up from the swirling cloud that began to form as the dust hit the floor. The soft, indistinct murmur seemed to be warning of a doom that lurked in the very air she drew in with each breath. The shadows around her began to waver as though they too could sense the calamity that lingered in the darkness. Stacie dropped her handful of dust and looked all around. At once the whisper faded and the shadows ceased to flicker. All became unnervingly silent.

That was when Stacie saw it: the dim, ghostlike figure of a man.

The wavering apparition stood in the obscurity at the other end of the aisle, its form slightly blurred and indistinct. The man's clothes were old and tattered; all about him clouds of dust swirled in an unfelt wind. His hair lay thin, gray, and wispy, like the dust that surrounded him. But the thing about him that caught Stacie's attention most was his neck. It protruded swollen and twisted at a grotesque angle; his head bent to one side. His face bore the blank, expressionless stare of the grave, and his sunken eyes gazed directly at Stacie.

The man was clearly dead.

Stifling a scream, Stacie leapt to her feet and ran back to where her friends were gathered.

"There's someone back there!" she cried.

Travis, Jon, and Katy turned and looked at her. "What?" Jon said, confused. "Who?"

"I don't know," Stacie said. "An old man. He was—he was—dead."

"What do you mean, he was dead?" Katy asked, trying to clarify.

"He was just standing there, at the end of that aisle..." she turned and looked back toward where she had been sitting. But the ghostly man wasn't there anymore.

"What are you trying to pull, Stacie?" Jon challenged. "Is this supposed to be a joke?"

Stacie whirled around to face him. "You of all people should know," she barked. "I swear; I saw somebody!"

"It was probably Mike," Jon scoffed. "It'd be just like you to exaggerate and see things."

"I just decided I don't like you, Jon," Stacie said coldly.

"That doesn't surprise me," Jon retorted.

"Shut up, both of you," Travis said. He turned toward Stacie. "Are you sure you saw someone back there?"

"Positive," Stacie responded, eyes narrowed and glaring at Jon.

Travis took a step toward the dark aisle where Stacie had been. "I don't see anyone there now, Stacie," he commented, squinting into the blackness.

"But I'm not kidding," Stacie protested. "There was an old man standing..."

A muffled shout rang out from one of the aisles behind them. Mike's flashlight beam danced across the ceiling of the supermarket, the circle of light waving and darting in erratic motions. Mike began screaming as though in mortal agony. The flashlight beam continued to slice through the hazy dimness, throwing flickering shadows across the length of the store until finally the light vanished and Mike became frighteningly silent.

All turned uneasily still, like icicles in a spider's web on a frigid winter morning.

The four friends stood motionless for several seconds, staring toward the now-dark aisle where Mike had been. A huge mushroom-shaped cloud of dust unhurriedly rose toward the ceiling, as if taunting them.

"Mike, quit messing around!" Jon hollered.

"Yeah," Katy added, setting the crowbar on the checkout counter. "We know you're just trying to scare us!"

There was no reply. Stacie felt a sick feeling rise inside her. What was going on over there?

Travis stepped toward the dark aisle. "Come on," he said, turning and motioning for his three friends to follow him.

Jon and Katy did so directly, but Stacie held back. An ice-cold fear gripped her heart, making her want to turn and run. But at the same time, she didn't want to be left alone—if there was anything worse than being in a haunted supermarket at night, it was being by herself in a haunted supermarket at night. So, she followed Jon and Katy over to where Travis waited at the entrance to the aisle.

Amid the gloom and dust that filled the hallway, Mike was nowhere to be seen.

Katy looked every direction before asking, "Where is he?"

Jon sniffed. "Probably hiding somewhere."

"No," Travis said, walking further into the corridor. He bent over and peered between two rows of shelves, then turned back around. "The only place where he could possibly be hidden out of sight is behind these racks, and he would have needed to move them to get back there. We would have heard that."

"Whatever," Jon said, brushing the comment away. "I think he's just trying to mess with our minds."

Katy took a step forward into the blackness and called out, "Mike?"

There was only silence in response. Dust gently drifted down toward the aisle floor, swirling and blowing among the shadowy shelves. Katy sneezed, then said, "What's with all this dust in the air?"

"Good question," Travis agreed.

He pulled a laser pen out of his pocket and depressed the button. A beam of bright red light shot out of the tip, faintly illuminating the corridor and the dust that slowly billowed through the air like smoke. Travis turned and looked at Jon.

"Well?" he asked. "How did Mike manage to kick up so much dust in so little time?"

"Who cares?" Jon ridiculed. "He maybe knocked a box off a shelf or something, and when it hit the floor, it made a cloud of dust rise. It's that simple."

"If that's what happened, where's the box that fell?" Travis said, shining the laser at the floor.

"I don't know; maybe he picked it up again," Jon shrugged.

Stacie felt she needed to say something. "Even still, Jon, there would be a print in the dust on the floor where the box landed."

Stacie froze, realizing what she had just said. She looked at the floor near her feet. Then she turned her head toward the entrance of the supermarket.

There were only four sets of footprints leading into the store, and only four sets leading into the aisle.

"Travis," Stacie whispered, "Mike's footprints are gone."

Travis glanced at the floor. He didn't say anything.

"What is this, a joke?" Jon muttered, noticing the footprints—or lack thereof—for himself. "What's going on here, Stacie?"

"What makes you think I know?" Stacie reacted, a hint of nervousness in her voice. "I don't know where Mike is, and I don't know why his footprints are gone. Amos didn't say anything about footprints disappearing…"

"Who's Amos?" Jon ordered.

Stacie remained silent, the sound of her rasping breaths sounding like thunder in her ears. At the edge of her senses, faint in the distance, she could barely distinguish an eerie tap, tap, scrape. It repeated. Tap, tap, scrape. It seemed to be coming from somewhere on the other side of the store.

Stacie only heard it for a few seconds because Katy shouted, "Mike!" and broke into a run toward the end of the aisle, disappearing into the darkness.

"Katy!" Jon shouted, taking off after her. "Where're you going?"

Stacie and Travis hesitated only a second before doing the same.

They found Katy standing motionless near the end of the hallway, staring into the gloom.

"Katy," Travis breathed, "what's the matter?"

Katy didn't say anything but continued to gaze into the shadows.

"What did you see?" Stacie probed, almost afraid of what the answer might be.

"I-I thought I saw somebody, but he's gone now," Katy stammered, still staring into the darkness. Then her eyes grew wide, and she pointed into the dimness. "There—there! Look! Don't you see it?"

Stacie peered in the direction Katy was pointing, but though Travis aimed the laser light everywhere, nothing could be seen except dusty shelves.

"I-I don't see anything, Katy," Stacie said, puzzled.

But Katy had begun to back up, her outstretched hand still pointing straight ahead. "It's coming!" she screamed. "Coming—closer than ever now, and what darkness lurks beyond this I dare not guess!"

Katy never spoke again in eternity.

She fell to the ground, screaming and writhing as though in great pain. Suddenly a huge cloud of dust engulfed her, rising from the floor. In a split second, Katy's screams were cut off, and the deathless sound of silence pervaded the stillness once more. The billowing wisps of dust began to dissipate.

Katy was gone—and only three sets of footprints led into the aisle.

V

Stacie's eyes stayed fixated to the spot on the floor where Katy had been only moments before. Now two of her friends were gone. A wave of fear rippled up her back. Her skin tingled; she felt as though something were watching her from the darkness that prevailed everywhere. The faint light of hope that had, for the past few minutes, been flickering slowly out like a dying candle, completely vanished in the horror that engulfed her.

But she had been expecting this. She knew all along, in the back of her mind, that Amos was right. So why had she let her friends walk so casually into such grave peril?

Stacie continued to stare at the floor. The dust that had been drifting through the air began to settle on her shoulders. A faint whisper seemed to float down with it; a deathly murmur of a terror that she couldn't begin to comprehend.

By chance then, she looked up, toward the entrance of the store.

There, faintly illuminated by pale moonlight glimmering in through the open doorway at the front of the building, stood some twelve human figures. Or were there thirteen of them? They were vague, almost invisible, standing motionless just inside the doors of the supermarket. They seemed to be made entirely out of dust; their sightless eyes gazed mournfully at nothing. The bodies seemed almost suspended in space, wavering ever so slightly in the faint light that glistened on the wisps of dust drifting through the air. The sight chilled Stacie to the bone with a horror she had never felt before.

Suddenly she heard Jon shout, "Let's get out of here!" He took off running toward the back of the store, leaving a trail of footprints in the dust.

"Come on, Stacie!" Travis shouted, grabbing Stacie's arm. "We've got to go, now!"

Stacie wrenched her eyes away from the corpselike sight before her and turned to look at Travis. His face remained calm, as it always did, but there was an intensity that burned behind his eyes; a fire of anxiety kindled by the desire to protect his friends. Stacie saw this and knew that she could not succumb to the will of fear that had been ever growing within her. She must survive, if not for her sake, then for Travis'.

Following Jon's footprints, the two friends began running toward the back of the supermarket. The dust on the floor swirled up around their feet, and the shadows seemed to jump out at them, but they didn't stop until they reached the back wall of the store. Jon was already there and turned to head down another aisle when Travis grabbed his arm.

"Jon," Travis said, "We've got to get out of this store, but we've got to use common sense as well."

"I'm not next!" Jon shrieked, wrenching his arm away. His eyes were wild, darting madly in every direction. "I'm not going next!"

He started running again, screaming, "I'm getting out of here! It's not going to take me!"

Travis sprinted after him, this time grabbing him and throwing him down onto the floor. Jon tried to get up, but Travis pinned him on his back.

"I'm not next!" Jon whimpered. "Get me out of here!"

"Shut up!" Travis commanded. Then he turned to Stacie, who was standing silently at his side. "Jon *is* right. We *do* have to get out of here." He squinted back at Jon. "But we can't just run like maniacs toward the nearest door. We've got to think this through."

"Ok then, man," Jon said, beginning to calm down. "Think it through for us."

Travis let Jon get up then stepped back and leaned against the wall. "Ok," he said. "We know that there's a front door—we came in that way. But that door is clear on the other side of the store from us. And those things, those shadows were there. I still might have headed that way originally if *someone* hadn't taken off running in the opposite direction."

"Whatever," Jon sneered. "Just shoot me now, then."

Travis didn't reply; instead he looked up and down the hallway. A large door that read "Employees Only" stood part way open at the other end of the hall. Somewhat closer, a smaller door that led to the store manager's office remained closed.

"There might be a way out through here," Travis said, stepping toward the office door. He tried the knob, but the door was locked.

"Oh shit, man, guess there's no way out after all," Jon flopped his arms, starting to walk away.

But Travis kicked at the door—once, twice, three times. On the third kick it broke from its rusted hinges and began to fall inward, but halfway to the floor it hit against something, causing it to remain at a slant.

Stacie watched as Travis grabbed the door, lifted it up, and pulled it out into the hallway. He shined his laser pen into the dark office.

Now Stacie could see what the door had landed on.

A huge stack of boxes, crates, and bags stood in the doorway, like a barricade to keep the door from opening. A few cartons had been knocked from the top of the pile and fallen on the floor behind it.

At that moment Stacie realized there was no dust in this room—at least, no dust that shouldn't have been there, only the amount that one would expect to find in an old building. This seemed very odd.

"Doesn't look like there's any exits in here," Jon said, peering into the room.

But Travis stepped in, his laser light scanning across the walls, the floor, and the ceiling. He jumped back, aiming the light at the desk—or the chair near the desk, to be more precise.

There, illuminated in the bright red light of the laser pen, sat an old, dry, human skeleton.

Jon gaped, "Is he, is he...?" Gathering himself he looked at the others, forcing an unconvincing smirk onto his face. "Don't," his voice waivered despite his attempted bravado. "Don't worry, Travis, I think it's dead."

Stacie stared at the corpse. It rested covered in moldering cobwebs—as though it had been there for many years. The dried lips folded back in a perpetual grin; the empty eye sockets gazed continuously forward.

Travis walked over to the skeleton, examining it with the laser. "Must have died of starvation, or something."

"Died of *starvation*?" Stacie repeated. "How? He's the manager of a *food* store."

Travis aimed the laser light at the desk, illuminating a stack of papers, a tattered leather folder, several pens, and a rusted metal key. Travis picked up several of the papers and leafed through them.

After several seconds, he said, "Stacie, look at this."

Stacie stepped into the office and joined Travis at the desk. "What is it? A way out?"

"No. Maybe. I don't know." Travis showed her one of the papers.

"A newspaper article?"

"He kept it right here on the desk. It must be important somehow."

The headline read, *"Town citizen dies in construction accident."*

Stacie skimmed the following several paragraphs, then looked up at Travis. "This is about an old man who died during the supermarket construction," she explained in hushed tones. "It says he was part of the team that set about filling in the mine shaft so the store could be built over it." She paused. "That's what Amos said—then, the mine shaft must be real..."

"Is there anything else?" Travis asked as he continued to search the desk.

Stacie glanced down at the paper again. "He fell into the mine shaft, and—and died of a broken neck—but before the other workers could retrieve the body, it disappeared."

She remembered the mysterious figure that she had seen earlier of the old man with the broken neck. Could he be the person who died in the mine shaft? Stacie glanced back at the paper and kept reading.

Stacie stared up at Travis again. "The man's name was Amos Martin."

Travis didn't say anything. Stacie didn't blame him. She, too, couldn't find the courage to speak the thoughts that came crashing down on her. *"Amos? Amos was* dead*? Then that must be why he disappeared as soon as I got back in the van—he was never really there at all!"*

There came a loud crash from some far-off aisle at the other end of the supermarket.

Stacie heard Jon shout, "Hey, an entire row of shelves just fell over, and I didn't do it!"

Stacie peered out of the office door and into the hallway where Jon paced with an anxious motion. Sure enough, clear on the other side of the store, a huge cloud of dust surged into the air. Stacie turned back around to where Travis was standing. Travis had already picked up the leather folder and began flipping through it.

"Stacie," he said after several minutes, "this guy—" he gestured at the skeleton "—wrote a journal during the time that he was locked in here." Travis handed the book to Stacie. "Take a look at this."

Stacie began reading, whispering the words aloud.

*"July 14, 1978. Last night I got very little sleep, as usual, and this morning I am tired. But alas, I cannot shut my eyes! All last night I heard sounds—horrible sounds from outside my tiny room-from other places in the store. I know not what caused the noises, but the fear of it looms over me like a storm cloud—yes, I fear it! I shall never get away from it. All my efforts to subdue it are for naught; it only becomes more determined to claim my fate!"*

After that, the writing became unintelligible for almost half a page, as though the writer had become frantic. Then, near the bottom of the page, the words became clearer again, and Stacie was able to continue reading.

*"My barricade has managed to keep it out for two months now. I am running low on food—though my water supply is still practically full. I shall die before I let myself be taken! It is at the door; it is waiting for me. I hear it day and night, tapping, tapping whispering through the cracks. I cannot shut out the voice, it torments me—alas, I can write no more today, for I am weary."*

The journal picked up again a day later.

*"July 15, 1978. Oh, what a horrible spectacle! Last night, as I struggled to fall asleep, I saw a dead man, standing in my room! His neck was broken; his eyes were sunken. He stared at me for two hours; I could not draw my eyes away from his! It was terrible! But that is not all; there were more. There were dead things—dead things, everywhere! Horrible dead things in the dust! They were all around me, all of them unmoving and staring. If they come back tonight, I am afraid that I shall be driven mad!"*

Once again, the writing became indiscernible. Stacie flipped to the back of the folder.

*"February 3, 1979. I awoke this morning to the sound of a car's engine on the road outside the building, but the vehicle did not stop. I am much lonelier now. For quite some time I had nearly forgotten that the outside world existed, but the sound of the car reminded me. Oh, what a terrible torment! Wait—I hear something tapping against my wall."*

Here it seemed as though the man had stopped writing for some time, for when the words resumed, they were quickly scrawled in barely legible print.

*"The tapping anguishes me! It has been there constantly for almost an hour! Wait—now it spreads to the door as well! I hear something tapping at the knob and scratching at the cracks—I cannot take this any longer!"*

The diary ended there, but Stacie had read enough. She closed the folder and turned toward Travis.

She mouthed, "We've got to get out of here."

## VI

Stacie and Travis joined Jon in the hallway outside the office. Stacie carried the leather folder with the journal in it. Travis held his laser light, shining it at the floor.

Jon stared into space.

"Jon? Are you all right?" Stacie worried.

Jon remained motionless, continuing to stare at seemingly nothing. After several seconds, he whispered, "Don't you see it?"

"Is it dust? Ghosts?" She squinted into the darkness. "Where? Where is it? I can't see anything, Jon."

Jon froze, transfixed. "Oh, it's there alright." He stretched out his hand and pointed. "Just to the left of that big rack of canned vegetables." Then he repeated, "Don't you see it?"

In an instant her eyes locked onto something. Stacie *did* see it. Hidden in the shadows, but still faintly illuminated by light from the moon, stood what appeared to be a human figure. She only caught a glimpse of it before it unnervingly vanished.

"It's gone now," Stacie said, turning and looking at Jon. "A we need to go. Come on."

But Jon didn't reply. He kept pointing into the near blackness. "There! There; it is coming! Coming for me! I shall be blind all of an eternity, for what darkness is not darkness but in truth a void where light cannot pass!"

Jon fell to the floor, screaming. This lasted but a second, however, for without warning, he was enveloped by a huge cloud of dust. It surrounded Stacie as well because she had been standing so close to Jon. She could no longer see; the swirling plume blocked out all light. She tried to breathe, but only inhaled a mouthful of dust. Gagging, Stacie fell to the floor, choking and trying to find some air. She rolled to one side and out of the dust cloud. She lay on the floor, gasping and coughing, blanketed in a layer of dust that clung to her skin and clothes. Everything reverted to quiet for several seconds as the dust began to dissipate.

Stacie scrambled back in the direction from which she'd came and looked at the floor where Jon had been.

He was no longer there.

Stacie felt a tight grip on her forearm, tugging at her. She flinched, a scream escaping her throat, her eyes wild and searching.

"Hey, it's me. It's only me." Travis' voice reassured.

She shuttered and let him pull her to her feet.

Travis, too, was covered in dust, although he still held his laser pen. "Are you all right?" he coughed.

Stacie nodded, trying to brush the dust from her shirt. She turned and gaped in horror at Travis. "What do we do now?"

Travis hesitated for several seconds, thinking. "I guess the only option is to try and get out the back door."

"Are you sure we'll be able to make it there?" Stacie worried.

"We have to try..."

A section of racks crashed over somewhere else in the store. Stacie whirled around. A huge cloud of dust drifted up from between two rows of shelves.

Everything in the building remained quiet—for a few seconds. Then, again, the eerie tap, tap, scrape; tap, tap, scrape whispered like a distant omen from one of the aisles near the front of the store.

A chill rippled up Stacie's spine. Something alive began moving and tapping at the floor away out of sight in the darkness. The tapping became more distinct, as if whatever ghoul that made the sound was coming closer.

Then Stacie remembered she had heard the sound once already that night—just before Katy disappeared. If she had been listening, perhaps she would have noticed it when Mike and Jon vanished, too. Wait, she did. She had. Hidden in the background, but there, nonetheless. *"That must mean that this sound is somehow associated with the disappearances,"* Stacie thought.

Stacie turned around and looked at Travis, then quietly urged, "Let's get out of here."

"Good idea," Travis agreed.

## VII

Stacie picked up the leather folder, and she and Travis began running toward the large door marked, "Employees Only." It stood ajar at the other end of the hallway, about fifty yards from them—close enough. Or maybe it was too far. The dust that drifted slowly through the air hit their faces like raindrops as they ran.

Seconds later, Stacie and Travis pushed through the big doors and found themselves in the storage room and receiving dock. Just ahead of them invitingly loomed a huge roller door, the size of a semitruck. And it stood open, a gaping hole in the wall. It made a perfect exit— except for one problem.

Standing just in front of the doorway were three rows of huge storage racks, lined up as if ready to receive the next delivery. They were seemingly two stories high, reaching from the floor to the ceiling, and about twenty feet wide. They formed a perfect barricade, their slatted shelves and screened backing too small to squeeze through.

"What do we do now?" Stacie gasped, staring at the huge things.

"We'll have to crawl under and between them. It'll take too long to climb over," Travis barked as a noise echoed in from the far end of the line of racks. "And there's something at the edges."

"Let's go through them," Stacie said, eyeing the top of the shelves. "Those things are kind of high."

Travis walked forward and squeezed himself into the tiny crawl space between two of the racks. Stacie followed him. The pair of them were crawling on their hands and knees between the towering shelf units.

About halfway through, Travis, who took the lead, stopped. He turned around and stared back at Stacie. They made eye contact, and he raised his hand and pointed behind her. Stacie tensed, and all of a sudden, she could hear it: a faint tapping sound, coming from just outside the entrance to the crawl space.

Whatever made the sound was very close.

Travis said to Stacie, "You go in front of me. I'll bring up the rear."

Stacie agreed, and hurriedly squeezed past Travis. As she did, Travis stopped her and handed her something.

"Here," he said, "take this."

Stacie looked down at what he placed in her hand. It was the laser light.

"Thanks," Stacie said. "Now let's go!"

She began crawling toward the end of the tunnel once again. Travis scrambled right behind her.

The tapping from near the opening became louder and more frequent.

Stacie kept crawling. The end of the hallway was close.

The tapping sound grew more distinct.

Stacie still didn't look back; she kept moving forward. Travis remained at her heels.

Then, suddenly, he wasn't.

A huge cloud of dust exploded from underneath Travis, swirling all around in the tight space. Stacie whirled to see what had happened, but she gagged, choking and coughing as her tongue and throat were covered in mud due to the dust. She pulled her shirt up over her mouth and nose so she could get air without inhaling any dust, then activated the laser light and shined it where Travis had been.

The red beam only illuminated murky, dust-filled emptiness. Travis had vanished.

## VIII

The ominous silence returned. The tapping had ceased. Stacie was alone, by herself, between the two massive shelf sections. Dust swirled around her, drifting steadily down toward the floor.

Stacie leaned back against the side of the shelf, the laser pen resting in one of her hands and the leather folder in the other. The tunnel became filled with the ghostly light of the moon that shone in through the gaping back door, which wasn't more than 40 feet away.

But Stacie didn't get up, her motivation falling like the particles around her. She no longer felt the will to continue. A gasping sob tore through her parched throat. All her friends were gone—she would be taken next. Then, at least, she would be free from the misery she was feeling.

Stacie pointed the laser pen upward, absently fingering the button. Inadvertently, she pressed it, and a beam of red light shot from the tip of the pen. Out of the corner of her eye, Stacie noticed something swaying above her ever so slightly. She looked up.

There, dangling by its neck from the roof of the tunnel, hung the rotting, dead body of a man. It was suspended by an old rope, tied to a metal pole that jutted out near the top of one of the huge shelves. The pale moonlight illuminated the imperceptibly swaying corpse, giving it a grim, cadaverous appearance. The sunken, empty eye sockets gazed into nothingness with a deathly expression.

Stacie didn't even flinch when she beheld the apparition. Instead, she simply stared at the dead, hanging body for several seconds, taking in every gruesome detail. She glanced down at the leather folder in her hands. Flipping it open, she skimmed the pages, looking for any information about the body that hung above her.

Finally, Stacie came across a paragraph that appeared promising.

*"Shawn has hung himself; I saw him jump from the top of the shelf as I was running to the office. I could hear his neck snapping as the rope went taught; I could see the skin and muscle stretching and tearing. The veins in his neck popped with an audible sound as his head was nearly severed from his body. But still, he has endured a much kinder fate than the others have! Alas, those of us who had not the competence to take our own lives are doomed to suffer something much more terrifying—a destruction of unimaginable horror. I do not yet know what lies beneath the dust, for dust is but the residue of passing time. Time is the one calamity which man cannot comprehend or destroy; man has not the power to determine where it has begun— likewise, he cannot govern where it shall end.*

*"All of life is bound by time, but the dust is not. For the dust neither lives nor dies. Just as the earth remains wet after the rain, so the dust remains after time has passed on. Forever it shall lie, stagnant like a pool of rainwater, until someone awakens it, and is taken by the dust—down, below, to a place where time has passed and been forgotten. In this place, there is no existence, for both life and death are brought about by time—and not even time endures within the emptiness that lies beneath the dust.*

*"Just as the residue of time remains visible to those who are bound to life, so a shadow can still be seen of all those that have gone down beneath the dust. Merely a shadow, and that is all. For while the dust erases the existence of those it consumes, so it also erases all evidence of the existence. The footprints, the clothes—all of this disappears as well so there is no trace of the being ever having existed at all."*

Stacie stopped reading and gradually closed the folder, setting it down on the dusty floor beside her.

But then she felt the laser pen, which still rested in her hand. Travis had given it to her. Now Travis was gone, but the laser pen was still there. That meant that the dust must not erase *every* trace of the person...

Then Stacie realized why not.

*She* had not been taken yet. The pen was now bound to *her* existence or nonexistence. Likewise, she figured, were the memories of her friends. After all, memories were evidence of an existence.

*"Memories,"* Stacie thought absently. *"Memories that I don't want to lose."*

That made up her mind.

She became determined to get out of the store. She was going to survive. She was not going to be taken "down, below, to a place where time has passed and been forgotten." Life was precious to her—she was not going to part with it easily.

Leaving the leather folder on the floor, Stacie immediately crawled to the end of the narrow tunnel. Then she stood up and stepped out of the confined space.

The back door was near.

Stacie heard a sound: a faint, barely audible scratching—coming from behind her.

She slowly turned around, peering back into the tunnel. Back toward where the corpse still hung. Back toward where the leather folder sat. Back into that dark emptiness past the opening of the tunnel, beyond where she could see.

The tapping returned, beginning to grow louder.

Stacie whirled around to face the back door again. Outside the moon was shining down upon the rocky ground and shrubby bushes. Everything appeared bathed in a pale glow. It was an unnerving sight, compared to the darkness within the supermarket.

But even dim light is better than darkness.

Stacie at once began running toward the door. The tapping and scratching intensified behind her.

Stacie kept running.

In a split second, it happened. Stacie felt a dull, numbing pull on her left foot. A cloud of dust exploded out from beneath her—but at the same time, Stacie's other foot caught the hard soil outside the door. She wrenched herself away from the huge cloud of dust, and found herself falling forward...

## IX

Stacie blinked opened her eyes. Night had not yet ended, as evidenced by the darkness that continued to enshroud the Arizona desert, but the moon had nearly disappeared from the sky, and the eastern horizon was beginning to show the faintest traces of morning light.

Stacie hesitantly sat up, wincing from a pain on the side of her head. She could feel a large bump at the spot, her hair matted with blood.

But she stayed alive. She survived. The dust hadn't taken her...

Stacie quickly glanced in the direction of the supermarket. The loading dock door remained open, revealing the darkness inside. Nothing moved; no sound came from within the building. Still, however, Stacie didn't feel safe.

Slowly, painfully, she brought herself to her feet. Dizziness swept through her but passed in a few seconds, and she found the strength to stand without wobbling. She began walking toward the parking lot at the front of the store, making sure to keep a good distance from the structure itself. Something about the place mystified her. It seemed too silent.

Stacie guessed it was probably because time somehow became altered within the building. The dust caused some sort of cavity in time—either that or some cavity in time caused the dust—and that was why Mike, Katy, Jon, and Travis had disappeared. They had been stolen from time itself, into an empty void of nonexistence.

It wasn't until Stacie rounded the corner of the building and saw her old van sitting in the parking lot with the hood still up that she realized she had no way to get home.

"Oh, no," she spoke out loud, to herself. "This is not good."

She walked across the parking lot to her inoperable vehicle. The door on the driver's side remained open, just as they'd left it. Stacie climbed in and sat in the seat, gripping the steering wheel with both hands. Her keys dangled from the ignition slot, so she turned them and pushed the gas pedal down.

No sound came from the van's engine. The vehicle was definitely not working.

Stacie leaned her head back against the seat and closed her eyes, exhaling a long sigh. She would have to walk home.

X

Six hours later, the sun hovered near its zenith and the outside temperature had long since passed 100 degrees. Stacie had been following the flat dirt road ever since some time before dawn. Now, panting, drenched in sweat, she stumbled into the shade of a gas pump—at the same service station where she had met Amos the night before.

The old man wasn't there now, though. Stacie collapsed onto the hot pavement; her face streaked with blood from the wound on her head.

She was covered in dirt and grime, and she hadn't had anything to eat or drink since the night before. Now, as she lay staring up at the sky, she thought about how stupid it had been to go driving out into the middle of nowhere. Not only were her friends gone, but her car wasn't working either, and now—here she remained, a likely candidate for heatstroke, lying on the ground at a gas station. This turned out so much different from the happy partying, the independence, she wanted to share with her friends.

Stacie staggered but managed to stand up again. She dragged herself over to the little food mart. There, near the bench where Amos had been sitting the night before, was a telephone booth. Stacie walked over to it and immediately reached into her pocket for some change.

She had two quarters. Inserting them into the phone, she quickly dialed her home number.

After several rings, her mother answered. "Hello?"

All Stacie could say was, "Mom."

"Stacie, honey, where are you?" her mother blurted out. "We've been looking for you all night! Are you all right? Where are you?"

"Mom, I'm—I—a lot of stuff has happened. I-I don't know where I am, really. It's a gas station somewhere."

"Where, honey? What happened? Are your friends with you?"

"No, Mom, they—" Stacie couldn't say any more. "They're gone."

"What? How?" There was a long pause. Finally, Stacie's mother softly said, "Stacie, can you tell me where you are? Please, think hard. You're the only person who knows. Are you in the desert?"

"Yes."

"You're on a pay phone, right?"

"Yes."

Stacie's mother sighed. "Are you near any roads?"

"There's a dirt road that runs in front of the gas station."

"Is it that one road that runs right off the freeway—near that restaurant where your father and I like to go?"

Stacie thought back to the prior night, trying to remember whether she had driven on a freeway or not or whether she had passed any restaurants. "Yeah, I think so."

"Ok, I think I know where you are. If I give you directions, can you drive home?"

"Mom," Stacie said quietly, "I-I don't have my van."

### XI

Stacie sat on the bench at the front of the food mart. Two hours churned slowly by since her phone call to her mother, who was now on her way to take her daughter home. There would be police, too, she supposed. And questions, a lot of them. But what could she say about haunted buildings and the like?

The store clerk had given her water and a prepackaged sandwich. She'd probably looked a horrible spectacle, stumbling in like she did.

The soft desert breeze swept over the sand and rocks, kicking up tiny clouds of dust and swirling them around before they finally dissipated into the air.

The sight frightened Stacie.

The sun shined down hard onto the pavement, causing heat to rise in rippling waves and making the atmosphere seem to waver ever so slightly. It was through this haze that Stacie saw her mother's green sedan crawling down the bumpy dirt road toward the gas station. Stacie moved her eyes away from the car and glanced at the road, following its dusty curves with her eyes until the path disappeared beyond the horizon. Somewhere that way waited the supermarket where she had spent the most terrible night of her life.

Somewhere that way, the shadows of what had once been four human beings, her friends, would lie, undisturbed, beneath the dust, until once again it was stirred from its dormancy.

Somewhere that way, a place existed where time had been forgotten and was but a memory. A place that held a secret that would forever rule the destiny of all life.

Somewhere that way.

# The Abduction

Don't. Don't be afraid. You've nothing to fear. Not from me. I love you. And you, you love me, too. It's true. I know. I understand. It's hard to wake up. The drugs make you cloudy. It will pass. I won't use those on you again. But they were necessary. Needed to help you stay quiet. Sleeping. Until we were out of town. Now you're with me.

Hush. It's no use. Nobody can hear you. Not here. Not all the way out here. Not even screaming. We're so far down, under the mountain, alone. Finally, alone. And you love me. You – You don't believe me? You do love me. You just don't know it yet. And I'm going to show you exactly how much.

But there are rules. Of course. There must be. Or there could be no order, no respect. Shhh. No crying, beautiful one. Eyes like yours should never be sad. Never. I can kiss away those tears. Yes. And I will. I will. I promise.

First rule. I take care of people I love as long as they love me, too. I'm a romantic in that way. And I know you are as well. Simple, right? Do you understand? Do you? Speak up. Louder! Mumbling and blubbering is not respect! It's not love! Yes. That's better. I thought so. I knew you'd agree.

And rule two. Are you ready? This is important. I don't take care of people I don't love. And I don't love people who don't love me. You don't want to be there. You don't. I swear. Because those others— those other girls, the ones before you—well, they didn't love me. They didn't listen. Even when I said please! No manners! No respect! But—but—it's ok. We won't have to worry about that one, all right? Because you love me. We both know you do. You'll see. You'll see so very soon.

Don't be concerned. I want you to be happy. See what I've done for you? This used to be a cave, or mineshaft. Maybe a civil war bunker. I found it out in the middle of the forest. Abandoned. Completely empty! Set aside as a treasure for us by the universe. But I made it nice. Pretty. I-I, see? I built this table from an old stump where you can put your brush and, and jewelry. I stole the candles and those lanterns, too. When two people love, they reveal thoughts and dreams and pleasures. My mother taught me that. She showed me that. You are so very completely like her. And now I'll show you, too. Teach you how powerful emotions really are. And the bed, ours, we can share, I found that mattress. Perfectly clean back down near Memphis. The sheets I got from a Marriott.

Wait. Stop. Stop! No pulling away. Not here. Not the two of us together. Not during our cherished time. I might think you don't care. And you don't want that. You don't. Those other girls, they-they—it's their fault. Them. I only want to hold your hand. To feel your skin, your fingers entwine with mine. Slowly. Yes. See? You want me to be happy. And I, you! Precious angel. You-you doubt me? You should never, never doubt the one you love!

Mmm. Your fragrance. Lavender is my favorite. You wore that special for me, didn't you? Don't stare at the dirt when you're speaking to me. Unless you think I'm dirt. Do you? Do you think I'm dirt? Or some bug? We'll see. You're not the first one to think that. Where did you get it? The perfume. Where? A gift? From who? Must be from someone who treasures you. What? It just showed up in your room? Imagine that! Your hair on my cheeks, under my nose. I could breathe in all of you. You smell so good.

I took these pictures. Of you. And some with us together. Just us. And you never suspected! At the park. School. The mall. See? I'm in the reflection of that window right next to you. We look good together, don't we? Don't we? And here, this one, you're so beautiful when you sleep. Dreaming of me? Sometimes you smile in bed. I could have taken you then, last year, when I was there beside you. I knew you wanted to share your affections for me. Back then, you wanted me. But I didn't. I wanted things to be perfect. Like they are now. We've only officially met today, but I've been with you so long. I know you so well. I know things. Secrets. Your secrets. I know them all.

The fragrance you're wearing. I bought it for you. After you sampled it at the store. I put it on your dresser. Right next to your stuffed bear. And you found it. Found me—us.

Beautiful one, I've waited an eternity to be this close to you. To touch you, smell you. To feel the warmth of you against me. To, to—to taste you.

No whimpering. No, stop! Be quiet! Quit struggling!

I feel as if you haven't been listening to anything I've been saying to you. This is a happy day. A new beginning for you, for us. A new reality. Your new life. Our new life. Together always.

You're-you're shivering. Can I hold you? Do you mind if I hold you? See, there, yes. Yes. It's time. Time to learn, to experience, how much you love me...

# September 30<sup>th</sup>

It's unnerving how feeble and few are the strands with which I cling to sanity and how frayed they have become of late. Hanging. Exposed. One small push, a single tug, the whisper of an unexpected breeze and tumbling, tumbling down I'll fall. And the pit has no bottom. It is interminably dark. The possibility of endlessly plummeting frightens me to my core. But oftentimes I feel the inviting temptation. Like a warm bed of woolen blankets on a cold winter's night beckoning me. Voices in the depths muttering my name, calling, calling. They want me, and I'm drawn to them and their forever promises. Their ever-enticing promises.

I walk the razor's edge. On either side, all is lost. But razors cut. It's what they do. Their Devine purpose. Surgical steel honed to so fine a blade no flesh can possibly resist. And my shoeless feet are bleeding, bleeding in crimson torrents. There is no healing from these wounds. Your wounds. If I bled out, would anyone weep? Would you notice? Dying alone is a terrifying fate. But at least it's a pathway when all else is brambles and cairns. And there are so, so many who've gone before that I can't imagine I'll be lonely. I can literally hear their welcome reaching across. Their seductive welcome reaching across the eternal chasm.

They mean well, those peddlers of false optimism. Their exhortations to find strength and gain perspective cripple me. The foolish assumption that madness is my preferred choice, that the desiccation of hope is something I actively seek. I'm a shriveled branch, broken off and swept along by an unyielding current. Forever carried away away to a gruesome destination. And I'm tired. Struggling in vain to regain a control I never had so I can return to a place I've never been. Forgotten by my past. Unwanted by my present. But those evil, evil eyes of my bitter future, they are piercing me. Ruthlessly piercing me with foreboding delight.

I fear I'll never finish this entry. There's something moving in the room. A jagged shadow. And it's coming. Coming for me...

# The Center Ring

I

Raphael tried to concentrate but couldn't. The deserted circus grounds kept tugging at his thoughts. The snapping of the shredded big top canvas in the wind, the grating creak of the rusted metal welcome sign over the collapsing entryway, and the tumbling rustle from the littered detritus of a performance gone bad skittering across dying grass all conspired against him.

But it was the animals, the angry growls of abandoned beasts, creatures unkempt for three days waiting and plotting in the thickening darkness, that consumed his attention.

The gas lantern struggled in a losing fight against the shadows of the ancient trailer. Raphael inhaled, the air steeped in dried sweat, moldering wigs, and a century's worth of spilled make-up. He'd been raised in it, spent a mindless childhood hiding beneath dressing tables and closets of flamboyant costumes, but over the prior days, it had turned rancid and stale.

"See, now," Mr. Bevecko shook a spindly finger at the mammoth form blotting the shuttered window, "I certainly don't think it's best to talk about recasting." He swallowed, trying to straighten bowed shoulders. "When my great-grandfather Elias first had the show outside Stillwater back in '42 and the strongman was murd—" his voice tightened, "Well, when he died, great-grandfather could have panicked. But he didn't. No sir, he didn't." A thin smile trembled beneath damp eyes, twisting his pinched face into the visage of a petrified weasel.

His gaze darted about.

Raphael shrugged, creasing his forehead. Sure, there'd been problems before, plenty of them, but this, this was different.

The air in the trailer seemed to chill.

"Listen, Bertok—" the hulking shape across the room turned through the blades of powdery white light that cut between the slats of the chipped window louvers.

"Mr.," the first man interrupted with a whine. "I'm to be addressed as Mr. Bevecko." He glanced away. "I'm in charge. My father…"

"Mr. Bertok Bevecko, Berty, your father ain't here, is he? Went off to, where was it? Australia? Left you, didn't he?" The shadow stepped into the feeble circle of illumination, fists leaning onto the table. "But me," he twitched, a tick in the muscles between his wide eyes and painted mouth visible beneath spattered face powder, "I'm in the center ring now." He pulled at strands of his dirty red wig. "My show, now."

"Y-you?" Mr. Bevecko stammered. "Center ring? Bedlam the Clown? Absurd. You're nothing but a second, part of the cheesy clown chorus, a prop in the background. And a poor one at that." He raised his finger. "You never excelled. 25 years you never rose to the occasion. Center ring? Hardly."

Bedlam splayed his hand and pounded the old wooden tabletop. "Remember El Paso? They were all rolling in the isles in El Paso!" His extra-large red lips pulled back, showing filed yellow teeth. "It was—I was—" He tugged a clump of fake hair, shouting. "You're always getting in my way. You yanked me from the skit. They were laughing in El Paso. They laughed."

From the cages, a cacophony of shrieks and growls rose, sweeping like a wave over the jackals, baboons, and lions.

"You? Laughing at you? It was the monkey, you fool. The monkey," Mr. Bevecko insisted, "not you." He glanced to Raphael. "Tell him. He sat on the monkey, and it bit him."

"Umm," he'd seen Bedlam like this before, the time in the mountains of Tennessee when they weren't able to refill his prescription for a week, "look, Juan hasn't come back from town, hasn't sent word. And no police. Nothing. It's been a while. Something's wrong out there." He extended his hands, palms up. "Maybe we can talk about the show, you know, later."

Mr. Bevecko sniffed and turned away.

Bedlam the Clown lifted his arms with clutching fingers, grasping above his massive head, scratching the ceiling. The lamp flame cast shadows across oversized eyes, smudged face-paint scuffed and ragged.

"I am the show now. There's nothing else left." His voice thundered as spittle flew from curled lips. "I am the circus!"

"What? This is the Bevecko Family Extravaganza! For generations we..."

Raphael inched forward. "Ok, ok." He kept his voice quiet. "I was just thinking with the power out and phones down, you know, with the cast and crew missing, maybe we'd have trouble getting people to come, is all." He tried to smile. "Just might need to figure out what's going on before we reopen. That's all."

Mr. Bevecko blinked. "I've never understood why my father kept you around, Raphael. Great grandfather Elias would never let such things stop a show. We have a reputation."

Bedlam spit on the floor.

"We've had no power for three days," Raphael reasoned. "Generators only." He looked back and forth between the two of them. "Don't you get it? Emergency lighting only. No power to the refrigeration unit." He swallowed. "The bodies are in there."

Wind slithered about the walls and floorboards as if in a derisive whisper. The hiss of the gas lantern seemed to echo the ridicule.

"There are protocols for that. People—the police—" Mr. Bevecko stammered.

"But they didn't come; Juan and the crew didn't come back..." Raphael's voice trailed off.

"Cry havoc," Bedlam mumbled behind garbled laughter, "and let slip the dogs."

The big cats raged against their cages nearby.

 "And there's animals, the animals." Raphael folded his arms as a shudder radiated from the base of his spine. "They haven't been fed for days."

"I consider it dereliction." Mr. Bevecko snorted. "When the hired help returns, I will issue a stern reprimand, count on that."

"I'm an accountant," Raphael adjusted his wire-rimmed glasses, "I don't know how or what to feed them, you know? So—" he shrugged.

Mr. Bevecko creased his brow, "You are an employee. Not by my choice, but, nevertheless. Your job is to serve where I need you..."

Bedlam spun and flailed wildly, "You think I can't do it? The animals? That I can't handle 'em?" His eyes bulged through purple make-up, his hand moving to his stained pants. "You, you think 'cause of this I'm some sort of a coward?" He tapped his stiff left leg, pacing the length of the trailer, each awkward step accompanied by the hollow thump of a prosthetic limb on the aged wooden floor. "You ain't holding me down again, Berty. No creature gets the better of me, and neither will you!"

"Calm down, calm down," Raphael soothed. "He wasn't talking about the accident, really."

"Said the ant to the boot," Mr. Bevecko pointed at the clown. "You fool!"

"Accident?" Bedlam lunged at Raphael, lifting him from the floor by his collar. "It was murder, or at least that was the plan!"

Mr. Bevecko gasped.

"Breathe, Bedlam," Raphael choked. "Remember your therapist. Slow down."

"No accident the big cats gettin' out just as I went past."

Raphael gagged, struggling for breath. "Sorry, you're right. Mur–der." He kicked, searching for a foothold. His vision fluttered into crimson hues.

"I was just a punk kid," he dropped Raphael, "we all were. Over behind the tent rigging and winches. My mother had run away to quit the circus." He paused, shaking his head. "My dad had beat me good, figured it was my doing."

"A long time ago."

"No! All night, every night! You think I don't see it? I live it, feel it! Flesh, my flesh, tearing from bone." His nails clawed the length of his grimaced face, gouging and drawing fresh blood. "Lion teeth in me. Tendons, muscle, shredding." He covered his ears and stumbled against the wall, his voice shrill. "I can still hear the sound of my bones shattering..."

Raphael reached toward him, "Remember your therapist. There was no lion. You fell into the machinery. Your leg was caught. An accident, that's all."

"Who says?" Bedlam glared, "Him? His precious ancestors?" He pointed his chin at Mr. Bevecko. "They're the ones who opened the cage doors. Ain't that right, Berty? Even then you had it against me."

He began to move around the table.

"You've gone mad—" Mr. Bevecko recoiled. "C-consider yourself terminated."

"I told you, Berty, I am the circus now. You can't hurt me anymore." He lifted a slow, dark grin. "In a way you done me a favor. A sick, malicious favor. I'm one of them now, the beasts. That's what happens when they eat you. We've got a bit of an understanding." He backed against the door and laughed.

Raphael moved toward him. "Bedlam, let's find your meds, ok? Everything's going to be fine. No need to leave. He didn't mean anything."

The clown turned the knob, stepped out, and looked back. "Shadows and blood" He stumbled into the darkness, his voice a twisted laugh. "Shadows and blood!"

"Who does he think—" Mr. Bevecko licked trembling lips. "He's insane. Go find him and send him away. He doesn't work here anymore." He waved in the direction of the door. "Go on!"

"Try and understand," Raphael stepped toward the exit, "the carnage at the last show must have triggered something in him. An emotional break. He was there, witnessed it all."

"The Bevecko Family Extravaganza is bigger than that. When my grandchildren are born and take over, they will look to this moment for inspiration." Mr. Bevecko straightened his shoulders and raised his chin as if he'd morphed into a portrait on a salon wall.

Raphael had been in the ticket office the night of the last show, keeping track of the incoming receipts. The evening had been still, the humidity broken by the Iowa sunset and mild temperatures. Under the big top the calliope wheezed as the acrobats flew above the heads of an appreciative crowd. It had been nearly a full house. The act one finale was nearing, and he'd wandered toward the entrance to watch. A sudden thunderous wind swirled like jet wash. He covered his face reflexively as dust and hay peppered his body. He staggered forward into the tent.

It was then the canvas groaned, popped, and tore, releasing tons of fabric and sending steel girders plummeting into the crowd. Blood. Dismemberment. Like an explosion. It crushed the ringmaster and performers live in the center ring.

Panic gripped the masses, hundreds of people fighting to escape.

As the power flickered and died, Raphael had seen an oversized clown trembling in the wreckage, encircled by an onslaught of broken bodies, screaming as if the blood spattering his face was his own.

Raphael stopped at the entrance of the trailer. "You weren't there Mr. Bevecko. You don't know." He turned. "Now get out here and help me find him before he does something truly harmful to great-grandfather Elias' legacy."

II

The emergency lights blazed halcyon white across carnival attractions and sagging rooflines while gouging dark crevasses of shadow in the leeward alleys. Sphinx moths circled high in the humid air, glowing brilliantly as they neared the uncovered bulbs, only to spin violently and tumble into the dirt below, thrashing in their death throws.

Raphael motioned toward the door.

"You can't tell me what to do." Mr. Bevecko stood, frozen like a winter statue.

"Look, he's sick, unpredictable. We need to help." He descended the rusted iron stairs, stepping into the dust.

"No. I'll stay until the phones are functioning and contact the authorities in town."

"You probably don't want to be here alone when Bedlam comes back." Raphael faced the residence trailers.

"Wait." Mr. Bevecko caught his breath as he hurried to catch up. "We will drive into town. Talk to the sheriff face to face. My car is near the midway."

"Don't you understand? I can't just walk away. I've known him," he stopped and glared at the weaseled man behind him, "we've known him since we were all kids."

"I'm not a child anymore. I have responsibilities..."

"We've all changed. All of us."

A cacophony of beastly shrieks and cries rolled from the zoo carts like waves atop an irresistible tide. Raphael turned, straining to see past trailers and bandstands and into the menagerie. His lips thinned into an uncertain grimace. "It seems he's over there."

Mr. Bevecko stepped backward toward the trailer, hand reflexively moving to his throat. "Why, do you suppose..."

His voice trailed off as three forms cloaked in shadows slipped into darkness on all fours just beyond eyesight. Their fur rustled against faded paint and canvass walls. He pointed, silent, mouth moving like a gaffed tuna.

The light tower amongst the cages went dark.

"Not much to be done of it," Raphael muttered. "Let's go."

"Certainly not. I'm in control here..."

A throaty growl from a charcoal form crouching in the murky recesses interrupted.

"They're scared, hungry." Raphael stepped into the blackness. "We've got to find him, Bertok. Stop all this."

"H-he." Mr. Bevecko swiveled wide, bulging eyes. "He can rot in prison for all I care. No clown forces Bertok Bevecko to do anything." He slunk away into the dimness toward the midway.

The breeze was cool against the perspiration beading on Raphael's brow. As a treat on his 8th birthday, his father had let him sneak in to watch the animal trainers in action. Elephants, bears, and tigers with no bars to interfere. He was entranced—until the tigress spotted him in the ring. She lowered her ears and held him in her predator's glare.

Fangs bared, she had swatted at him with a paw larger than his head. He ran, pants soiled and wet, as her snarl mixed with his father's echoing laughter.

He paused, the memory feeling far too relevant at the moment, then squeezed between the cotton candy and corn dog booths, his shirt momentarily snagged by a rusted nail. He froze. An aged black bear was licking stale sugar from the pink tabletops.

"Good Daisy." He flattened himself along the wall and moved away. "Like sweets, don't you?" His breaths were birdlike, shallow and rapid. "Good girl."

He slipped around the corner. The swinging door of an open cage was sketched in black against the ebony sky. The menagerie. Raphael inched closer, pressing his vision deeper into the night. Not one set of swinging bars, but rather row after row of unlatched openings as if the occupants had simply turned the knobs and walked away.

Raphael gasped and looked about. "No…"

The lights of the second tower above the arcade went dark.

Only the big top remained illuminated.

"You always wanted to play in center ring…"

In the darkness, a scream. It was Bertok.

Raphael couldn't breathe. Fingers of ice had reached into his body, grasped his lungs, and squeezed. Nausea swept over him.

A chorus of guttural grunts and howls seemed to roil in an invisible hoard from the midway, through the gift bazaar, and toward the big top.

The sign on the crumpling entrance creaked as the breeze spun a path of withered grasses like breadcrumbs leading to safety.

In the distance, the calliope wheezed to life, morose and out of tune.

"Ok, ok, ok," he muttered to nobody. "Are you hearing this?"

A shudder radiated from the small of his back, circling up to his brow. He swallowed, stepping forward.

"Get him the meds. Save Bertok."

His pace quickened toward the cacophony, the gasping music, the big top.

### III

The giant tent sagged, its grandeur eroded by the gaping wound ripped into the southern roof and wall. Fallen rigging had degraded the structural integrity, leaving it with the appearance of a double scoop ice cream cone dropped onto the sidewalk on a blistering summer afternoon.

The calliope wheezed an ancient circus tune, a melody from years gone by sounding of cobwebs and dust. Raphael squeezed his eyes and hesitated, the vision of skeletal clowns performing in a field of coffins spun through his strained imagination.

Bertok screamed. Close. From inside the slumping fabric walls. Cut short by a hollow thud.

Laughter rolled, deep, thunderous, like a tornado eviscerating a house. Bedlam's voice, thick and vacant. It echoed about the grounds until melding with the ravenous howls of the lions and tigers.

Raphael grasped the loose canvas door, pushed it aside, and proceeded in.

Sawdust swirled through the half-light and shadows, stirred up by unseen paws. Eyes, orange and yellow, glinted from the pitch beneath the bleachers on either side.

Raphael stepped forward. "Save Bertok. Help Bedlam. Get out."

He didn't recognize his own whispers.

Ahead, the center ring. Chalky pale light flickered down through the shredded canvass awning. The ragged edges jittered in the breeze, making the red and white circle strobe like a giant blinking eye.

A voice screeched beside him as a cold grip clawed his leg. Raphael stumbled, reflexively swatting, and turned in time to see a band of chimps break toward the center post. They climbed to the trapeze platform, hanging from the railing, eyes unblinking.

The calliope paused, the music fading in a torturous rasp.

From the ring, the sound of breathing. Large, voluminous, on edge. Like an angry mob after chasing down a victim.

An angry feline mob...

The male lion, head of the pride, shook his vast mane, bared his fangs, and released an agitated roar. He paced, circling. The lionesses, with lowered heads and raised shoulders, swatted with claws extended, ready to pounce.

The tigers massed together, alternately standing and laying. Their broad tongues darting past curled lips, licking their whiskers, preparing to feed. Beneath their rippled torsos lay a broken form, unmoving, lifeless.

Bertok.

Raphael inched into the spattered light.

Movement. Across the ring, partially silhouetted in streaking darkness, an oversized figure loomed, maniacally swinging his powerful arm in downward chopping strokes. His eyes bulged and glinted on a face smeared with the blotchy remnants of smudged makeup. His wig was stiff and sprouting in misshapen spikes. Bedlam. In his darkened hand a cleaver, stained and wet. Each blow ending in a sickening squish.

"We have an understanding." Bedlam motioned his blade to the animals. "They only eat when fed." At his feet, ocelots and lemurs scratched, the python encircling his neck flexed powerful muscles, and scorpions clung to his sleeve. A sound gurgled from him, mottled laughter mixed with derisive glee. He tapped his prosthesis with the handle and returned to his labors, painted lips stretched into a twisted grin, face stained with fresh droplets of blood.

Raphael stared, transfixed, urgently deciphering the unnerving spectacle. "Bedlam, wha-what—" but his words trailed off with incomprehension.

"Shadows and blood."

Raphael raised his palms, "Buddy, is Bertok—is he—" his feet crept toward the center of the circle.

"Dead?" The cleaver descended harder, faster. The cracking sound of splintered bone shot like shrapnel. "You, you think I'm a killer? A crazed crazy maniac?"

He embedded the blade into the wood of his workbench, grasped a large object, and began to pull. Ripping, like a bolt of wet cotton fabric being torn oozed across the ring.

"I-I am the circus!" His voice tightened into a rending howl.

The calliope hissed back to life.

"I am the circus!"

In unison, the lions bellowed their collective rage, the sound echoing against deserted trailers and booths, circling the tent in a ravenous din.

The tigers rose, leaping forward in bluffing charges, screeching through exposed fangs.

Bedlam tugged the shadowed object in one final, horrendous jerk then lifted. Sickly beams of light streaked through, illuminating the pale cleaved appendage held high as if in sacrifice. A leg. A human leg. He tossed it to the cats, like a spare scrap of chicken at a backyard barbeque.

"They only eat when fed."

Raphael wretched as the animals scuffled for their meal. The world spun and shifted.

Bedlam wiped his palm on the fabric covering the plastic of his leg and laughed anew. "They prefer drumsticks."

"Your meds, let's get them. Please. Can we?"

"We make an unstoppable team," Bedlam yanked the cleaver from its rest and pointed it at Raphael. "You complete me." He laughed. "All this," he spun, "is you!" He wiped gore from his cheek with the back of his hand. "You said, 'We can't feed the animals. The bodies are in the refrigeration unit.' Brilliant!" He licked his lips. "You think. I do. Perfect."

Bertok twitched and groaned.

"He's alive." Raphael motioned to the bloodied form. "Let me get him to the hospital. We'll all go. Together. Like old times."

"All? All? Am I some sort of cripple to you?" he stepped around the legless torso. "Me? Some sort of freak show?" He hovered over Raphael, eyes wide, teeth bared, red hair in filthy disarray, white face paint scarred and spattered. "I am the circus—and the circus is life!"

He turned away, bowing to the empty stadium seats. "Ladies and gentlemen! In the center ring the master of mayhem, Bedlam the Clown and his astounding animal show!"

"Bedlam, no." Raphael rushed toward the cats and the limp body of his friend.

The tigress lowered her ears and glared, swatting with massive paws, fresh blood on her jowls.

Raphael pulled Bertok's leg, moving him toward safety.

"Look!" Bedlam continued. "We have a volunteer from the audience." He pointed his weapon at the prone man. "Now watch as this worthless, untrained weasel of a man performs for the first time with this team of starving lions."

He shoved Raphael away and knelt beside Bertok's splayed leg.

"No!" Raphael regained his footing and pushed past the circling cats.

Bedlam the Clown raised the cleaver above his head and swung it down with a thundering stroke.

Raphael dove, covering the fallen body with his own.

The lions roared with approval at the sound of the sickening impact.

# The Stench

The descent into madness is not a meandering staircase of gentle turns and mild slope but rather a rocket sled on steeply inclined rails.

I

The hound barked incessantly.

Rhyce sandwiched his skull between pillows and sheet, struggling to clutch the last fraying strands of a fading dream. A dream about Kitty. "Shut up, shut up. For the love of God, shut up!"

His shouts would do no good. He knew they wouldn't. They hadn't for the past two weeks. All hours of the day and night the dog charged between the abandoned grain mill and the house. Back and forth, a half mile or more each way, through sage and bristle as if trying to breach an unmarked and ill-conceived barrier.

Rhyce kicked off his covers, cursed the predawn pitch, and tottered down the stairs. He flipped on the porchlight and opened the door to the side yard. He saw nothing save clawing shadows, the neglected lawn, and a broken gate.

"Come here, boy," he called, squatting down with his hand extended. "It's ok."

A deep throated growl emanated from the darkness beyond view as bedeviling eyes, tinted red, reflected the insufficient light.

Rhyce checked the food and water bowls he'd left out. Both remained full.

"You'd better eat this stuff before the coyotes do. I don't want Kitty coming home to find you nothing but bones."

The barking resumed, angry and fierce.

Rhyce leapt up, stumbled back into the house and slammed the door. "You're an idiot, an idiot for agreeing to watch that thing," he muttered to himself, tugging fingers through his knotted hair. "Lucky the neighbors haven't called the Sheriff. Or shot the mutt."

The next nearest ranch was over a mile south, but sounds travel far across the Wyoming plains.

"I may shoot him myself, if this keeps up." He regretted the thought and looked about as if checking to ensure the house remained vacant. "I'm sorry. I shouldn't be thinking like that. For you, Kitty, anything. Anything and more! That's what a proper fiancé would do, right?" He rubbed an errant blush from his warming face.

He went to the kitchen to start some coffee, scraping the last of the grounds into the reused filter. He hadn't been to the market since Kitty came into his life. No need. She took care of all the frustrating trivialities, only wanting him to be safe and happy.

Filling the pot with water from the aged and rattling faucet, he paused and wrinkled his nose.

"What's that?" He sniffed. "Come on, I cleaned this yesterday." He clawed at the air in frustration. "Kitty likes things clean. Not much to ask. Pure. She's pure, like winter snow. Wants the house the same if she's going to visit. Or move in." He grinned. "Move in with, no, marry me."

Pulse surging, he spun about as the dog thundered on the rear deck.

He emptied the pot onto the counter and sprinkled it with Ajax. Grabbing the dishcloth from the basin, he scrubbed until every inch of the surface had been scoured and rinsed.

"Better," he thought. "More better."

He stretched his tired shoulder.

The sky beyond the window transitioned from black to grey to fiery orange, and the snarls began to fade as the dog sprinted away again across the rangeland.

"Run, you miserable creature," he shouted. "And stay gone for a few hours this time."

He went into the bathroom to shave and shower. He needed to be ready, just in case.

II

Rhyce hurried down the stairs after dressing and splashing his face with aftershave. Turning the corner, he almost crashed into a figure crossing the room. His spirits leapt.

"Rein it in, Romeo. I'm not your little squeeze."

Rhyce sighed, "Damn, Corky, you about gave me a heart attack."

His friend laughed. "I take it today's the special day? When?"

"Soon, I think."

"Let's hope so. You've got enough stink-pretty on to choke most of the cattle this half of the state."

Rhyce cocked his head, creased his brow, and opened his mouth as if trying to speak.

"Never mind. I'm happy for you." A condescending, doubting smirk twisted Corky's lips.

"Can't you really try to be? For reals? Just this once?"

"Of course. I am. Seriously." His eyes darkened as he forced a worried smile. "We've been together most your life. I know you. The real you. The one you never share."

"You think you know me so well?"

Corky winked and stepped toward the kitchen. "Hungry? I had my hopes set on eggs and sausages."

Rhyce jumped forward, blocking his path. "Cooking? In there?" He gaped and pointed toward the stove.

"Unless you want to build a fire here on the parlor floor. Relax."

"It needs to stay clean. No spills or splatters or drips."

Corky studied his friend. "What are you talking about? You're the messiest person I know. At least you used to be."

Rhyce, crossed his arms, fists clenched, eyes darting from Linoleum to stove. "Cooking leads to spatters and splashes. Food, pieces, fragments, and crumbs falling and rotting all over the place. Rotting, making everything stink."

Corky raised his palms, placating. "Ok. Nothing to get riled about. I thought you'd want to eat, is all."

"Corn Flakes." Rhyce hurried to the cabinet. The cabinet in the kitchen. The one above the counter. The counter he scrubbed, scrubbed because of the smell. "Not going to let you mess things up when there's no need."

"Are you kidding? We've got a full day planned. Corn Flakes?"

Rhyce stopped. "Wait, what?" He breathed deeply.

"A full day. You needed to ride out to check the well first thing. I'll go along. Then we could do some gaming. Maybe down a few suds if you've got any left. Hang out like old times, at least until Princess Wonderful gets here."

Rhyce wrinkled his nose. "Do you smell that?"

"Smell what?"

"Right here in this corner. It's sour, bitter."

Corky checked the bottoms of his boots. "Well, it ain't me." He gestured to the window. "But you do realize one of the largest free-range cattle herds in the country wanders around right out there, right? They're not noted for hygiene."

"I know what manure smells like," Rhyce seethed. "This is different, worse." He lowered his face to the Formica and inhaled, searching, before moving to the stove and sink. "Where is it? I can't find the source." He peered at the clock. "There's still time, still time. I can do this."

He fumbled in the lower cabinets, knocking against the groaning pipes, and retrieved a half empty bottle of ammonia cleaner. Like an old west gun fighter, he pulled the trigger again and again, spraying the contents over the counter and cabinet doors. Grasping a rag, he pressed against the surfaces, leaning his whole bodyweight into the cleansing.

"Hey, buddy," Corky said, "take it easy."

Rhyce blew a wayward lock from his face and continued his efforts.

"You're making a big deal of nothing."

Rhyce glowered over his shoulder. "What? You, you don't think I'd rather do something else? That I want to scrub this mess? Kitty says the worst thing I can do is have a filthy home, and she's right. She's right! The thought of moldering food makes me nauseous."

From a distance, the baying of the mongrel began drawing near, sounding agitated and raw. It circled the house, snapping and barking as if in a rabid fit.

Rhyce peeked through the window glass. "It's back, the fool thing."

"Something's sure troubling it. What do you suppose?"

"Damn dog, leave me be!" Rhyce threw his cloth against the wall and buried his face in trembling hands.

"Kitty can control the thing," Corky consoled. "She'll be home today, right?"

Rhyce nodded. "Soon, I think." He retrieved the rag and returned to his work.

"Ok, ok. Then let's have you finish all this," Corky waived at the kitchen fixtures, "so we can hang out for a bit."

III

Luminescent figures circled, punched, and kicked on the screen as animated crowds cheered their efforts.

Corky pressed buttons on the controller and leaned left as his avatar threw its foe out of the ring. "Gotcha again," he laughed. "You really suck at this today."

Rhyce tossed his handset on the sofa. "My minds just not here."

"I know, I know, Wonder Woman's got your privates in a vice."

Rhyce smirked, "Maybe."

"Has she called? Texted?"

"I don't think so." He checked his cell. "Nope, nothing. Where is she?"

"Women, right?"

Rhyce leaned back and crossed his arms, tapping nervous fingers against his biceps. The relative warmth of noonday caused the roof and walls to pop as the old building equalized temperatures. The floorboards creaked both above and below.

He sighed. "Sometimes I'd swear this place is alive."

"Life on the western frontier, I suppose. My place does the same."

The plumbing behind the sheetrock grumbled and knocked, sounding as if an angry bear was crawling through the pipes.

Corky rolled his eyes. "Maybe you two should find a new place."

Rhyce laughed. "Naw, Kitty likes it here. We'll be staying, I think."

From outside, the sound of digging claws and snapping teeth interrupted.

"Even with the devil dog from hell living with you?"

"Kitty can control him. She can do pretty much anything."

A morose howl circled them, as if in agreement.

Rhyce jumped to his feet and pounded against the wood paneling. "Stop it, please! Just for a few minutes! You're driving me crazy!"

The sounds continued, unrelenting.

Rhyce turned, hands over ears, frustration etched into the creases about his eyes. He paused mid motion, lifting his face.

"I don't believe it." He moved toward the kitchen. "There it is again!"

"What?"

"The scent. That horrible stink."

Corky stood and shrugged. "Come on, for reals?"

"And it's worse, it's worse!"

"There's nothing. All I smell is cleanser and ammonia and maybe the breath of your canine tormentor. Drop it. Come back over here and play another round."

Rhyce gaped. "There's something wrong with you. The stench is everywhere."

He bounded past the settee, the one his mother loved until she died, and the brass frames holding long forgotten faces of ancient relatives, crossing the room, nostrils flared.

He wagged his index finger as if solving a great puzzle. "And beyond the bitter rot, more. It's subtle, hidden beneath the surface, in the depths, where only I can smell it. Only me. Just for me."

He plucked about his face with fanatical pinches, eyes darting between nowhere and nothing.

"Hey, compadre," Corky interrupted. "You ok?"

"Something, something. What is it?" Rhyce flicked his tongue between thinned lips. "Like violets and vanilla—mutilated, strangled, and stressed, but there beneath." His knee began to tremble beyond control. "It's like the shower would be after Kitty has finished if she bathed in a crypt or grave." He spun in a circle, brushing his palms over his body like a person being swarmed by fire ants.

"Rhyce?"

"But Kitty will come. You'll see. You'll see!" He covered his ears, blocking the echoes of the barking dog, and ran to the kitchen. "She'll be here. She'll know what to do."

Seizing a clump of rusted steel wool, he set upon the counter, sink, wall, and stove. The pipes groaned and rattled each time he twisted the faucet, the drain bubbled and clogged.

"Clean. I need this place clean!"

Corky stopped on the Linoleum.

"Damn you, don't just stand there! Help me!"

"Help with what? What in God's name are you doing?"

Rhyce glared, chin squared as he placed a pot of sterilizing water on the stove to boil. "Are you blind? You know very well..."

From across the room, a knocking on the front door interrupted his rant.

Corky looked to the floor. "And that will be Lemmah, no doubt."

Rhyce turned.

Corky leered, "This ought to be rich."

## IV

Rhyce smudged his dripping palms on his jeans as he approached the entryway. He saw the movement of a feminine shape silhouetted on the other side of the stained-glass pane that adorned the doorway on either side with images of descending angels. He unbolted the lock and rotated the knob, breaking a dusty spider web hanging across the corner of the frame as he pulled.

Lemmah stood on the welcome mat, smoothing her pink floral dress, small clutch in one hand.

Rhyce stared, unspeaking. The dress, with delicate flowers, was the kind his mother used to fancy.

"You said I should stop by next time I was in town." She smiled tantalizing lips, lightly painted and sparkling with fresh gloss.

"L-l-lems," Rhyce stuttered.

"Got back from UW last night. The semester's done, so I'm here for the summer."

Rhyce stood frozen, like a computer struggling to open a saved file while fighting off a corrupting virus. "Lems," he said again.

"Is everything ok?"

He blinked.

"Are you going to ask me in?" She coaxed him with her eyes.

Corky cleared his throat. "You might want to think about that before you answer."

Rhyce discounted the warning, instead focusing on the powder blue of Lemmah's eyes. "Yes, yes, of course. Come in." He stepped aside.

"It's been forever. I've not seen you since—" Since when? He couldn't remember. From long ago. From before Kitty.

In the distance, the baying of the hound returned, waking him from his confusion. He grasped Lemmah's hand and tugged her into the house, slamming the door behind her.

"Welcome," Corky nodded. "For whatever it's worth."

Lemmah ignored him, turning instead to Rhyce. "So, how have you been?"

"Good, good," Rhyce fumbled. "Yes, all good here." He glanced to the floor and wall. "Umm, you want to come in and sit?"

"Thank you, yes." Her lashes dipped as she spoke, and she made her way toward the parlor.

"Have you lost your mind?" Corky whispered in staccato syllables after Lemmah rounded the corner. "Need I remind you she's a demon or devil or something. Whatever she is, she surely ain't real."

Rhyce waved him off with a dismissive gesture.

"She lives in your head. She's not of our world. Does that not disturb you? Because it scares the hell out of me!"

"Would you please stop?" Rhyce scolded. "I know what I'm doing."

"Oh yeah? And what about Princess Perfect who could show up here at any time? What will she think of your imaginary friend?"

Painted nails slipped across the sheetrock partition between rooms. Lemmah peeked back, "Is everything ok? Are you coming?"

Rhyce smiled and entered the parlor. "You look, you look amazing, Lems. Like I remembered."

"Thank you." She surveyed the room. "You seem to be keeping the place up fine."

"He's a veritable cleaning machine," Corky interjected.

Rhyce shrugged. "Kind of important to stay on top of things."

Lemmah examined the old photographs on the mantle. "I remember these," she smiled. "It must be great to have so many memories. By the way, my folks send their regards. Said they haven't seen you around town much recently."

"I, um, really haven't gone in much."

Lemmah studied him. "Then how do you get supplies? Food?"

"I, well," Rhyce clenched a fist as his back stiffened.

He thought about mentioning Kitty but, how could he? Lems had been known to be jealous in the past. But still, it was Lems. They'd grown up together through school, 4H, and long evenings in the barn. They'd been together so long it seemed she was a part of him, like another appendage or an extra brain. She seemed to know his every thought. But that was before Kitty came and Lems started to fade away. The veins around his eye began to twitch.

"That's," his voice became clipped and curt. "That's, that's not important."

"Oh, ok." Lemmah blinked downward and grimaced. "I was only curious."

Corky motioned for Rhyce to join him near the settee. "Well played there, genius," he mumbled. "That won't make her at all suspicious. Why don't you simply tell her about you and Queen Squeeze and be done with it already."

Rhyce covered his mouth to shelter his words. "Shut up about that. I'll tell her when I'm ready."

"I don't get it. How does Lemmah live inside your mind and not know about Miss Marvelous?"

"Her, her name is Kitty," Rhyce objected. "Kitty. Not Squeeze or Marvelous or Wonder Woman or anything else. Stop making fun."

"Lighten up, damn."

"Kitty, just Kitty. Ok?"

The wall of the structure shuddered as the dog threw himself against the siding. Savage barking followed as claws tore into the wood, sounding like a pack of starving wolves were attempting to break in. Rhyce stumbled back to the sofa, fear constricting a scream in his throat.

"Holy cow," Corky whistled, "He sounds truly pissed."

Sweat beaded on Rhyce's temples and neck as the blood drained from his face.

"I hope you don't mind," Lemmah called from the adjacent room. "I'm going to make up a pitcher of lemonade. And I found an open bag of cookies."

Corky spun to look at Rhyce. "She went back out to the kitchen. That can't be good, right?"

"No," Rhyce struggled to stand. "No messes."

Outside the dog continued its assault.

"Send her away," Corky warned. "This is getting serious."

Rhyce rounded the corner and toward his guest as she turned on the faucet to fill the pitcher.

In the walls, the pipes clattered and groaned, knocking against the sheetrock.

"Wait, stop!" He cupped his ears to block out the cacophony as he stumbled forward. He shut off the tap and emptied the pitcher down the drain, which sputtered and bubbled in reply. "No, not now. No messes."

Lemmah stepped back, bracing herself by placing a hand on the counter. The one he'd scrubbed and scoured. The one in the kitchen. The kitchen with the awful, terrifying, belittling smell.

"What are you doing, Lems? No!" He flailed at her. "Get away from there. That's mine, my business."

She caught her breath, startled, raising her arms to deter his momentum.

"You, you shouldn't be touching. Stop looking at me like that. Stay away from me!" Rhyce felt his heart exploding as waves of adrenalin flooded through his veins. "Get out of my brain and leave me alone!"

V

Lemmah retreated from the kitchen, eyes rounded. "What's going on? What do you mean?"

"I-I don't know. It's just," Rhyce smoothed his arm across the counter, caressing the surface, "just that—it's personal, ok? Private." His pupils dilated and quivered.

She glanced at the front door, hesitating.

"Yes, please go," Corky goaded. "We don't want you here. You're not helping."

Rhyce glared at him, "No, stop!" He turned his gaze to Lemmah. "Don't go."

Corky lifted his palms with an exasperated sigh.

"Something's wrong," Lemmah said. "Let me help."

Rhyce's voice became chopped, panting, like the beast outside the window, in spurts and stutters. "Oh, oh." He swallowed and gaped. "I think, I do think." His hollow cheeks turned ashen as he thrust his palms against his nose. "Oh, I think it's me. This reek, yes." He lifted his face staring at Corky and Lems with disconcerted eyes, lips drawn and thinned over bared teeth.

Lemmah reached for him, "Good, yes. Something inside you." She touched his sleeve. "We can fix that. We can find help. Make it go away."

Rhyce blinked at her.

"For the love of God," Corky complained, "don't listen to that thing. Wake up, man! Lemmah isn't real. She isn't of our world. She's trying to steal you away to a place where you'll be forced to live with the stench for eternity!"

A shrill, wounded laugh began convulsing through Rhyce's lungs, echoing out through his splayed mouth. He looked toward the ceiling as if in search of angelic intervention. Hiding behind riven claws, he gouged his face, shredding mottled flesh and leaving behind hemorrhaging crimson gashes.

"You're not real, neither," he screamed. "It's me, I am. It's me!"

Lemmah grasped his wrists. "Stop it! What are you doing? There's nothing." Her eyes teared. "I don't understand. I'm here. Let me help you."

"No! Shut up!" Rhyce writhed. "It's not the counter or the sink or the kitchen. It's me. Only me. I'm the smell." He spun about, facing the stove and the cauldron of steaming water. "It's me who needs to be sterilized!" He stumbled forward, thrusting his hands into the pot.

The thunderous pain rocked him, and he collapsed to the floor, blistered fingers already swollen and peeling.

"Hey, stop!" Corky yelled.

Lemmah stood, eyes frozen with horror.

## VI

Rhyce thrashed, a ghastly mask pulling his face taught, exposing yellowed teeth as his body convulsed. "It's me. It's me! I'm the smell!"

"Oh my God," Lemmah rushed to him, kneeling. "Why did you do that? I don't understand!"

"She can't know. Can't know it's me!"

"Hold still," Lemmah insisted. "Let me see."

"No, no! She can't, can't know!"

"Who can't know? What are you hiding?"

Corky tapped Rhyce with his boot. "Be careful. Dangerous ground, my friend."

Rhyce forced himself up on his elbow, clutching his injuries close to his chest.

He glared at his partner. "Shut up, Corky! Just shut up!"

He pushed himself against the cabinet into a slumped seated position.

Lemmah stood, following him with confused eyes.

"Buddy," Corky pleaded, "look at her. She isn't real. She doesn't exist. She's only a figment of your imagination. Kind of like this mysterious stench only you can actually smell. And now see what you've done to yourself! You're losing it!"

Rhyce flinched at the words. "Stop it! You're not helping!"

"What am I supposed to do?" Corky replied.

"Just make it go away. That awful stink. Corky, please."

"What do you mean?" Lemmah stammered. "Who?" She turned. "Corky?"

Corky shrugged.

"Kitty will be here soon," Rhyce wailed. "She'll know what to do."

"You're not making any sense," Lemmah said. "Who's Kitty?"

His eyes went wide.

A demonic shape crashed against the kitchen window, fangs exposed, froth dripping. It clawed and tore at the casement with its teeth, viciously trying to break in.

Rhyce jumped and scooted away toward Corky, who himself had recoiled in fear.

"There's something more to this creature," Corky snapped, glaring at Lemmah. "Rhyce, look. She didn't even blink. She's not even startled."

"She's, she's not?" He shifted petrified eyes to her. "She isn't. How...?"

"Because she controls that thing, that hell hound. She's evil, I told you. She's in your mind, and she's driving you mad!"

The beast hurtled itself against the glass anew, mud and dirt from its snout mixing with its own blood, distorting the view.

Rhyce mewled and cried.

Lemmah inched toward him. "Rhyce?"

"She's the devil," Corky gesticulated and raved.

Rhyce pushed himself to his feet on trembling legs, gagging at the smell gouging his senses. "Stay away from me!" He fumbled in the drawer for a knife, grasping it with fingers shrouded in hanging flesh.

Outside, the hound became rabid as the pipes rattled and the drain in the sink began to groan and bubble.

"Kill her! Kill that devil!" Corky sounded frantic.

Rhyce staggered forward. "I will, Corky. I'm trying!"

Lemmah raised her hands, as if about to cast a spell. "Rhyce, stop! It's me! Lemmah!"

"You're evil, the devil. Corky says."

"Who's Corky? There is no Corky. Not here. Not now!"

Rhyce looked at Corky as the walls pounded and the sink moaned like a chorus of spirits in a storm. "What—"

"Don't listen to her, buddy. She's playing with your mind!"

"My mind—she's tricking me?"

"Yes," Corky screeched above the hysterical cacophony of noises. "Now do something about it and get rid of that bitch before she drags you into the flames with her!"

Rhyce set his jaw, eyes wild, lurching toward Lemmah. "To hell, to hell with you!"

"There's nobody here but us," she cried. "You're talking to an empty room! This Corky isn't real!"

The drain in the sink backed up, the basin filling rapidly with a viscous sludge as if the underworld were vomiting its malevolence in a reverberating convulsion.

Corky covered his ears against the onslaught. "Make her stop! I can't take it any longer!"

Rhyce raised the knife over his head, mouth gaping, eyes glazed.

Lemmah screamed, stumbling away.

The vile liquid from the sink began spilling to the floor as the window above it shattered.

The dog, rabid and wild, burst into the kitchen, snapping and barking with ferocity.

Rhyce turned to the invader, the beast, dirt and gore caking its jowls. He slashed the knife downward, drawing canine blood.

The mongrel crouched, enraged, a malignant growl shaking the house. It its jaws, strips of fabric.

"No," Rhyce gasped.

Fabric from a dress.

Rhyce recognized the print.

A dress he'd given Kitty.

Corky laughed.

A dress that had been buried.

Rhyce stumbled, eyes rolling into his head. He slipped in the spreading sludge.

Buried on a corpse.

"Rhyce, what is it?" Lemmah begged. "What's happening?"

Corky cackled in derision, pointing a distended finger as shadows darkened his cheeks and brow. "Your mind is completely gone! You're mad! Insane!"

Rhyce lifted the cleaver anew as the dog lunged. Rolling into the pool of sludge as the house ridiculed with pops and snaps and the pipes continued to spew their fluids, Rhyce brought down the blade again and again and again. Into his own throat, severing his jugular and trachea, until he could no longer move, and the beast began feasting on his flesh.

In the distance he heard Lemmah scream.

He looked about. In his final moments, he saw, and for the first time, he understood. There at the end. There was no sludge. There were no noises from an angry house. There was no Corky. There was no devil dog. No scraps from a corpses dress because, when all was said and done, there had been no Kitty.

And, in his nose, there was no longer any stench.

# You Made Me

The sound of wood splintering, breaking. The muddy thwump of a baseball bat gouging flesh on impact. That is my sound, my special. In the shadows, behind the feted dumpsters, I stalk. I wait. I pounded nails through my bludgeon so, so that my angels, dark angels, might scream before they die. In a squishy, bloody sacrament, they vanish into the next world. Free at last, free at last. By my hand, they are free at last. I am the night. The tormented end of days.

Pain is the great purifier. I wield it. This world is a smelter. I stoke it, burning away the just and the unjust. In the end, we're ashes, all. The piled corpses wear collars and not. All under the same dying sun. Don't thank me. No! It was my pleasure. Flesh is your weakness. I free you from it. Sometimes slowly, very slowly. In that way, you can pass through to forever refined, pure, and lovely. I am darkness. Without me, you would never miss the light.

My leathers, black, pocked, and stained, conceal me. My scars. Filthy wounds. She cut me, cut me, the little shit! Buried now behind a curtain drawn. In the dark of embers, the memories fester. In a searing rot, malignant. My cancer, my cancer, my growing, burning, killing gash. But I have a blade, too. A Morgul blade. It will eat you from the inside. I will consume your soul. Leaving you a shriveled husk. I am desolation. No good thing survives me.

I pierced her, spilling her gore. Splattered blood on my boots. And again! I crushed her bones, her skull. Her stoned and wasted self spilling down the same storm drain where I'd recently pissed. And she writhed, helpless. She knew. From the first ripple in the darkness as I crept near, unseen, unheard, but felt, she knew! Pain had come. Misery is an unrestrained mistress whose kiss is irresistible. I am agony. You secretly desire me, and I am eagerly waiting.

Churning, my guts, inside. Seething. I didn't deserve this! This was not my dream! You pushed me into the blackness and blocked all the exits. Prey for monsters with lurid jaws and jagged teeth. Until I learned to hunt, to kill, to feed! My blood boiling now in a molten vengeance. And you blame me? Me? Hide if you must, although no hope remains. The howling wind is filled with razors! Churning clouds spill acid that no shelter can resist! I am the storm. No penance can assuage me.

Do not scoff! Never doubt! Look in the mirror!

I am the night. I am darkness. I am desolation. I am agony. I am the storm.

And you made me.

You made me...

# The Razor

Where the bedroom wall should have been, Brandt saw only darkness. It seemed to stretch forever, away into a desolate abyss. A silhouette falling into gloom being consumed by despair. He'd killed the lights and sealed the drapes hours before, like a premature death.

Brandt preferred his surroundings to match his hopes. Crushed, cheerless, and bleeding.

He shifted his emaciated body on the sagging twin mattress he now called a bed. The rusted springs protested. A far cry from before. The queen he'd shared with her. The one with the ornate bedposts. Gone, of course. Like her. Like his life.

He squeezed his eyes shut, pressing his palms against them, struggling to staunch the wetness that spilled across his cheeks. Like so much in his existence over the years, he failed in his efforts again and again and again. Guilt and frustration gnawed, relentless like termites burrowing into his psyche.

He looked back to the void, trying to see if anything was there, straining to find the slightest semblance of a future.

"Not even a flicker? Is there nothing anymore?"

On the floor he noticed—what?

He wasn't certain.

Behind where the table would have been if his world hadn't been obscured. A faint silver shadow. Less of a glint then a menacing blink from some hideous, unseen monster. It was thin, polished, and evil.

At one-point, Brandt had crafted model planes. Gliders with wingspans to harness the twisting thermals that developed in the mornings along the central California coastline. He carved each strut and cross beam from the most delicate of balsa strips. He birthed masterpieces; he created flight. All with his imagination, a bottle of modeling adhesive, and a razor...

...a razor he lost when she turned her back on him, forcing him to move out of the home they'd built together. A razor that had fallen behind the table in his pathetic rented flat. A razor that now winked ominously through fraying seams in the night.

Brandt struggled to breathe, such was the weight that pressed against him all day and doubly so during those desperate hours when blackness reigned. Gone were the playful days of flirting and whimsy, the promise of endless tomorrows, the warmth of a new sunrise each morning.

In their place, he found only anguish.

He kicked at the natty blanket, uncovering his arms, chest, and thighs in a sad effort to find comfort. But all it did was remind him he lay abandoned in the murk, unwanted and unloved.

"I'm by myself, again." His grating voice cracked. "It's almost four in the morning. I'm tired, very tired, and so, so alone."

The razor agreed, silently taunting. From across the room, it pointed toward Brandt, his forearm, where his radial and ulnar arteries labored in an uneven rhythm.

"Damn you—" he spat toward the emptiness.

It traced the ridge between his chest and neck mercilessly while prodding his carotid.

He struggled to remember those magnificent aircraft. He couldn't. They were gone. All seven. Where? Off flying, soaring on their own? Lost to him?

The cutting edge explored the back of his thigh, searching for his femoral.

Brandt swallowed, resigning himself to the inevitable calling and wept. "I never imagined things would end like this."

But the blade remained insistent.

Brandt slipped to the floor, crawling as if through a quagmire of India ink until he felt the table.

He reached behind it.

The surgical steel was cold, sharp, and lethal.

It came all so easy then. A pathway. A future. A freeing thermal rising. It took only a stroke, just a single stroke, and he spilled into an ill-boding eternity.

# He Still Felt

When a soul is cut off and buried, memories become obscured relics; not that Larom spent much time recounting those. They hurt. Savage wounds picked at and torn open, over and over again. He found no value in them. In fact, quite the opposite. They always came with a cost: screams, and tears, and the unspeakable guilt of failure. Countless doctors and years of therapy had never brought improvement. Nor had the priests, the self-flagellation, or the exorcisms. Despite his best efforts, he still felt agony poisoning every remaining cell of his body as if woven into his DNA, just like always.

"Bad—you're bad." He slapped at his dirty, crusted hand, not recognizing it was his own. "Go away."

How long had it been since even the faintest blush of warmth from the fading sun brushed his skin? Larom didn't know. He stopped counting when he boarded up the lone window in his hovel and sealed the door weeks, possibly months, prior. That's what they wanted. Or was it him? He couldn't remember. He only understood a storm was building anew outside, or perhaps in, but it was coming back for him nonetheless, and this time it wasn't going to leave unsatisfied.

"Ready, pure—the voices—stronger now," he mumbled, incomprehensible, to no one.

# Maxx's Well

For an instant, the parched corner of his lips quivered and lifted before drooping once again.

The dilapidated structure around him sagged from the weight of the darkness it concealed within, looking as though tons of malignant slag hung from the aged rafters and pocked walls. It protested with shudders and groans as if the last breaths of life were being cleaved from a dying man.

And perhaps they were.

But as far as he could recall, it was the only home he'd ever known. The stench and rot were familiar; the excess junk in every foul crevice, comforting. His rational brain, such as it was, recognized he should clean everything out before it brought the entire building down, but he feared—what, exactly? He wasn't sure. He just feared.

Larom shuffled across the dirt floor, dragging his wounded foot in the unstable murk, his cadence a tortuous thump, scrape, thump, scrape with each belabored step.

"I don't—don't need them—it."

Searing pain in his ankle and leg almost caused him to pass out.

"Yes," he whispered. "Good. Away—pure."

The inadequate sputter of an ancient kerosene lantern puddled an erratic red glow on the stained butcher block. It scarcely illuminated the extent of Larom's residual universe: pliers, blades, and metal shears jumbled together with ropes, vices...

...and bandages.

Piles of those. Some still coagulating in the corner past the feeble edges of faded light and the boundaries of his sanity.

He leaned against the table, his remaining fingers gripping, as he fought a wave of nausea. The shadowed dimness caused the scar running the full length of his forearm to appear mottled and purple. A remnant from his childhood, along with so many others, for years concealed beneath the starched cuffs and collars of his Charles Tyrwhitt button down shirts but now laid bare.

"You're weak. Look at you." The voices were back, crisp and firm. Male and female in a tangled cacophony. And as always, they spoke with the authority of disappointed certainty.

Larom spun about, peering, searching the fissures and flickers of his fetid mausoleum. Nobody. Only the enigmatic shadow of a charcoal rat, scurrying along the far wall, what appeared to be a desiccated phalange in its mouth. Beyond that, he was alone, lost in the deepening gloom.

"Pathetic."

Outside, the skeletal branches of the eucalyptus trees began to slap the clapboard in derisive agreement.

"I-I'm sorry." Larom swallowed. "I did what you asked. I tried—tried hard."

"Did you?" The hauntings scoffed. "Did you really?"

The fire in his foot and leg radiated anew. Larom cried out. "I'm here, aren't I? Like this?" He waved his scabbed and gauzed hand in a hopeless gesture as his voice broke into a sob.

"And still so weak."

He fumbled amongst the detritus, grasping the first handle he could find. With a slashing move, he swung a heavy meat cleaver at nobody, at nothing, at only the darkness.

"Leave me—" he shouted. "Leave me alone!"

"But you're already alone."

Larom grimaced and stumbled back.

"And still so unclean."

"What—" Larom trembled. "What do you want?"

"Strong."

Rain began pelting the tarpaper roof in buckets.

Larom shook his head. "No. Please."

"Pure." The swarm of voices grew in fervor.

Larom clutched the weapon, feeling dried gore beneath his grip.

"Severing ties with the putrefaction and filth holding you back."

The house rumbled and quaked, engulfed by peels of thunder.

"I—" Larom's words slurred and mewled. "I can't—can't."

"There's weakness in your very flesh," the spirits condemned. "You know this. Every inch. It's sickening!"

The deluge intensified, demanding tribute, moaning for a sacrifice.

Larom looked to the floor and the bloody trail smudged behind him, past the knot of soiled and seeping bandages, his truncated foot, and his missing toes. "Not-not again."

The voices bellowed, "Do you think anybody cares?"

Larom knew the answer, knew it fully. It had been well rehearsed throughout his life. Nobody cared. And why would they? He wasn't yet good enough. But, maybe this time. Maybe this time he would free himself from his vile filthiness. Maybe he could become clean enough to be loved. He placed his left wrist beneath a bloodied clamp and tightened the handle, pinning it to the splintered tabletop.

"What are you waiting for?" His spectral tormentors screamed with blood lust. "Purify!"

The gale howled against the shattering walls. The beams above snapped under the added burden of the onslaught. The crippled structure began to collapse in on itself.

Lightning flashed and winds swirled through new holes torn into the ceiling. Larom's hair blew wild across his splayed eyes.

"Now!" The voices became omnipotent, one with the storm. "Do it now!"

In a single movement, Larom raised his free arm high above his head. "This time! This time!"

His raging cry morphed into a deathly shriek as he brought the cleaver down, down, fast and sure, atop his trapped hand. The heavy blade performed its duty flawlessly, sinking deep into the saturated wood below.

Crimson streams spilled to the floor past his severed flesh. Larom laughed, spontaneous, wild, like a drunken addict on a new high and he felt—he still felt—as everything he thought he knew crumbled into rubble.

# The Stoplight

At an intersection, he waited as the stoplight bled crimson through a deluge of pouring rain. A hundred miles from nowhere. He sat even though he'd not seen another vehicle since before night erased the scenery. Two abandoned roads, perpendicular and separate. Each leading no place. He kneaded his creased brow with unsteady fingers.

He remained because he should. Not that anyone cared if he simply drove on through. Nobody was there to see. Nobody but him, of course. And that seemed significant somehow, despite feeling so desperately alone. But choices made a difference, he thought, except he recognized this one was unrequited. He sighed a futile breath, sinking, lost, into the frayed upholstery.

The GPS blinked nonresponsive as the cell signal died hours earlier. He didn't own a paper map, hadn't gone anywhere in forever. Stopped dreaming a lifetime ago. He only knew left, right, or straight ahead mattered not. All led to places he didn't want to experience. And he couldn't go back. She'd made certain of it. His lip trembled as his eyes began to water.

It would solve a million problems if he could vanish. Drive the rusted sedan off a bridge and into a river. Or sell himself to black-market organ harvesters. They'd put him to sleep, rip out his guts, and he'd drift peacefully away. Improve the world and be done with it at the same time. Who'd know? Who'd care? He hunched forward, hitting his head against the steering wheel.

And why should he stay? Because some archaic rule said so? Why shouldn't he dream of something more? Something beyond? Why did any of this matter when she stopped caring and when humanity would be better off without him?

But still the light dripped red.

He no longer gave a damn.

Pressing his foot on the accelerator, the tires spun on the slick asphalt. The old car lurched forward into the intersection going no direction in particular, rejecting inaction and doubt. He whooped aloud, for some reason feeling strangely empowered.

And then came the blaring of an airhorn, the screeching of ineffective brakes, and the glare of a semi-truck's headlights hurtling, unable to stop, only inches from his head.

He placed his palm upon the window—and smiled.

## The Tamerlane Bridge

Rowone was nine when he found Daisy out past the meadow in a swale not more than three quarters of an hour hike downslope from the family cabin. She'd run off, as mongrel dogs do, likely driven by the madness of a full blood moon. She always came back. But not that time. Not the summer when he was nine. He'd smelled her first. What he discovered beneath the wild prickly ash bushes was a few splotches of her mottled red fur, the collar he'd made from a broken piece of halter, and a teaming mass of maggots, flies, and worms in what had become the putrefied remains of her carcass.

He ran, terrified and crying, all the way home.

"That's the way of life, honey," his mother tried to comfort. "Gonna happen to us all one day. Nothing to be done of it. We all die. Just be sure to hold onto the times you had together. Memories stay in your brain for a lifetime. Nobody, nobody can take them from you."

"Dumb as a stump," his father said, voice scalding. "Two miles from the house and can't find her way back. And what the hell were you doing down there anyway? I told you not to stray. You get lost, and there'll be no finding you... 'cept maybe in a ravine like that stupid mutt. These mountains will eat you alive."

But Rowone did stray as he grew. Bullied at school, beaten at home, he'd run away five times before he was 15. He always came home, though. He couldn't leave his mother there unprotected.

Until one day he found her dead near the Tamerlane trailhead, half eaten by insects and worms. His father had never even reported her missing.

Rowone didn't utter a word for a month after that, even while being institutionalized. And when he ran again all he took with him was a tangled hive of images, twisted and knotted in his scarred mind.

For decades, he'd never found his way back. Despite a lifetime of disconsolate wanderings through grief and loss, disappointment and death, therapy and medications. And the accident. Especially that. But he had to. They were becoming too strong, the images. After fifty years, he had to now or he never ever would.

If he could only get past the memories.

Rowone fell against the knotty trunk of a hemlock pine, catching himself with a splayed and bony hand. Flecks of bark and moss adhered to the cuts and scrapes suffered as he fled through the thorny brambles of the underbrush. The last whimpering dimness of a dying sunset struggled to pierce clouds that hung like tattered banners from a morose sky. He shivered, the damp cold piercing his aged body completely to the bone, and spun about, searching with wide, skittish eyes.

Rowone was alone. At least he hoped so.

But, but, no. Of course, he wasn't. He hadn't been for months... or had it been years? Or decades? He couldn't recall anymore.

He first sensed and then heard a muddled scuffing marginally beyond his sight in the gloom behind a blotched osoberry shrub. Rowone flinched, crouching back to the relative shelter behind the tree. In the wild mountains of central Washington, it could be almost anything. Cougars, coyotes, bears.

"Or those—those other things," he mumbled, "the slimers. Or worse, the ones with the giant fangs."

Movement, almost imperceptible, caught his eye. A slithering motion like a firehose being dragged through obscurities at the edges of his awareness. But not simply any firehose. One that might be found in an ogre's lair. Huge and long, black and slimy, and very much living. It could have been a Giant Gippsland earthworm but on steroids, lots of steroids. It stretched easily 20 feet in length with the circumference of a heavy branch and slipped along the edge of Rowone's perception.

He rubbed his gaunt, stubbled cheeks. "Damn beast. Tracking me. Always chasing me."

He squatted low amongst the vegetation and began inching away from the creature. But from behind came the snapping of branches and the scraping of leaves. A second and third worm, monsters, both, slimed and entangled their pointed heads together, jagged teeth exposed behind ringed segment bands.

Rowone tried to run but tripped and fell on his back as the sky above the treetops continued to darken and the creatures moved closer.

"Just let me down to the cabin. Please!" His voice trembled with an agitated whine. "Please. Let an old man go home and die in peace."

As if in response, another worm approached from below. This one dwarfed the others, like a full-grown pine toppled and slipping through the forest. It blocked his escape and, along with its mates, seemed to be forming a noose about him, driving him up toward the ridge and the bluffs and, beyond, the Tamerlane Gorge.

He scrambled to his feet, clawing his way up the slope.

"You're worms... worms! You're not supposed to eat me until I'm dead!"

Rowone glanced behind as he hurried. More and more of the repulsive creatures joined the pursuit until the mountainside resembled a malign, writhing mass of monstrous demonic noodles coated with puss and tar... each a twisted memory, a tortured emotional scar, a bitter disappointment.

"No! No!" His horrified voice echoed across the wilderness, unheard and abandoned. "I don't, don't understand. Why me?"

He gripped the rocks as the incline increased, dragging himself ever higher.

It occurred to him the sun had been setting for weeks but never actually reached night. He realized with the continued dimness came a sullenness of heart. He hated the evening mist and the sound of the encroaching darkness. It left him feeling vulnerable, naked, dangling by a single fraying strand.

Rowone knew, somehow, he wholly understood, buried in the depths of his brain, when that last fiber finally snapped, there would be greater terrors awaiting. He'd already glimpsed them before, obscured, hazy, loitering in the recesses of his troubled mind. Red glowing eyes, gaping mouths, and long treacherous fangs dripping with blood... near mortal gashes, all. Gouges in his misshapen psyche.

He struggled the final steps, the commotion of the pursuit near behind. He cleared the summit, the bottomless wound of Tamerlane

Gorge spilling away below, sheer cliffs falling into a thousand-foot drop.

"Not possible, I can't… Trapped…"

He twisted around; the surging boil showed no signs of slowing. He thought again of the family cabin, the one where his father had raged, the one where Daisy had died, the one where his mother had always waited for him with loving eyes until she was stolen away.

The cabin so near at that moment. The one he so desired but couldn't reach.

"Because worms, giants. They'll catch you. Devour you," he said to himself. "These mountains will eat you alive."

The first of the horde wriggled a dark greasy head on the rocks at his feet, lashing against his ankles. A second rose, looming over his shoulder as if to crush him.

Their smell reminded him of Daisy. Poor Daisy. Dead rotting Daisy.

He saw in the distance, scarcely above the tips of the windswept trees, the towers and cables of an enormous suspension bridge. It crossed the ravine. If he ran, maybe, just maybe, he could still reach the cabin. Reach his mother. Find his peace.

"You don't need to keep straying anymore, Dad."

Seth's voice.

Seth.

Rowone felt his sanity tumble into freefall, the breaking of his final solitary thread. The vastly overwhelmed cohesion of his mind chose that moment to fail.

Shadows intensified about him. He lept forward, narrowly avoiding trunks and branches as he descended at breakneck speed, unsure when he might find himself hurtling over the ledge and into the chasm.

"The bridge. Over the gorge." His breaths came hard, the cold air burning his lungs as he labored for oxygen. "Then circle back. To the cabin. To home."

From somewhere close, too close, a rumbling commotion shook the earth, causing him to fall.

He screamed. He knew.

He'd seen them before.

Daisy, the stink of putrefying Daisy choked him as enormous snake-like phantoms began to blot the dwindling light. To the side, a violent thrashing as dagger fangs sliced through a giant worm, a gaping maw swallowing it down down in one long perverse motion.

Hell's elite guard had been freed. A legless combination of leach and lion, razors and rage. Where they hunted, thunder and terror reigned.

Rowone understood they were after him. He waivered, leg gashed and hurting, before stumbling forward anew.

The bridge was near, so very near.

"Dad! Wait!" Seth called.

Rowone froze.

"Seth?" He couldn't fathom. He'd not heard that voice since... "Not possible..."

Crashing, roaring came from behind as trees began toppling before the invertebrate onslaught.

Rowone started forward again.

"Dad, please! Don't!"

In his mind the memory of screeching tires, grinding metal, and his teenaged son's frightened eyes as their Buick was thrown against a tree by a drunk driver in an oversized pick-up.

"Dad, look at me."

"No, no. You're dead. All these years."

"I'm here. Dad, come home."

Home? Rowone so wanted to be there. With his mother. With Daisy.

Glowing red eyes closed the space behind him, monstrous jaws snapping. A second set, giant worm carcass still hanging limply in its mouth, appeared to his left.

"Cross the gorge. Circle back. The cabin." He hurried onto the structure, dragging his injured leg as the voice of his dead son implored him to stay.

The bridge shook as the worms and their demonic, bloodthirsty cousins slipped atop the deck to the rear.

Without the impediment of brush and trees, Rowone found he was increasing the gap.

"Across. Circle. Home," he gasped. "Gonna make this. Gonna..."

But the night had at last come in fullness, the darkness entombing like a long-buried crypt.

He'd made it halfway across.

Only half.

The wind through the Tamerlane Gorge cracked like the stained end of an executioner's whip. It snapped about his emaciated frame, draining him of the last vestiges of will. Twigs and pebbles were blown past the suspender cables of the center strand and into the depths below.

Before him, on the far side, Rowone saw red glowing eyes mount the bridge and approach, hurrying in his direction.

He spun about, hoping for escape. But there was none. Eyes, jaws, teeth, all still there with the decomposing reek of Daisy clawing at his senses.

"I want to go home. I want to go home. Mother!" His body became racked with sobs. "Please. Please. Leave me be."

But the creatures, repressed fears that they were, remained relentless. Worms, in an effort to avoid their own certain demise even as they still sought Rowone's, slithered up the support cables, entangling themselves, stretching and wrapping their lithe forms around the pylons and peaks.

Soon the entire span was a bleak congealed heap of leathery bodies, smoldering eyes, eager teeth, and the anticipation of death.

His death.

"Dad," Seth said, his voice near. "What are you doing?"

Rowone scrambled to the edge, clutching the rail for support. His eyes searched the dark, looking for... for what? "No, you're dead. Seth, you're dead."

"Not true, I'm right here. Look."

Rowone tried but couldn't see. He shook his head, rubbing wet eyes with his bloody palms.

"Dad, you're hallucinating. Imagining things." The form of a young man emerged from the murk. "Your depression, Dad, it's got you again."

Rowone recognized the face, not of a teen boy, though, but a fully-grown man with familiar features.

"Seth?" He gaped and swallowed. "Not possible. You're a boy, should be in high school."

He twitched against the supports as the wind howled.

"Remember? I survived the accident. You know I did. Your therapist explained." He reached out a hand. "Dad step away from the side. Come on, now."

The bridge shuddered as the seething mass of worms slimed their way up and over and around. The fanged horrors, snatched them, swallowing them whole or tossing their cadavers into the depths, all the while hungrily watching him.

"Stay away!" Rowone climbed over the railing, foot slipping as he clung to the slickened edge. He thrashed his free arm about as if shewing a swarm of flies, like those he'd seen around Daisy. "All of you! Demons! Slimers! Leave me alone!"

"No, wait! Come back over to this side," Seth pleaded. "You're loved on this side."

Rowone shook his head in staccato bursts. "I... I... I don't understand it. Death, Death himself is coming for me. Somehow, he left his iron gate ajar. And, and, as he tried to drag me in, you must have gotten out."

He looked down, unable to see the depth of the chasm beneath him.

"What are you doing?"

"If you really are my son... Seth, if it really is you..." A cry clawed his throat. "I won't let those things have me. I can't be eaten. Not while I'm alive."

"There's nothing, Dad. It's only you and me. Please. Come back over."

"If it truly is you, son, you need to go back. Dead all these years. The grave can't be cheated. Death keeps his own." He looked down again. "Join me. We can go together."

"No, no. That's your depression. Fight it! Please, step back over, just right here." Seth's voice began to tighten. "Watch, I'll stay away. Alright? Please. Please! I'm begging. Come back to this side, to the light. Ok?"

Rowone watched the snake-like forms thrashing about him. He caught the hissing of their malevolent breathing. He felt them inching ever nearer, preparing to snatch him back into a detached past. "No. No. I don't, don't have a choice. And you, you need to come with me."

"Dad! Wake up! You're lost in your own memories. Wallowing in your own misery. Listen. If you jump, you're going to die. Now, please, climb back to me. We can talk about this. Just talk for a minute."

The cold pointed head of a worm stretched from the underside of the bridge, brushing his legs and side. Rowone flinched. "I don't have time! They're going to eat me!"

"You're imagining."

"Like they ate Daisy. And your grandmother, like they ate her, too." His words tightened and slurred into a screeching mewl. "Like they ate you in your coffin. I'm sorry, I'm sorry! I shouldn't have killed you! Buried you! Your eyes! Your lips! The worms, those worms, they ate you, they ate you!"

"No, Dad! They didn't!"

"We've talked enough."

"Wait..."

"Come join me on this side of the cable, son."

"Promise me we can talk about this. Alright?"

Rowone looked around him. "Can you promise Death will call off his minions?"

"I don't know what you're talking about. There's nothing here. Only you and me, the wind, this damned bridge, and the deep, deep chasm. We're facing it all together."

"You need to trust me, son."

"No, Dad. I can't." Seth touched the cable near his father's hands. "I need you to think of Mom and your grandkids. They're all waiting back at my place. They're hoping to see you."

"Your mother, she left. Left right after. Blamed me, always blamed me, for the accident, for you, for everything. She want's nothing to do with me. It's what I deserve. She left me." His words choked. "She left me. I'm all alone."

"No, no. She's at the house. Wearing the heart necklace you bought her on your anniversary. Remember that? Cost you a month's pay. Remember?"

Rowone shook his head. "I love you, son."

He slid his feet back until only his toes rested on the railing.

"Oh no, no. Don't do that!" Seth shouted above the pummeling wind, moving closer. "Look at me, Dad. Listen! You're loved. Loved. By a lot of people."

"Not true. It's not." His eyes faded. "Gonna happen to us all one day. Nothing to be done of it."

"Dad! Damn it! Don't do this!"

"You get lost, and there'll be no finding you... 'cept maybe in a ravine like that stupid mutt."

A worm wrapped about his waist, tugging at him as another tightened around his throat.

Rowone let go...

...as Seth lunged and grabbed his flailing wrist, holding his father in a dangling grip.

"Dad, no!"

"Come with me, son. We can be together."

"Dad! Fight this! Stay with me!"

From the tower, a hulking shadow with glowing red eyes lunged, fangs bared and mouth cavernous.

Rowone struggled, freeing his arm from Seth's grasp as dagger jaws closed about his body...

...and he fell. The worms, his son, and the Tamerlane Bridge disappearing into the darkness above him.

# Section 7: Finem Suum

"I wonder if that's how darkness wins, by convincing us to trap it
inside ourselves, instead of emptying it out.
I don't want it to win."

Jasmine Warga, My Heart and Other Black Holes

"He in his madness prays for storms, and dreams that storms will
bring him peace"

Mikhail Lermontov

# Floating

J amie's emergency scuba tank contained only three minutes of air
when fully charged. His body might hold another minute or two
of oxygen in blood and muscle tissue, slightly more if he
happened to be in frigid waters. Two important reasons to always
dive with a partner.

But the tank wasn't fully charged; it was fully spent. And the water
wasn't cold; it was balmy in the geothermal caves of the South Pacific.
And Claire? His partner? Jamie didn't know. They'd become separated
after the walls crumbled and their lights failed.

It didn't matter anymore. Nothing did. Nothing ever would again.

He found himself floating, as if in a tactile vacuum. All his senses
dimmed to the point of worthless static.

Undersea caves are among the very few places on earth where rays
from the sun have never penetrated. And without the 1,100 lumens
from his lost OxyLED lantern, he'd never find the passage back to the
entrance. He was hopelessly cut off. Even if he had 100 tanks of air at
his disposal, when cave diving, darkness equals death.

He pulled in the final breath from his expended reserve and hung in
the inky black waters, waiting for the inevitable.

Claire is the one who'd encouraged him to try his first cave dive. She'd
been before. Jamie had been eager to learn. Together, on the ragged
outer edge of survival, they'd shared experiences deeper and more

meaningful than those who'd never embraced true danger ever could. The reward? Undisturbed caverns of crystal, intricately carved crevasses, and a bond between them so close as to be seemingly unbreakable.

Until they went too deep. Until the rock fall knocked out the lights, sentencing them to perfect blackness. Until she drifted away...

...and Jamie found himself alone.

Sound doesn't travel well under water. A few feet from the surface and all that remains is the gurbled sucking of lungs through the regulator and the escaping bubbles from the exhalation. Beyond that, a vacuous cocooning, save for the occasional propeller or whale song. Scant chance of either of those finding their way into Jamie's noiseless cavern. And with his air gone, there was overwhelming silence. He may as well have had no ability to hear at all.

Except for the thundering of blood coursing through his ears, slowing exponentially with each passing second, and the ever-diminishing rhythm of his rapidly failing heart.

Cut off from the surface, by design. That's the reward of underwater caving for those who need escape, need to run away. All that world with its leashes and connectivity and stress and demand is left behind. Hundreds of feet down swimming among massive growths of gypsum and selenite while encased in caverns of polished granite provide solitude and an opportunity to experience uncontaminated wonder. In truth, being entombed beneath the sea is one of the most freeing and mind-expanding experiences possible as each fin-stroke takes you deeper into unexplored dangers.

Unless you can't get back out.

Unless the world above forgets you and cares not about your struggles.

Unless you are abandoned to the nothingness that is swallowing you.

It stared at him, the void, as if a million judging eyes looked through his body and directly into his being. Jamie felt their derision, their malice, and their overpowering will that he simply succumb.

A price would soon be paid, and he'd begun to accept the terms. It was as if he'd stumbled and fallen down down down into a never ending well, splashing finally into water so dark as to feel malignant, and sinking further still until his mind became detached from reality. He assumed he'd panic in such a situation. Instead, he felt at peace, an unexpected resignation toward his own fate.

But not hers.

"Claire," he thought, "I'm so sorry. Oh God, please let her be safe. Take me, not her."

The absurdity of a man with mere seconds of life remaining trying to negotiate a deal with God to take those moments in exchange for someone else struck him as beyond pathetic.

But desperate times allow for such things.

The gentle currents in the water inched him deeper. He could scarcely feel the motion or the infinitesimal nudges against the neoprene of his wetsuit. He hadn't the strength to resist it any longer and no direction to go even if he did. His final journey, destination unknown.

And there he floated, feeling neither warmth nor chill, suspended in midnight, no sound or taste or smell. Cut off, a million miles from anything or anyone.

His fingers and toes began to tingle as hypoxia set in. Soon his legs and arms felt as if he was cocooned in a wool blanket.

"Claire. I love you so much. I can't let you go."

But he knew that wasn't his choice.

The tepid sea pressed in on him, like muscles contracting in his mother's womb as he floated in amniotic fluid. This rebirth didn't frighten him. Not at that point. Not as he lingered on its doorstep.

Slowly, slowly, now unaware, he curled, knees to chest, into a fetal position as his fingers gently removed the ineffective mouthpiece from between his teeth.

It became all so simple. One with the unending darkness.

Words with no form and fragments with no meaning softened his mind in scattered electrical impulses.

"Cl-Claire?"

And in that concluding flicker of life, that mortal instant when one's mind clings to the echoes of past blessings, she wasn't there...

...and a deathly pall consumed him.

He'd entered the world alone and would now leave it in the same way.

But it didn't matter.

Quietly, peacefully, eternally, ...

he fell asleep...

as the waters...

carried...

him...

away.

# Section 8: Après

"There's got to be a morning after. We're moving closer to the shore. I know we'll be there by tomorrow. And we'll escape the darkness, we won't be searching anymore."

Maureen McGovern, There's Got to be a Morning After

# Going Home

The lights of the terminal faded as we taxied away into the darkness obscuring London Heathrow Airport. In the distance, strands of mist, silver in the predawn hours, covered the ground like woolen blankets. I stared at my reflection, cold and one dimensional on the thick glass of the window; my gaunt companion, transparent and hollow, tired eyes wet behind a sagging face.

At that moment, I wanted nothing more than to be home.

The lights in the cabin flickered, and my mind blinked in the transitory darkness. I saw my love in that instant, her countenance outside, an apparition in the red and blue beacons pulsing beneath extended metal wings. I lifted my hand, reaching toward her. She was gone. The wound of prolonged separation tore anew, and I shuddered.

Chestnut strands had swept across Marie's face as she lay beneath the comforter of our shared bed the morning I'd left. I sat at her feet, watching as a dream lifted the corners of lips so soft they could caress away any sorrow. Her eyelids fluttered as she rolled onto her side, the delicate motions of a rose petal in the breeze. With a longing finger, I brushed the hair from her cheeks, looping it behind her ear. The base of her neck curved like a porcelain swan to the smoothness of her shoulder. The strap of her gown had fallen, and I marveled, transfixed, at the beauty of the woman who so richly blessed my life.

Too soon, the horn of the waiting cab had torn me away.

It had been over a year.

*A year.*

A year on a journey I never wanted to take. A year stolen away in a forced purgatory. A year of searching and scrambling amid the wreckage of loss and pain.

*A year.*

A sigh filled my lungs and echoed. I twisted the ventilation knob above my seat, releasing a breath of air that spilled down from the fuselage in a cottony whisper. I drifted in the sensation, waves pulling me from shore. The plane, the cabin, the passengers about me all dimmed, and I became lost in a vast, warm pool with no horizon.

Marie muttered, close, her voice throaty. She smiled at me and bid me come. The door to our room was latched. A candle on the nightstand glowed with ribbons of crimson beside empty glasses dappled with droplets of Pinot. Lace slipped from feminine curves, tanned skin gently illuminated. I touched her, feeling heat. Perfume encircled me, tugging at my senses. I inhaled, long and slow, holding every drop. Her nearness was an opiate. It pushed away the outside world and sheltered me in the security of a love divinely constructed. Her nails circled. A hand on...

...my shoulder. "Mr. Jackson?"

My muscles seized, and I jumped, wrenching my head about and clutching the fabric armrest.

The flight attendant leaned closer. "I'm sorry, Mr. Jackson," she smiled. "You need to fasten your safety belt. We'll be lifting off in a moment."

"Yes, of course." I swallowed and fumbled with the straps. "Been a long trip."

She patted my arm. "You're near the end, now. Going home. Let me know if you need anything."

"I need to know what I'll find when I get there."

Her expression softened, caring and concerned. "You'll know soon."

I nodded and glanced at my wristwatch. Six thousand miles away, Marie was climbing into bed, her day just concluding. Opening her Bible to the marker, she would focus on the Word.

A familiar passage surfaced in my mind, and I recited with her. *I gave orders for all of us to fast and humble ourselves before our God. We prayed that he would give us a safe journey and protect us, our children, and our goods as we traveled—and he heard our prayer.*

She would close her eyes in a silent appeal, lifting me up and weeping for strength.

I bowed my head and joined her, beseeching our Savior to reunite us anew in our loving union.

Outside, the waning moon descended, and the stars glistened. The same as they did in California.

*Our God is greater than these.*

A warmth bathed and freshened me as my mouth drew into an assured smile.

The engines roared, causing the plane to tremble as it accelerated along the runway. I relaxed as I was pressed against the cushions, content in the machine's ability to power my journey but trusting God to shepherd the way even as he prepared hearts for my return. Through the window, London shrank beneath me like a receding galaxy. The eastern horizon began to glow as we banked over the Atlantic toward home.

# Maxx's Well

~~~

In the end, sunset is either a beautiful gift in the moment,
the seed of a bright new tomorrow,
or the onset of oppressive, interminable darkness.
We each have our personal monsters who get to decide.

~~~~~~~~